the Season
W9-BHJ-025

THE SEASON

SARAH MACLEAN

SCHOLASTIC INC.
New York Toronto London Auckland
Sydney Mexico City New Delhi Hong Kong

This book was originally published in hardcover by Orchard Books in 2009.

ISBN-13: 978-0-545-04887-3
ISBN-10: 0-545-04887-7

12 11 10 9 8 7 6 5 4 3 2 1 9 10 11 12 13 14/0

Printed in the U.S.A. 40

First Scholastic paperback printing, December 2009

For Lisa,

who believed

For Eric,

who reminds me that love is real . . .
even if boys don't brood about it
quite as much as I'd like to think

and

For the women in my life,

who will find themselves in these pages

prologue

January 1815
Blackmoor Estate, Essex, England

The rain fell steadily on the slick rocks marking the edge of the Essex countryside, where the land fell in sheer cliffs to a frigid winter sea.

His horse was uncertain of its footing, shying away from speed and direction in favor of steady ground. The creature's fear would ordinarily irritate him and mark it for sale or slaughter, but today the wet cliffs made him equally cautious. He hadn't planned to make this particular journey today — but some things would not wait.

He had received word by messenger early that morning — critical information that pointed to the possibility that the scheme he had set in motion was about to be compromised. Someone was determined to ruin everything . . . and that someone had to be stopped.

He had done all he could to keep his work a secret. But the earl had somehow discovered everything. Well, not exactly everything. He didn't know how closely his precious earldom was tied up in the whole plan. Wouldn't that be a surprise? He couldn't wait to see the look of shock on the earl's face. That would make this whole miserable trek in this godforsaken rain worth it.

He turned his gaze to the ocean, where a ship was anchored not far from the bleak Essexshire cliffs. Thirty yards ahead, the path split into two. To the left began the steep descent to the sea — too dangerous for a horse, barely wide enough for a man. To the right, the passage continued along the tops of the cliffs and, not far from the fork, offered the perfect spot for anyone interested in watching the events taking place below. There, he would find his prey.

He dismounted just before the split and left his horse, continuing to the right on foot. Without a mount, the advantage of surprise was his. On foot, he moved by instinct. He knew every inch of these cliffs, having traveled them hundreds of times before. They provided the perfect cover for the work he was doing, the perfect rendezvous point for his partners, and, coincidentally, the perfect place to dispose of someone.

The earl had, at long last, made a mistake. And now he would pay.

one

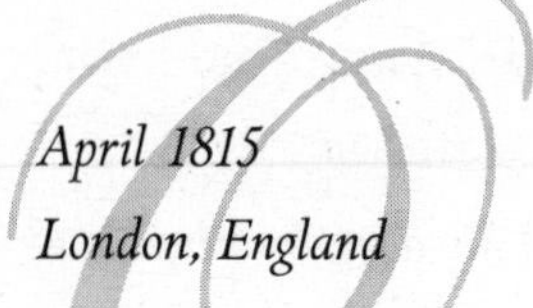

April 1815
London, England

"Oof! I've been stabbed!"

The Duchess of Worthington did not look up from her needlepoint. "Perhaps that will teach you to fidget while at the hands of your dressmaker." She cast a sidelong glance in the direction of her youngest child. "Besides, I highly doubt that Madame Fernaud 'stabbed' you."

Lady Alexandra Stafford, only daughter of the Duke and Duchess of Worthington, heaved a sigh and rolled her eyes. She rubbed the spot at her waist that bore the mark of London's finest dressmaker's needle. "Perhaps not stabbed — but wounded nonetheless." Garnering no reaction from either her mother or the unflappable *modiste,* Alex slumped her shoulders and muttered, "I fail to understand why I must suffer this fitting anyway."

The duchess continued with her needlepoint. "Alexandra, there are plenty of young women who would happily assume your position, standing on that platform, 'suffering' through a fitting for that dress."

"May I suggest any one of them take my place?"

"No."

Alex knew when she was fighting a losing battle. "I didn't think so."

The Duchess of Worthington had been waiting seventeen years for her daughter to be released, finally, into the social whirlwind of a London season. For the last three years, Alex's daily lessons had been shortened to accommodate hours of ridiculous tutorials designed to make her most marketable to those unmarried men whom her mother deemed to be "good catches" — which is to say, titled, wealthy, and *thoroughly dull.*

Perfectly useful time in Alex's days had been taken up with a rigorous schedule designed by her mother and her governess to break her of all her quirks, that is, anything about Alex that someone with a thimbleful of intelligence might find interesting. From "Poise and Posture," a torturous half hour designed to keep Alex's back straight and chin tilted just so, to "Proper Conversation," a playacting session designed to help Alex understand what to say and what not to say to the various men she would be meeting over the course of her first season, to "The Subtlety of the Dance," during which she learned the quadrille, the waltz, the cotillion . . . and any number of other dances that would give her a chance to try to "appear graceful and lovely" while practicing all she had learned about Proper Conversation, the lessons were a precious waste of time as far as Alex was concerned. Unfortunately, she didn't imagine anything short of Napoleon's army marching straight through the drawing room of Worthington House would steer her mother from the course of marrying off her only daughter and, even then, she didn't put it past the duchess to question the Captain of the French Guard on his lineage and inheritance before surrendering.

After all, a carefully won marriage was far more important than affairs of state.

The lessons *had* taught Alex some of the rules of the London aristocracy, however. *Do*: pretend to be interested as men regale you with the boring details of horses, hunting, and themselves. *Don't*: reveal any amount of intelligence. Evidently, it scares eligible gentlemen off. Also, refrain from suggesting that there must be men who are looking for a woman who knows the difference between Greek and Latin. That particular remark sends governesses into hysterics.

Without considering the repercussions, Alex let out a deep, resigned sigh. And received a needle in the backside for it.

"Ouch!"

Madame Fernaud may have been considered the most renowned dressmaker in all of England, but Alex knew better. Clearly, the Frenchwoman was waging a quiet war against her British enemies by poking the young maidens of London to death.

This was the final fitting of the most important of Alex's new gowns — the one she would wear to her first ball at Almack's in a little over a week's time. An appearance at Almack's was essential for any debutante. Here, London's most revered aristocrats — collectively referred to as the *ton* — were given a good look at the fresh young faces of the season. *Like livestock going to market,* Alex thought to herself, a single eyebrow rising in wry amusement as the corner of her mouth kicked up. The simile was too apt. Of course, most of the other girls who would join Alex for her coming-out had been dreaming of the moment their entire lives. Alas, there was simply no accounting for taste.

A quiet throat-clearing came from the door of the room and Alex, being careful not to move too much for fear of being skewered again, craned her head around to look at Eliza, her lady's maid.

"Excuse me, Your Grace," Eliza directed her words to the duchess while dropping into a quick curtsy. "Lady Alexandra has visitors . . . Lady Eleanor and Lady Vivian are in the downstairs sitting room."

"Thank goodness. I'm saved," Alex muttered under her breath and snapped her head around to send a pleading look at her mother. "Please? I've been standing here *forever.* The dress must be *perfect* by now."

Madame Fernaud stepped back from her work and spoke for the first time. "Perfect is right, Mademoiselle." She turned to the duchess and said, "*Et voilà.* Your Grace . . . she is a masterpiece . . . do you not think?"

Alex pounced on this statement. "A masterpiece, Mother. I rather think we shouldn't fuss with such a tour de force, don't you?"

The duchess, ever a perfectionist, stood and walked a slow circle around her daughter, casting a critical eye at a seam here, a detail there. After what seemed like an eternity, she raised her gaze to meet Alex's. "You are lovely, Alexandra. You're going to set the *ton* on its ear."

Alex knew she'd won. Her face broke into a wide smile. "Well, with a mother like you, how could I not?"

The duchess chuckled at her daughter's blatant flattery. "Rather excessive, Alexandra. Off with you."

Alex clapped her hands and hopped down from the raised platform where she had been standing, throwing herself into the arms of her mother and planting a kiss on the duchess's cheek. "Thank you, Mama!" Alex bolted for the door, tossing back a complimentary, "*Merci, Madame Fernaud!* The dress is just gorgeous! *Oui, c'est magnifique!* Thank you!"

Behind her, Her Grace spoke to no one in particular. "What am I going to do with that girl?" If Madame Fernaud hadn't been caught up in her own indignant sputtering at the atrocious treatment her creation was suffering at the hands of Alexandra, she would have detected a hint of laughter in the duchess's voice.

two

Alex bounded down the wide staircase of Worthington House and skidded to a halt in front of the sitting room doors. Harquist, the long-suffering butler who had been with the Stafford family since Alex's grandfather held the dukedom, was standing at the ready. As Alex's heavy skirts swirled to a stop around her legs, he opened the door to let her into the room.

Casting a twinkling glance at the butler, Alex stiffened her spine and offered her most ladylike "Thank you, Harquist" in his direction as she exaggeratedly flounced into the room.

His somber "my lady" was still hanging in the air when two sets of giggles exploded from across the room. Alex's serious expression dissolved into a grin as she threw herself most indelicately onto the nearest chaise — across from her closest friends in the world, Ella and Vivi.

The three had been friends since birth. Their fathers' boyhood camaraderie had carried on into adulthood and fate had given them each a daughter, born in three consecutive weeks of the year. It was only logical that the girls would become friends, confidantes, and partners in crime.

Lady Vivian Markwell, the only daughter of the Marquess of Langford, was the eldest of the trio — tall and slender, with her father's dark hair and violet eyes, Vivi's beauty betrayed a sharp mind and a strong will also inherited from her father, who was not only wealthy and charming but also a national hero and a high-ranking member of the British War Office.

Vivi's mother had died when Vivi was only seven years old and her father had never remarried. Instead, he had poured his energy into raising Vivi and her twin brother, Sebastian. While Sebastian spent his days at Eton, studying to inherit his father's title and become a peer of the realm, Vivi had grown into a perfectly mannered, distractingly exotic beauty.

The youngest of the three by a mere five days was Lady Eleanor Redburn, the eldest daughter of the Earl and Countess of Marlborough. Ella's delicate features and petite frame, combined with her corn-silk-blond hair and blue eyes, afforded her the exact features that most ladies of the *ton* would have sold their souls to have for themselves. Ella's personality defied her porcelain looks — she preferred books to balls and had even less interest than Alex in the trappings of London society. While Ella recognized and embraced the fact that her interests would likely leave her without a husband, Ella's mother was beside herself with horror at the prospect of such a life for her daughter. Not that such a reaction bothered Ella in the least . . . in fact, Alex had a sneaking suspicion that her friend considered irritating the countess an added bonus.

Vivi and Ella had been with Alex for every step of her life and she couldn't imagine a day without them. And, at that particular moment, she couldn't have been happier that they were there.

"I am thrilled to see you! You've saved me from history's longest dress fitting. What perfect timing!"

The girls cast sidelong glances at each other.

"That would explain your odd attire," Ella said drily.

Alex looked down at herself with a groan. "I was in such a hurry to get out of that room, I forgot that I was still wearing the gown." She sat up on the chaise and fluffed her skirts. "I'll change in a bit. I'm not venturing back up there until Madame Fernaud has gone. She takes pleasure in my pain."

"Your mother will have fits if she finds you lying about in your coming-out gown," observed Vivi. "But since you're here . . . stand up so we can have a look at it."

Alex stood, curtsied, and twirled for her friends. Vivi smiled broadly. "It's beautiful, Alex. The color is perfect on you. Cruelly or no, Madame Fernaud knows how to wield a needle."

Alex grimaced at the memory of the needle in question and spoke wryly. "Alas . . . if only she were as careful with skin as she is with silk." The girls shared a laugh — they'd all been on the receiving end of the *modiste*'s needle — and Alex looked down at the dress she'd been wearing for most of the afternoon.

She had to admit that it was beautiful. A rich emerald silk, the perfect color to highlight her bronze complexion, green eyes, and auburn hair, the gown was perfectly fitted to her body from shoulders to neckline to waist — a style Alex had never been able to wear before, her age prohibiting her from donning something so revealing. At the waist, the dress fell in rich waves of luxurious fabric down to the floor. What made it truly remarkable, however, were the hundreds of tiny handmade rosebuds that were meticulously affixed to the fabric in a diagonal cascade. The flowers, in the same green silk, appeared sparingly at the top of the bodice and gradually spilled down the dress, increasing in number. The design played on Alex's uncommon tallness, elongating her form and accentuating her height.

It really was a masterpiece.

Ella interrupted her study of the gown. "If you think you're going to be able to steer clear of marriage in *that*, you're sorely mistaken."

Alex cast a scowl at her friend. Ella never minced words. And she was almost always right. Unfortunately, this situation was no exception. The gown was designed for one reason only . . . to catch her a husband. For more than a year, her mother had been in a whirlwind of preparation for this, the spring of 1815, when Alex would turn seventeen and be "introduced" to the world. Not that she hadn't been introduced to the world for seventeen years. But this was different. This was her first season, when she would be paraded like a piece of horseflesh in front of every unattached male in London who happened to have a sizable inheritance and an acceptable title. Her mother's goal was to have Alex married off by autumn.

Did anything sound worse?

"I'm simply going to have to try *not* to do this dress justice." Alex's tone was filled with resolve. "My mother has her heart set on making my life as dull and boring as she possibly can. I mean . . . who on earth wants to end up married in Surrey? What a nightmare!" she said to no one in particular.

Ella leaned back against the soft upholstery of her chair and looked up at the ceiling with disdain. "No one. At least, no one with a mind to think for herself."

"My brothers are all years older than I am — does my mother pester them to settle down and get married?"

Vivi interrupted, "Yes."

"That's because my mother enjoys pestering her children. But they don't listen to her! The only reason they've agreed to attend any balls this year is because they want fodder with which to mock their little sister!"

Ella this time: "Well, you can't blame them. You are exceedingly mockable."

Vivi chuckled as Alex shot her friend a withering glance and carried on. "It's atrociously unfair! Men our age aren't even asked to *attend* balls. The idea of boys marrying at eighteen is unfathomable for our set. It's what happens in the country! And yet, we are paraded around like . . . like . . . cattle . . . to be sold . . . to the highest bidder!"

Ella interrupted again. "Well, to be fair, perhaps it's best men aren't married off at eighteen. Have you *met* the average eighteen-year-old male?"

Vivi's dry remark followed. "Mmmm. I'm still trying to avoid taking offense at being compared to livestock. Go on, Alex. . . ."

Alex sighed. "I'm just being silly, I know. But that's how it feels. *Especially* when you grow up with three older brothers who seem to have an entirely different set of rules."

"You're right," Ella spoke seriously, "but it seems that we don't really have a choice. Our options are rather limited."

And Ella would know. As the eldest in a family of girls, Ella had a familial obligation to marry and marry well, setting the standard for her younger sisters . . . unless she could figure out a way to take herself out of the running. Ella had considered any number of options to render herself unmarriageable. The girls had discussed every possibility and come to one conclusion: The fastest way to be set "on the shelf" and ignored was to have one's reputation ruined.

Unfortunately, being ruined was not an option, however tempting it was, for it seemed that ruination was the punishment for anyone daring enough to try something exciting. Girls in London society could have their reputation destroyed in any number of ways, but the biggest offenses were clear:

kissing (or something more scandalous) on the lips (or somewhere more scandalous); dancing three or more dances with someone at a ball; or visiting a man at his home unchaperoned.

Ella had considered these options again and again, even going so far as to make lists of the men she felt she could convince to aid her ruin, but she simply couldn't commit to bringing gossip and criticism down upon her family. After all, ruination didn't stop at the young lady. Polite society could be devastatingly cruel to her loved ones as well.

"Unless I decide to give my mother a case of hysterics and destroy my sisters' chances of ever being matched, I have to settle for remaining unnoticed," Ella said to no one in particular.

Vivi chuckled and shook her head at her friend. "You make it sound so easy! You're beautiful and come with a sizable dowry. Spinsterhood isn't exactly guaranteed, Ella."

"Ah, but you've forgotten my most hideous trait. No one wants an intelligent wife." Ella gave a mock shudder. "Too terrifying a possibility."

Alex laughed. "Sadly, I think you're right. Reveal just enough of your intelligence and you're safe from being courted. Especially by any of the ninnies who will be asking us to take a turn about the room at Almack's."

Her friend smiled. "Let's hope so, because that's the best plan I've got. It's the only way my novel is ever going to be written."

It wasn't simply that Ella found the idea of a proper marriage to a proper man distasteful, it was that she found it in direct opposition to the one thing she had wanted to do for as long as she could remember. Ella had dreams of becoming a great novelist and writing the sort of book that told the story of her time. She read anything she could get her hands on and was rarely seen without her notebooks, which held any ideas and observations she thought would be useful when she finally had a chance to tell her tale.

Of course, the challenge of being a woman who writes loomed over Ella's head. Of all the respectable novelists in the past fifty years, few had (at least publicly) admitted to being women. But Ella was well aware that the small odds of her being an unmarried female author were slightly higher than the minuscule odds of being a married one. And she was willing to bet on them.

"That reminds me," Vivi interjected, "I have an idea for your book that I think might be just perfect." The girls were always trading concepts and plots to be recorded in Ella's notebook. "I overheard my father discussing the impending capture of a series of spies — English spies — who have been trading secrets to the French."

Alex leaned back against the chaise and pulled her feet up under her. She *loved* hearing tales of Vivi's eavesdropping. "Oooh . . . go on."

Vivi leaned forward, a natural storyteller with a gift for making anything sound interesting. "From what I could gather, the Royal Navy have had some trouble with their secret movements being intercepted by the French. It's apparently quite vexing for the men at the War Office. With Napoleon's escape from exile last month, they've obviously been preparing for a full-scale push to unseat him; they've considered a number of possible ways that their coded instructions to naval ships might be intercepted and decoded, but it seems there's only one conclusion. English spies."

Alex had a choice and unladylike word for any Englishman who would sell state secrets in wartime. Ella already had her notebook out and was scribbling. Ignoring her friend's crude language, she spoke without looking up, "Fascinating. Who?"

Vivi shook her head and waved a hand. "They don't have any idea at this point. It must be someone fairly high up in the War Office who has access to this kind of information. My father was recently placed on the case, along with William." She made eye contact with Alex at the mention of her friend's eldest brother. "Between the two of them, I'm sure it will be cleared up soon enough. But I'm certain that if anyone can make it more interesting, it's you, Ella."

Ella was lost to them for a moment — focused entirely on the words in her journal. Chewing daintily on the end of her lead pencil, her mind was turning over the story she might weave around such a loose collection of information. Leaving her to her reverie, the conversation turned to Vivi and her own preparations for entering society.

The three girls would attend Almack's for their official coming-out on Wednesday evening. Vivi, the only one without a mother to pester her, had the least amount of animosity for the event. It wasn't that she didn't feel the pressure of society's will as much as her friends. As the ravishing only daughter of a wealthy and decorated marquess, it was simply expected that she marry and marry well, considering that she couldn't inherit her father's title. She'd been hearing this from meddling aunts and the parents of her friends for years, but she had one thing in her favor — her father thought it was a terrible idea to marry for marriage's sake.

While the ladies of the *ton* had spent years worrying about Vivi and her twin brother being raised by a widowed father and encouraged the marquess either to deposit his children with any number of female relatives or to quickly remarry, the marquess had flown in the face of convention and flatly refused to do any such thing. Vivi's parents' marriage had been a love match (something that would have been considered disgustingly common had the marquess not been just that — a marquess), and he had showered his daughter with the same caring and affection that he'd given her mother, encouraging her to marry for the same reason he had. Love.

"You unbelievably lucky chit!" Alex spoke. "You have parental permission — nay, parental expectation! — to avoid all versions of limp-necked, pasty white, simpering dandies who might come calling for your hand in marriage. Are you sure your father wouldn't like to assume charge of me as well?"

"I'm not sure my father could handle you." Vivi laughed. "But, in all honesty, I'm not planning to avoid anyone's simpering wish for my hand. My plan is to gain as many proposals as possible. I need to hone my flirting skills if I'm going to catch The One."

The One. Vivi had always been the only girl in the threesome who believed in "The One." Ella speculated that it was the result of her being the product of a love match. Alex felt she knew better, however, and could never shake the idea that Vivi had already set her sights on the man she wanted. Vivi, ever mysterious, refused to respond to any prodding or cajoling for more information on the subject, leaving her friends with a simple: "Everybody has a One. We just aren't all willing to wait for Him."

Alex snorted indecorously. "I don't think it is unwillingness to wait, Viv . . . I'm more than willing to wait. Years! Decades even!" Her eyes twinkled with laughter.

Ella chimed in with, "Centuries! Millennia!"

"There is just one problem." Alex leaned forward and, with a wink to Ella, she spoke with grave seriousness, "Mothers." All three girls burst out in giggles.

"ALEXANDRA ELIZABETH STAFFORD! WHAT DO YOU THINK YOU ARE DOING?"

"Uh-oh."

"Speaking of . . ." Ella said drily.

Alex's feet came off the chaise and she sat up. "Mother . . ."

For a petite woman, the duchess could appear as regal and enormous as her title suggested. "What did I tell you about that dress? What would possess you to come down here and lie about in it as if it were your nightgown and this your bedchamber? Leaving aside your unladylike behavior for the moment . . . do you have any idea how long it took Madame Fernaud and her assistants to turn that dress into something worthy of your coming-out? It is a ball gown . . . not a riding habit!"

"But . . ." Alex tried to get a word in.

The duchess was not in the mood to hear her daughter's feeble explanations. "No buts, young lady. March up to your chamber, apologize to Eliza for her having to bother with you at this hour of the day, and Remove. That. Dress."

Ella was suddenly and vastly interested in the weave of the upholstery on the armchair in which she was seated. Vivi could have been searching for treasure in her tiny reticule for the amount of attention she was giving to the contents of the bag, likely a handkerchief, some lip rouge, and a traveling comb. Neither girl wanted to be the next recipient of the duchess's wrath.

"And you two." The two in question looked up, then stood. "Do you think I haven't noticed that you were both encouraging her ridiculous behavior?"

Vivi's mouth opened. She thought better of it. It closed.

"Excellent choice, Vivian. I rely on the two of you to keep Alex from losing hold of *all* of her decorum. I do not expect to be disappointed by you."

Ella risked speech. "Yes, Your Grace."

"I feel confident that I will not be disappointed in you again . . . especially during your first season." Contrary to the wording, this was not a theory the duchess had shared, but rather an order she had decreed.

Vivi spoke this time. "No, Your Grace."

From behind her mother's back, Alex gaped at her friends. "Traitors!"

The duchess did not turn to look at her daughter. "Good friends know not to cross mothers, Alexandra." There was a merry glint in her eye as she studied her daughter's closest confidantes.

Vivi knew the storm had passed. "Especially when the mother in question is a duchess."

Alex groaned. The duchess smiled.

"Are you girls staying for tea?"

three

When Alex returned to the drawing room, she was in more suitable attire for an afternoon with her friends. The Empire gown she wore was a lovely shade of pale blue, falling to her matching slippers. It was comfortable and fashionable — another one of her new gowns, designed to make her seem more adult and less ungainly.

Of course . . . no dress could actually *make* Alex more ladylike — she burst through the door of the room with a "What did I miss?" . . . only to realize that her friends were no longer alone.

And they were outnumbered.

Alex's brothers had arrived. Towering well over six feet — all broad shoulders and long legs — the boys never failed to dwarf even this larger-than-average room.

With satin-covered chairs and dainty chaises, the room was designed in the most fashionable of ways; which, of course, meant it was designed for a more foppish and less . . . enormous group of men. Not that the men in question seemed to care. They were sprawled out, long legs extended, leaning back on the petite furniture with no notice of its size — or their own.

For generations, the Stafford men had been known throughout the *ton* for their appearance — the epitome of tall, dark, and handsome. Alex's father was a mere six feet tall, and was teased relentlessly by his brothers and cousins as "the diminutive duke." His sons did not suffer the same fate — all standing taller than six feet, four inches, proving that the next crop of Staffords would reclaim their statuesque heritage. The sons in question — William, twenty-three, Nicholas, twenty-one, and Christopher, nineteen — shared other familial qualities with their father, however: They were devilishly handsome, with the dark-as-midnight hair, strong jaws, regal noses, and full lips that had made the Staffords legendary since the early days of the kingdom.

But it wasn't their good looks that stopped women in their tracks. It was the famous Stafford eyes. For as long as anyone could remember, Stafford men had been blessed with eyes the color of clearest emeralds. One could get lost in those eyes — they were windows on emotion, glittering with humor, flashing with anger, fiery with passion.

These were eyes that wreaked havoc on the women around them — unless the woman in question was a sister. In which case, they served to simply exasperate.

"Ah. Talk of the Devil."

Alex moved farther into the room and perched herself against the edge of the chaise, leveling her brothers with a cool look. "What has you three so amused?"

"Just the fact that, even on our most difficult of days, we have never infuriated Mother the way you seem to with virtually no effort. An admirable trait, to be sure." William Stafford, already the Marquess of Weston and heir to the dukedom, spoke wryly from across the room.

"She merely holds you three to a different standard, Will. She manages her expectations of you — a trio of mediocrity. Aren't you three, as gentlemen, supposed to stand when a lady enters?" Alex was beginning to regret returning to the sitting room.

Christopher shot his sister a questioning glance. "A lady entered?" At his sister's withering look, his face broke into a broad grin as he made himself more comfortable in his chair. "Come now, Allie . . . just because you're about to have your first season doesn't mean you have to lose your sense of humor."

"On the contrary, Kit, my sense of humor is very much intact." She shot a conciliatory look at Vivi and Ella and spoke frankly: "You're simply not that amusing."

A deep, rumbling laugh came from the doorway. "She has a point, Kit."

Alex spun around to face the newcomer with surprise, followed by delight. "No one told me you were back! Of course . . . with this lot" — she nodded to her brothers, none of whom seemed moved by the new arrival — "I shouldn't be surprised."

Gavin Sewell moved across the room toward her to bow low over the back of her hand. "It would seem that I am indeed back . . . and that you're still making as much trouble as you were the last time I saw you." His eyes met hers with a smile.

"Not on purpose," Alex defended herself. "How am I supposed to remember all the silly rules of the season?"

Ella piped in practically, "In fairness, it seems not wearing your first ball gown in the front sitting room in the middle of the day is a fairly simple rule to remember."

Gavin chuckled over Alex's glare, unable to resist teasing her. "It does seem that way, although never having had to wear a ball gown myself, I can't guarantee I wouldn't be confused as well."

"It's a good thing, too. I'm not sure you'd survive the corset."

He cocked an eyebrow in response to Alex's retort and moved to greet Ella and Vivi. As Gavin bowed over the backs of their hands, Vivi was the first to speak. Her "Good afternoon, my lord Blackmoor" surprised Alex.

"Oh," said Alex quietly, remembering her manners and falling into a curtsy, "apologies, my lord, your new title slipped my mind."

Gavin turned back toward Alex, surprised. "No need to stand on ceremony, Alex. I forget that I'm the earl myself most of the time. I cannot seem to get comfortable with the idea that I carry the title now. Besides, I don't see how it would change much. Nick has been an earl your whole life and that doesn't seem to change the way you treat him." He shot her an odd smile and nodded in the direction of Alex's middle brother.

Nick, as always, was quick to chime in. "That's right! You lot have never respected my title," he said, puffing out his chest in a false air of pompousness. He added a thickly arrogant tenor to his blustering. "Why should Blackmoor get any respect? I've been the Earl of Farrow since before you were born and it doesn't earn me an ounce of esteem!"

Everyone laughed and, with that, the awkwardness of the situation had disappeared. Gavin moved to sit by Alex's brothers, throwing himself into their conversation about a horse auction they planned to attend the next week.

Alex rejoined Vivi and Ella, who resumed their discussion about a novel that the three girls had recently read, *Mansfield Park*, but she couldn't shake the odd feeling she'd had during the scene that had just unfolded. She hadn't missed the fact that, even when Nick was making light of his own title, he'd casually referred to Gavin as Blackmoor — the name that was now rightfully his, along with the earldom and all its privileges — as though it were the most natural thing in the world. But when she'd seen him in the doorway, Alex hadn't even registered that Gavin was any different, that anything had changed. With one ear on the girls' discussion, Alex stole a glance at the object of her thoughts.

Gavin's father had been her own father's closest boyhood friend — something that was bound to have happened, considering the fact that Blackmoor and Stafford lands bordered each other both in the Essex countryside and in London, where the townhouses shared expansive back gardens on Park Lane. Proximity and age had made Gavin a natural companion of the Stafford sons. The four had climbed trees together, been schooled together, and wreaked general havoc together.

For all the afternoon teas, suppers, and dinners that Gavin had been a part of, Alex thought of him as a fourth brother, equal parts exasperating older sibling and wonderful protector. When, at the age of seven, she had climbed a tree in the back garden trying to emulate her brothers and become stuck in its branches, it was thirteen-year-old Gavin who had come to rescue her — talking her down to a low branch and convincing her to let go and trust him to catch her when she fell. Of course, once it was over, Gavin went back to teasing her; he had never let her forget that she "climbs trees like a girl."

To her surprise, she had missed him in the past few months, and the short time had changed him. She had seen him last in January, three months ago, at the funeral of his father, the late earl. The earl had died tragically from a fall from his horse on a rocky cliffside path on the Blackmoor estate in Essex. The entire *ton* had mourned the loss of Gavin's father — a wonderful, intelligent man who had been liked and admired by all.

Alex could remember watching Gavin at the funeral as he

stood with sadness in his eyes, strong and silent next to his devastated mother. She had wanted to go to him, to speak to him, but in the crush following the funeral and in the days thereafter, she'd been unable to find a moment to tell him how sorry she was for his loss — not that those words would have held much comfort for a son who had lost his father so unexpectedly.

Now, as she watched him speak with her brothers, she noted his thinner, more serious face, the deeper set of his tired eyes. She was happy he was out of official mourning, that he had joined them in London for the season, and that he seemed to be surviving the shift from unburdened heir to earl, complete with all the responsibilities that came with the title. Yet she couldn't help but wonder just how much of a toll the last few months had taken.

As though he sensed her thoughts, Gavin turned and met her gaze. Several seconds passed and he winked, as if to assure her that her worries were unnecessary. One side of his mouth raised in a lopsided smile, he turned back to her brothers, and Alex refocused on Ella and Vivi's conversation, pushing her questions to the back of her mind for the time being, and promising herself she'd find a moment alone with him later.

"I didn't find it nearly as interesting as *Pride and Prejudice*," Vivi was saying.

"Of course you didn't! I've never read *Pride and Prejudice*'s equal," said Ella, passionately. "But better or worse is really irrelevant, Vivi. What's most tragic about this book is that, even now, after publishing three wonderful books — each one easily as brilliant as anything written by a *man* — the author cannot reveal her true identity for fear of repercussions! It's inexcusable that, as a society, we would show such a devastating lack of progress."

"It is disconcerting. But it cannot go on forever," Vivi pointed out. "This particular 'Lady' has garnered too much celebrity to remain anonymous."

"One can only hope that's true," Ella said, turning to look at Alex. "What did you think of the book, Alex?"

Before she had a chance to answer, the conversation was interrupted by Will's loud and exaggerated groan of anguish from across the room. "We can't go to the theater that night. It's Scamp's coming-out at Almack's. Mother will have our heads if we're not there."

Hearing the odious nickname her brothers used for her, she stopped the girls' talking with a raised hand and looked over at the boys. "I'm in the room, Will, in case you'd forgotten. And trust me — I don't find the thought of an evening at Almack's any more entertaining than you do."

"Nonsense," interrupted Nick. "All girls love the idea of Almack's. They spend the majority of their early years envisioning exactly what their first evening there will be like. They go all starry-eyed about the ruddy place, imagining just who will be the first man to steal their hearts."

"Not these girls," piped in Ella.

"I, for one, have no interest at all in having my heart stolen," Alex interjected, ire rising.

Gavin leaned back in his chair and studied the trio of girls, taking note of Alex's rising temper. "To be honest, Nick, I'd be surprised to hear these three speaking of having their hearts stolen . . . with an attitude like this . . . I'm guessing this lot is much more interested in who will be the first *man* to have his heart stolen — they don't seem the wallflower type."

Alex exploded in irritation. "Why is it that men believe that all women care to think about is the trappings of romance and love? You really don't consider the possibility that there's anything more to us, do you?"

The boys looked at each other and turned to the girls with expressions that clearly articulated the answer to her question — rendering words unnecessary.

"Fools," Alex mumbled under her breath. "In actual fact, gentlemen, I think we'd all much prefer to steer clear of heart stealing of any kind, victim or perpetrator," Alex continued. "Of course, you lot wouldn't understand that. You're never going to be forced into dancing with some namby-pamby so your mothers can feel better about your marriage prospects."

Will snorted in laughter. "Spoken like someone who has never been to a ball with our mother. I promise you, Alex, as difficult as she can be with you, she's just as impossible with us. The duchess wants a wedding . . . any wedding will do."

Gavin joined in. "I second that. Last season our mothers aligned against me — I thought for sure I was done for. I danced scores of quadrilles with any number of desperate young ladies before I realized it would be smart for me to beg off attending balls altogether." His tone turned thoughtful. "I had planned on doing the same this year . . . but seeing Alex take London by storm just might be entertaining enough to drag me to a society gathering or two."

"Be careful what you ask for, Blackmoor," Nick interjected. "It is I who has been forced to play partner to her during her dancing lessons. She's not the most graceful of ladies."

"Nor the lightest. Mind your toes, chap." Kit, as usual, delivered his barb with an impish grin thrown in the direction of an increasingly irritated Alex.

With a chuckle, Will interjected, "Ah, well, as brothers, we can rest easy from the fate of Alex's clumsiness. We'll never have to dance with her again. Wednesday evening, she shall be loosed upon the men of London. I'm sure someone in the mix won't mind partnering her."

With an exasperated groan, Alex leveled her gaze at the men in the room. "Well, I console myself with this: No matter who I end up having to dance with, he can't be more boorish than you three oafs. Lord save your future wives."

A noisy truce fell upon the group, and the conversation turned to the upcoming season and the ever-present gossip that would be the talk of the *ton* in the coming weeks: who had eloped with whom while away from town for the winter;

which notorious rakes were on the hunt for wives this season; which balls were certain to be filled to the brim with the brightest stars of the town. As the conversation went on, Alex noticed that Gavin became more and more quiet, retreating into himself. She was not surprised when he stood to excuse himself and leave the house. No one took notice of the fact that she followed him out of the room.

In the wide hallway of Worthington House, Alex placed a hand on her friend's arm. Gaining his attention, she asked quietly, "Are you well, my lord?" He noticed the caution in her words.

Meeting her clear emerald gaze, the corner of his mouth lifted in a half smile. He reached out and tapped her chin with his finger — a brotherly gesture he'd been performing for most of her life — and said wryly, "No need to walk on eggshells, Minx. I'm fine." He redirected his gaze to some faraway point and continued, "It feels good to be back in London . . . away from Essex and all that comes with it." He returned his attention to her. "And with you about to have your first season" — his half smile turned into a rakish grin — "I wouldn't want to be anywhere else. . . . I'm eager for the fireworks to begin."

Alex didn't miss the change in topic. She shook her head as though rejecting the whole idea of a season and turned a sympathetic look on Gavin. "My lord . . . if you should ever need to talk . . . about anything . . . I am here. . . . I hope you know that."

Gavin's grin disappeared, replaced by firm lips set in a determined line. His next words came out in a manner that brooked no rebuttal. "Once again, I'm fine, Alex. Thank you for your offer, but I assure you that there's no need for it. Now, if you don't mind . . . I have an important meeting for which I really shouldn't be late."

With a short bow he was gone, leaving Alex with the distinct impression that she'd been summarily dismissed. And Alexandra Stafford did not like being dismissed.

four

He took a long drink of scotch and leaned back in his chair, staring into the distance. To an unsuspecting onlooker, the paper held carelessly in his hand would appear forgotten and unimportant. The exact opposite was true.

Scrawled across the parchment were two lines of text.

Young Blackmoor is out of mourning.
Find out what he knows.

His mind was swirling with possibilities, turning over the various next steps that lay before him. While the young earl had been prepared for his new station since birth, it was guaranteed that he hadn't expected to assume it so abruptly or so early in life. The odds that he'd been apprised of any information by his father were slim, but even slim odds left too much of a possibility for discovery. He could not risk discovery.

As it was, the death of the elder earl had set his French associates on edge. They had been very angry about his actions, and he'd had to work tirelessly to prove that he was a worthwhile partner. It continued to cost him dearly as he struggled to regain their trust.

He swore harshly under his breath. His first thought was to do away with the new earl altogether, but he recognized that this would bring investigation and suspicion down upon them all, especially if there was information hidden somewhere in Blackmoor House. The dead earl had been loathsome but never stupid. Whatever he had known, he would have documented. If that documentation were found, they would all be in danger.

To date, he had told his partners that he did not believe them in danger of discovery, but they were beginning to doubt him. He could see it in their eyes, hear it in their voices. He had to tread lightly. The only way to ensure his safety was to do as they commanded.

He must discover exactly how much the earl's brat knew about his father's life — and his father's death.

"Bloody fantastic that you've got this entire house to yourself, Blackmoor." Christopher Stafford leaned on his billiard cue and looked across the table. "Who needs a men's club when your closest friend has a place like this right next door?"

The new Earl of Blackmoor glanced around the room, taking in the rich oak paneling, the deep green of the billiard table, and the weathered leather chairs that established this room squarely in the domain of men. He'd inherited the room and the London townhouse along with his title but found little pleasure in the knowledge that he was the master of it. Before he could reply, a crack from the table signaled a successful shot. Nicholas, the middle Stafford son, straightened from sinking a ball in the side pocket and addressed his younger, less tactful brother. "Christ, Kit. It's not as though he won it in a game of chance. Have some care."

Kit's face flushed as he turned a chagrined expression on Blackmoor. "Sorry, old chap. I didn't mean to suggest . . ."

Blackmoor saved his friend from having to finish his apology, with a dry interruption. "No harm done, Kit — you've never been the most tactful in the family. I expect such from you periodically."

William chuckled at his brother's expense. "I'm just happy that he's skilled with numbers — gives him something to do besides talk himself into a corner. Do you have any port in this house?" The future Duke of Worthington redirected the conversation artfully, the way he had been trained to do since birth, easing the situation for both his friend and his brother.

Blackmoor gave a last glance at the billiard table, recognizing that Will was poised to win as usual, and turned toward a section of bookshelf. "Port is a capital idea. Right this way, gentlemen." Throwing a hidden switch, the Earl swung a section of wall back, revealing the room that had been the seat of the male Blackmoor line for generations. The study was enormous, occupying a rear corner of the townhouse, boasting two full walls of floor-to-ceiling windows that framed luxurious views of the property's perfectly manicured side and rear gardens.

As Nick and Kit burst into the room, Will and Gavin stopped just inside the door to the study. Turning a knowing look on his old friend, Will said quietly, "It just doesn't feel right, does it?"

Blackmoor's expression shuttered. "No. Although I haven't much choice but to adjust to it." He followed the younger Staffords into the study, his gaze falling on the enormous mahogany desk and the man seated behind it — who immediately stood and began organizing the papers he was reading.

"Uncle Lucian." Blackmoor looked in his direction and waved an arm indicating the others in the room. "I don't believe you have formally met my friends. May I introduce William Stafford, Marquess of Weston; Nicholas Stafford, Earl of Farrow; and Christopher Stafford, Baron Baxter? Gentlemen, my uncle, Captain Lucian Sewell."

In turn, the young men stepped forward to shake hands with the captain, who, seemingly eager to escape them, greeted them each with a quick "my lord," and addressed his nephew curtly. "I will leave the four of you in peace, Blackmoor. Shall we speak tomorrow about my discoveries relating to the estate?"

"Certainly, Uncle. Tomorrow it is." Blackmoor offered his uncle a warm smile. "Good evening. And thank you."

"Of course. Until tomorrow." And with a short bow to the Stafford boys, the older man took his leave.

Kit took a seat in a soft leather chair. "So that was Uncle Lucian? He seems rather solemn."

Blackmoor moved toward the sideboard to pour several glasses of port. "He's a quiet sort. My father always said he was proof that still waters run deep. Apparently, they were never very close while they were boys, but Lucian rushed to be with us as soon as he received word of . . . what happened."

Will nodded solemnly. "No matter the differences between them, brothers are brothers. I would have expected nothing less."

Blackmoor crossed the room and handed his friend a glass. "That sentiment was never more true than three months ago. It was a remarkable show of familial loyalty. At the time, I was quite surprised. I hadn't seen Lucian more than a handful of times since I was a child. As a captain in the Navy, he's been at sea and at war on the Continent during much of the past decade. I never would have expected him to drop everything and join us so quickly."

He gazed into his glass, watching the amber liquid swirl inside the heavy crystal. Shaking himself out of his contemplation, he continued, "But he has been a remarkable boon, considering. Whatever I might think about his personality — for, in all honesty, he's not the most engaging of characters — he has helped me a thousandfold in the past few months. As you know, I was less than ready to assume the duties of the earldom — it's nice to have someone around who knows the trappings of the estate so well."

Nick broke in. "Lucky, too. Considering he's been at war. What happened that brought him home? Was he injured?"

Blackmoor shook his head. "To my knowledge, no. I was at Oxford when he returned, so I was not privy to the circumstances of his leaving his post. I know that he was a hero at the Battle of Lyngor. Will would know more about it than I would, I suspect."

Nick asked, "Lyngor . . . wasn't that in Denmark?"

Will nodded at his younger brother. "Well remembered. I'm afraid I don't know much about your uncle at all, Blackmoor. I began my tenure at the War Office several months after that battle. What I do know is that Lyngor was particularly bloody and one-sided. The Danes were roundly defeated there and lost more than their fair share of men that day. They pulled out of the war immediately, leaving Napoleon with one less ally on the sea."

"Unfortunately, that hasn't seemed to stop Bonaparte from pressing on. It doesn't seem like this war is ever going to end." Kit spoke this time, referencing the French general's recent escape from forced exile and the rekindling of the two-decade-long war. He shot a pointed look at his eldest brother.

"You know I'm prohibited from speaking about it, Kit. All I can say is that British troops are the best trained and British intelligence is top-notch. We have set Napoleon back once . . . we will do so again."

"One might argue that Napoleon has bested us before, and he might do so again," the ever-logical Kit pointed out — deliberately provoking his brother's ire. "He's already escaped from exile and overthrown King Louis, all while picking up troops and supporters from every corner of France. It seems we're not doing an excellent job of 'setting him back.'"

"If I didn't know better . . ." William began, warning in his tone, but was interrupted by Nick, who, recognizing the beginning of a political argument that he'd heard hundreds of times before, quickly brought the conversation back to safe ground.

"Well, it appears that London society isn't nearly as concerned with Napoleon or impending war as they should be. This season is shaping up to be more elaborate than any in recent memory. Judging by the number of invitations I have already received, the mothers are out in full force . . . husband hunting before the season even begins." Leaning back in his chair, he looked up at the ceiling. "I, for one, am running out of excuses to avoid the odious events."

Kit, following his brother's deft change of conversation, said, "Mmmm. It doesn't help that Alex is coming out this year. I've already given up the idea that I'll be able to avoid Mother's nagging." His tone shifted from resigned to inspired. "I've got it! Let's get Alex married off as quickly as possible. That will make it easier for all of us!"

Nick spoke with dry humor, "I'm not sure it would make it easier for Alex."

Kit feigned disappointment. "Nor her husband, I suspect."

"I don't expect many men will be too thrilled at the prospect of courting Alex, to be honest, what with having us to contend with," Will said, then added, "I confess, the only thing I am looking forward to is terrifying her potential suitors."

Kit chuckled. "It's an additional benefit that, in terrifying them, we shall infuriate her."

The three laughed, each in turn realizing that Blackmoor was silent, lost in thought and removed from the conversation. One hand propped on the window sash, his view into the dark garden obscured by the candlelight reflected in the glass, the young earl was miles away from his friends, distanced from their world and their conversation.

As the laughter died away, the three brothers looked at each other, and William leaned forward in his chair, propping his elbows on his knees as he called his old friend's name. "Blackmoor?" A quiet question, no response. "Blackmoor." Firmer this time, still no response. "Gavin." The given name sliced through the room and hit its target.

Blackmoor spun toward his friends, expression clouded and dark, with a curt "What is it?"

In the silence that followed, Nick rose and headed over to the sideboard to pour another glass of port. "You were worlds away from us." He moved to the young earl, offering the glass. When Blackmoor took the drink, Nick folded his arms and leaned against the window sash, leveling his friend with a look. "'What is it' seems like something *we* should be asking, chap."

Blackmoor swore silently under his breath and turned back toward the window. "Apologies. I seem to find myself with a great deal on my mind this evening. It makes me rather a rotten host, I'm afraid."

"I was going to point that out myself, what with the remarkable billiard room and the exceptional port," Kit spoke wryly from his seat across the room. "You'll have to improve upon that if you're going to have any success as an earl."

In forced appreciation for his friend's teasing, one side of Blackmoor's mouth kicked up. "Well, that's part of the problem, you see . . . I wasn't supposed to become the earl just yet."

Will leaned back in his chair and let out a long exhale. "No, you weren't. It was insensitive of us not to recognize how difficult it must be for you to come to terms with all that has happened. We should apologize. Not you."

The new earl looked at his friends and said, "No. You couldn't have known that I received word this morning. . . ." He paused, then plunged ahead. "The constable in Essex, along with several high-ranking members of the War Office, has concluded that my father's death was accidental." He stalked across the room to the desk, lifted a piece of paper from where it lay, and read aloud quickly and without emotion. "*The earl was thrown by his horse, which, in the findings of this commission, most likely lost its footing in the rain. There is no indication of any foul play, and the commission finds that the death of Richard Sewell, sixth Earl of Blackmoor, was a tragic mistake borne sadly of inopportune time and location. The investigative team sends its sincere condolences to the late earl's family, particularly the Dowager Countess and Earl of Blackmoor.*"

Blackmoor's movements were tightly controlled as he returned the letter to the desk. "That last Earl of Blackmoor, one assumes, is I." He exhaled with what, in other circumstances, might have been described as the beginning of a laugh. "So that's that, I gather."

Nick, always the most sensitive of the Stafford sons, spoke cautiously. "Had you expected the findings to be different?"

Blackmoor met his friend's eyes with a dark look and then redirected his gaze to the ceiling as he leaned against the desk. "To be honest? I don't know what I had expected. My father was a master horseman. I was there the day he rode out onto the estate — I heard him tell my mother that he was going riding. I heard him explain that he was checking on the drainage system in the rain. I saw his face as he left the house. He was a man on a mission."

In the silence that followed, William spoke. "Your father was a great man. He took every part of his life seriously. I believe he would have considered even that small task a vital one."

"Of course, you're right, Will." Blackmoor looked down at his hands. "I suppose I just want to believe there was a reason for his death — something more important than a soggy pasture.

"There was simply no reason for my father to be on those cliffs, no reason for his horse to be spooked, no way that, even if the horse had scared, my father would have lost his seat. In all our years of knowing each other, have you ever known my father to take a fall from the saddle?" He looked at the others, all of whom shook their heads.

"This report," he said with quiet conviction, "is wrong. I can't prove it, but I know it."

He looked at the others in the room, each quiet, each waiting for another to speak first. He saw the shock in their faces, their concern, their uncertainty, and he checked himself. "Christ, this whole thing is taking its toll, isn't it?" With a deep breath, he crossed to the hidden door that led back to the billiard room. Tripping the switch to swing the door open, he turned back to his friends. "No more macabre conversation. Fancy another game?"

There was a deep pause, as the Staffords considered the impact of the scene that had just unfolded and their own next steps. Will stood first and broke the silence; recognizing Blackmoor's embarrassment and desire to end the awkward moment, he spoke with his trademark arrogance: "Certainly, if all of you don't mind being roundly trounced . . . again." Taking their cue, Nick and Kit groaned in mock disgust and, matching their older brother's grin, stood up to follow Blackmoor back to the billiard table — just as friends should.

five

This whole process is really quite ridiculous, isn't it?" Alex stepped from her scalding bath, receiving a large linen bath sheet from Eliza, who, seeing her charge wrapped in the dry cloth, wasted no time in guiding her to sit by the roaring fire on the other side of the room.

"Head down." Alex flipped her hair over toward the heat of the flames, and Eliza went to work combing the long auburn tresses free of snarls and knots as the fire dried the wet curls. "Ridiculous?" the maid queried.

"Quite," Alex said, her voice muffled by the curtain of her hair and the strange contortion of her body. "I mean, how long was I in that bath? An hour?"

"No' even a quarter of that," Eliza said, unable to keep the humor from her tone.

"Well, it felt like an hour," Alex said grumpily. "I feel as though every inch of my skin has been scrubbed off. And all for what?"

"For beauty," the maid spoke, focused entirely on her

task. "The Prince shall think you the most beautiful lady he's ever seen."

Alex replied wryly, "Let's hope that's not the case, Eliza. History teaches us that things never end well when royalty set their eyes on 'the most beautiful lady' they've ever seen. Have a care; if you perform your tasks too well, I could be haunting the Tower of London without a head, alongside Anne Boleyn." She looked up through her tresses at Eliza, eyes dancing with amusement the maid did not share — and received another shove, reminding her to keep her head down.

"Fine. For beauty, then," she continued, waving one arm, her tone rich with boredom. She stayed quiet for a few moments, allowing the scent of the lavender soap Eliza had used so forcefully to envelop her before picking up her head and continuing, "Am I nearly done?"

"Nay. Head down."

Alex sighed. "I *hate* this."

"Yer in a funk."

"I am *not* in a *funk*."

Eliza made a noncommittal sound and Alex lifted her head to look at the maid, only to have her hair tugged. "Ow!"

"That wouldn't 'ave happened if you'd kept your head down."

Alex snorted in disbelief but kept her head still. The truth was, she *was* in a funk. Eliza was right. Eliza was always right. Just three years older than Alex, Eliza had grown up alongside the Stafford children in the Essex countryside, the daughter of the cook and the stable master at Stafford Manor. While the difference in their stations was always clear, when the two girls were alone, they were as equal as they could be. From their earliest days together, the young maid had always had the uncanny ability to understand Alex's moods — often before Alex understood them herself.

"Why don't you tell me why you're in such an ill humor?" Eliza prodded, continuing to comb Alex's hair, which was drying quickly in the burning heat.

"I don't really know," Alex admitted. "I am rather dreading this day, this presentation, this . . . pomp and circumstance."

"Whatever for? It's your first day as a real lady. I've ne'er seen your mother so . . . well . . . she's proud as a peacock. I should think you'd be excited. Up."

Alex sat up and spun around on the little stool upon which she was perched, repositioning herself to dry the rest of her hair. Eliza kept combing the long tresses until they shone brightly.

Alex scoffed. "My first day as a real lady. What on earth does that mean? And my mother is excited because I'm one step closer to being married off."

"You know that is no' what she is thinking."

"Not consciously. But it is there. Lurking in the background. A smart match is the future she's always wanted for me. And today is the beginning of that future." She paused, stretching out her legs and leaning back into the heat of the fire. "If only I wanted it as much as my parents do."

"Perhaps tonight you'll meet someone who'll make you want it that much."

Alex rolled her eyes at the idea. "It's a night at Almack's, Eliza, not an enchanted ball. Let's not get too carried away."

"You never do know, luv."

"*I* know."

"Up."

"Finally!" Alex jumped up from the stool and paced across the floor of the bedchamber, happy to be freed from the tedious task of hair drying. "Now what?"

"Well" — Eliza tilted her head and looked thoughtfully at Alex — "I'm thinkin' it won't do for you to meet the Prince draped in damp linen."

Alex grinned broadly. "Likely not."

"Stockings." Eliza pointed to two pieces of silk that were hanging over the top of the dressing screen, and Alex moved to pull them on while the maid went searching in the wardrobe for the rest of the garments necessary for this, the "biggest day" of a young woman's life.

Just as Alex had finished tying her garters at the tops of her stockings, Eliza emerged, an enormous stack of white cotton and linen in her arms. Alex rolled her eyes again, saying aloud, "The things we are required to do in the name of fashion."

Eliza was not considered to be one of the best lady's maids in the history of the Stafford family for no good reason, however. She took little interest in Alex's distaste for the process of dressing and handed her mistress a set of drawers. Alex pulled them on, letting the linen towel go and turning to give Eliza access to the tapes and ribbons on the pantaloons so they could be fitted to her waist and hips.

As the maid worked, Alex spoke. "Tell me something fascinating." Eliza always had some terrific piece of gossip that she'd been saving up to share at just such a moment.

"Well, I do have something, but I don't know how reliable my sources are."

"Gossip from unreliable sources is *always* better than from reliable ones, Eliza," Alex said with a wide smile. "Go on." She leaned forward toward the pile of undergarments and pulled the wide-shouldered chemise over her head, letting it fall around her in a voluminous swath of fabric. This particular piece had little shape to it, and Alex was always rather amused by how thoroughly unfeminine a garment designed specifically for females could be.

Eliza set herself to arranging the chemise to Alex's figure, folding the fabric here, pinning it there, as she said, "Well, it seems that John Coachman is smitten."

"Really?" Alex had trouble envisioning her father's coachman, an immense giant of a man who rarely spoke to anyone but the horses, *smitten*. "With whom?"

"Margaret, the butcher's daughter."

"Truly?"

Eliza nodded, snatching up a stiff whalebone corset from

where it lay on Alex's bed. From a small box on the dressing table nearby, the maid selected a large corset needle, threading it expertly with a length of cord as she returned to Alex. "I must say, he does seem to be more willin' than usual to drive the kitchen maids down to the meat market."

Alex took hold of the corset, centering it on her torso and passing the sides back to Eliza, who deftly threaded the two halves together as they talked.

"And does she reciprocate?" Alex held the rigid stays to the natural curve of her waist, waiting patiently for Eliza to finish her task.

"I'm no' certain, but Mary, the kitchen maid . . . ?" Alex nodded in recognition. "She says that Margaret always has an extra sweet for John when he's there, and that she always asks about him when he's not. Hold on."

"Excellent! Love comforteth like sunshine after rain! Oof!" Alex reached out and grabbed hold of the bedpost as Eliza began tightening the corset laces.

"I told you to hold on." Eliza kept tugging, the stays growing tighter and tighter as both girls began to breathe heavily. "I thought you didn't believe in love."

"I never said that!" Alex exclaimed, her emphatic tone lost as she struggled for air. "Of course, I believe in love."

"Oh? Breathe."

She took one last deep breath, feeling the stays tighten to the point of pain, and couldn't help herself from swearing roundly. "Enough!"

"Finished." Eliza turned to retrieve the next layer of clothing. "I'm goin' to forget that you just cursed like a dockside sailor."

"Blame my brothers." Alex gasped for air, perching on the edge of the bed. "It's too tight."

"It will loosen. You know that."

She did know that. "I hate fashion." Alex scowled.

"Tell me about this new belief in love," Eliza said, distracting Alex and holding open a circle of petticoats. This piece was more elaborate than any of the others Alex had donned, a Madame Fernaud creation in cambric and linen with a stunning swath of beautiful green fabric affixed to the bottom, designed to match the dress Alex would wear that evening.

Alex paused to admire the delicate rosebuds that had been painstakingly added to the undergarment before allowing Eliza to throw the piece over her head. "Not new. It's not love I'm opposed to. It's marriage! The first reminds women that they're free to be as they wish — because someone loves them for it," Alex said, her voice coming from inside a mass of fabric as she pushed her way through the petticoats toward the light of the room. "And the other takes away that freedom."

Eliza began securing the top of the petticoat, tying a small row of bows that ran down the bodice of the garment. "Seems to me that the right kind of marriage could increase that freedom, nay?"

Alex tilted her head to one side, thinking on Eliza's point. "I suppose so . . . but how many of *those* have you ever witnessed?"

"Yer parents have one like that, I'm thinkin' . . . and yer grandparents before them." The maid moved to the bed and lifted the rich green ball gown, giving it one final shake to loosen the folds of satin fabric before holding it out for Alex.

"That's different," Alex replied, stepping into the dress and helping Eliza to pull it up over her arms to fit her now perfectly shaped torso. Holding the bodice straight while the maid fetched a buttonhook and began fastening the long row of buttons on the back of the gown, she continued, "My mother and grandmother were notorious beauties with brains to match. And my father and grandfather were men who were not afraid to take wives who equaled them in intellect. There aren't men like that outside the Stafford family."

Eliza snorted, "Of course, you would say that. Yer a Stafford. But truly, Alexandra, I just cannot imagine that in all of history there has only been one man in each generation willing to let his mate blossom." Her fingers flew across the buttons, expertly closing them.

Alex then sighed, waving a long arm. "Fine. However, my point is that there aren't *many* men like that. And I am simply not interested in taking the risk."

"Look here." Eliza waited for Alex to turn to face her, then smoothed out the lush green skirts of the gown. "Well,

Alexandra, you'll be taking a risk this evening, I daresay — because any young man who sees you in this dress shan't know what to do with himself. Yer just as much of a beauty with brains to match as the Stafford women who came before you." Eliza pointed to the dressing table nearby. "Sit."

Alex sighed again, knowing that she was in for another long stretch while Eliza tamed her long, auburn curls, piling them just so on top of her head and applying the finishing touches prior to her presentation to the Prince. Before she could follow the maid's instructions, however, Alex caught her reflection in the looking glass next to the wardrobe. She was unable to stop herself from gasping at what she saw.

There she stood, bathed in the golden sunlight that poured through the windows of her bedchamber, hair shining like silk, cheeks rosy from the heat of her bath and the exertion of dressing, in a dress that had been made for her in every way — the cut, the color, the fabric, all of it. For a brief moment, she couldn't believe her eyes; *she* was the beauty in the looking glass.

Like it or not, this night was one she would not soon forget.

The Duchess of Worthington placed an elegantly gloved hand on her daughter's knee and spoke quietly, "We have arrived."

In the dim light of the large carriage that muffled the sounds of the street beyond, Alex took hold of her mother's hand. She turned glittering green eyes on the older woman and offered an uncertain smile. "And so it begins."

"Indeed. You will be wonderful."

And, as if on cue, the door opened to reveal a livery-clad footman, and the duke climbed down from his seat across from them in the imposing black carriage emblazoned with the Worthington crest. Once on solid ground, he turned back to reach up and hand the duchess down from the transport; she gave Alex's hand a quick, reassuring squeeze before accepting her husband's assistance.

Then, it was Alex's turn. She scooted across the velvet-draped seat, focused on her father's smiling, pride-filled eyes, and took his hand. His grip was firm and steady as he helped her down to the street, and Alex was encouraged by it — no matter how she felt about this day, making her parents proud couldn't be such an awful thing, could it? When her feet touched the ground, she found herself assaulted by all the sights and sounds of the legendary Almack's.

The first thing that Alex registered was the noise. There was a cacophonous din of chatter, louder than anything she'd ever heard out of doors, which enveloped her immediately. She couldn't make out much of the conversation for the sheer amount of it — punctuated with bursts of laughter and shrieks of recognition from ladies and gentlemen of the *ton* who were all enjoying this . . . the first major event of the 1815 season.

The building itself was unimpressive — a simple stone structure that, at most times, provided little indication of being one of the most important locations in the life of London's high society. Alex had passed this place dozens of times before and had never given it a second thought. It appeared, however, that on Wednesday nights during the season, all that changed.

Looking back at the coach, Alex felt an intense desire to return to it, to clamber inside and swing the door shut behind her and simply wait there until her parents finished making their rounds. Instead, she stood tall, revealing none of her trepidation, and looked down the length of King Street, jammed with carriages and coaches all with a common goal — to deposit the most well-respected members of the *ton* on the steps of the Assembly Rooms, leaving them to an evening of seeing and being seen. Light from the scores of carriages flooded the sidewalks and steps to the building, lending a dazzling brightness to the moment, as if even the sun couldn't stay away from the beautiful people who filled the street.

Alex drew a shaky breath, feeling a knot of apprehension twist in her stomach. She hadn't fully realized until this moment how much she dreaded this, her first official night in society. That afternoon, she had been presented at Buckingham House to the Prince Regent, a charming older man with a reputed eye for the most beautiful women and the best parties in London. And, while the ceremony had been filled with all the pomp and circumstance befitting a visit to the Royal Court, it hadn't made Alex nearly as uncertain as she felt right now, surrounded by throngs of London's finest, all pushing madly toward the entrance to the assembly. After all, everyone knew it was really the Lady Patronesses of Almack's whose opinions were most valued in matters relating to society.

With a sigh, she turned back and caught her father's quick smile as he leaned down and proffered his arm. "Terrifying, isn't it?"

"Quite." She took the offered arm and matched his grin with one of her own. "How do you ever survive it?"

With a brief, almost imperceptible nod toward her mother, who had turned from her position just steps ahead to wait for them, he answered, "'Tis a duke's duty to make his duchess happy, moppet."

Alex's smile broadened at his answer. Her mother spoke quietly as they reached her, her voice traveling only far enough to be heard by the two of them. "To your right, Alexandra, is Lady Jersey." Alex turned her head to get a look at the petite, rather unattractive woman who was nicknamed The Queen of London for her position as the most discerning of Almack's patronesses, before her mother added in exasperation, "Do attempt to be discreet, Alexandra. Ladies do not stare."

Alex snapped her head back and offered a sheepish apology to her mother, then lowering her voice to a whisper and speaking close to the duchess's ear, "*That* woman turned away the Duke of Wellington?" referencing the legendary piece of gossip that would certainly afford Lady Sarah Jersey a place in the annals of London's aristocratic history. The Duke of Wellington — a war hero of the first water and a *duke* no less — had been set down by this wisp of a woman? Denied entry to Almack's? A place made famous by satin flounces and weak lemonade? What kind of rules was this society perpetuating?

"Indeed. He arrived wearing trousers instead of knee breeches."

Alex couldn't help rolling her eyes at the ridiculousness of such a perceived infraction. Her father noticed and spoke drily, "Never fear, moppet. My understanding is that Lady Jersey's lesson has served him well in battle. He wouldn't dream of meeting Napoleon in anything less than the most current of fashions."

"And thank goodness for that," Alex responded, her feigned seriousness drawing a bark of laughter from her father.

"I do wish you wouldn't encourage her," the duchess said to him, covering her obvious amusement with an exasperated sigh before turning back to her daughter. "Are you ready for your debut, Alexandra?"

"Do I have the option of saying no?" she asked, the hint of sarcasm in her voice drawing a quelling look from her mother.

"Not in the least. I've been waiting for this moment for far too long. You are going to . . ."

"Yes, yes. Set the *ton* on its ear." Alex interrupted, taking a deep breath and shoring up her confidence. It was time, whether she liked it or not. "Well, then. I rather think we should get started, don't you?"

"What a crush!"

Alex took hold of Ella's hand and pulled her friend into an alcove off the main ballroom of Almack's, away from the mass of London's nobility. "And people do this every week?" Making sure they were tucked away behind a significantly sized potted fern, Alex leaned against a marble column. "I'm never coming here again if I can help it."

Ella chuckled and leaned close to her friend with an impish gleam in her eye. *"And now I am at Almack's, the more fool I; when I was at home, I was in a better place!"*

Laughing at her friend's rendition of a line from her favorite Shakespearean play, Alex then completed it. *"But travelers must be content!* Oh . . . what I wouldn't give to be in a forest far away from titles of any kind!" She lowered her voice to a conspiratorial whisper. "If I am cornered by Lord Waring one more time, I shall have to feign sickness. I may counterfeit a swoon to avoid having to speak to him again!"

"I shall keep my smelling salts at the ready." Ella peeked through the plant to be certain no one was listening to them. "I noticed him mincing after you. Your mother must have been happy to see it. He is, after all, a marquess."

"Indeed. The Marquess of Excruciating Dullness. Lord 'Waring' is right. He's wearing on my patience."

The girls laughed a touch too loudly, checked themselves, and grinned. Ella spoke. "You shall see us both into a grip of trouble if you keep on like that, Alex. What will our mothers say if we are discovered laughing too loudly! And mere hours after being presented to the Prince Regent!"

"I thought I heard you two laughing!" Vivi poked her head around the plant. "I was wondering where you were hiding." Taking note of the nook, she tilted her head in approval. She tucked herself into the small space and gave a mock appraisal. "Very nice. Quite spacious!"

"There is still more room than out there," Alex said with an unladylike cock of her head. "Is it getting any better?"

"Not remotely. But it's just eleven, which means no one else can enter — so that's something." Vivi peered through the leaves of the palm, scanning the room. "Why anyone would look forward to an evening at Almack's is beyond me. I've had my toes stepped on twice, the Dowager Duchess of Lockwood poked me with her walking stick — on purpose — and I narrowly avoided a lemonade mishap at the hands of Lord Waring." She sighed and looked back at her friends. "You don't appear to have been doing much better!"

Resuming her overview of the ballroom, Vivi took note of a tall, handsome young man and lifted an eyebrow at Alex. "However, I did happen to see you laughing with Lord Stanhope during a quadrille. Is there something you would like to tell your dearest friends?"

Alex shook her head. "I'm afraid nothing of note. I've known Freddie for years. He and Will were at school together. He was just being kind and making certain that I had my dance card filled." She peered over her friend's shoulder through the plant to see the object of their conversation offer one of the grande dames of the *ton* a glass of lemonade, with a bold grin. "He is charming, though." She paused. "And fun."

"And quite attractive," Ella chimed in.

Alex turned to her friends. "And an inveterate rake."

Vivi nodded. "Truer words were never spoken." The young Earl of Stanhope's reputation preceded him. "But if anyone's safe with Stanhope, it's you, Alex. Your brothers would have his head if he overstepped his bounds."

"Speaking of . . ." Ella was peering through the fern, "Your brothers have arrived. All of them." Laughter edged into her voice. "And they're being swarmed."

"Really?" Alex turned and joined Ella at her lookout post. And there they were, all three of her brothers surrounded by a gaggle of cloying mothers and decorated daughters, all clamoring for an introduction.

Nick, ever the gentleman, was doing his best to appear interested. Kit was looking terrified, eyes darting this way and that, obviously desperate to escape. It was Will, however, who caused a giggle to escape Alex. As the future duke, he was surrounded on all sides by eager females. But the eldest Stafford wasn't the young star of the War Office for nothing. Alex could see him working out a strategy for retreat even as he was *enchantée*-ing his way through the crowd. Within seconds, he had backed up to another gentleman, deftly shifted the attention from himself to his unsuspecting mark, and moved away toward their mother, who was waving him over.

"Remarkable," Alex whispered. It was a tactical disengagement that would have made Wellington proud. Taking a moment to admire her brother's skill at dealing with the *ton*, Alex made a mental note to ask him for a tutorial when next she saw him. Redirecting her gaze to the mass of femininity he had escaped, Alex waited for Will's replacement to turn his face toward her. She wondered who could so easily capture the attentions originally directed at an heir to a dukedom — or was Will just that skilled with such evasive maneuvers? Whoever it was stood at the same height as Nick and Kit, towering above the women around him. The way he was positioned made him impossible to recognize, but Alex couldn't help but notice his broad shoulders and blond hair falling attractively over the collar of his waistcoat.

Alex checked herself. *Since when did hair fall attractively?* Irritated with herself for noting something so inane, she turned away from her spying to resume her conversation with Ella and Vivi, who were consulting their dance cards.

"Are you ready to reenter the fray?" She asked a touch too quickly — hoping that her friends wouldn't notice.

The girls agreed it was time to come out of hiding, for fear someone might find their spot and ruin it for future nights. As casually as possible, Vivi exited the alcove, followed by Ella, with Alex bringing up the rear.

The madness began immediately.

"Lady Vivian! I thought perhaps you had left! I was nigh perishing at the thought." Vivi was virtually accosted by the eldest, and one would hope most dramatic, son of Viscount Sudberry.

Ella found herself instantly distracted by Lord Sumner. "My dear Lady Eleanor, I have been searching for you everywhere. Never say you haven't a free dance on your card?"

"Lady Alexandra! I believe this is my dance!" Alex turned toward the nasal voice and, hiding her grimace, pasted a bright smile on her face. "Why, Lord Waring, I believe you are right." Turning back to her friends, she mouthed, *Rescue me!* Vivi leaned in close and whispered, "Meet us on the other side of the room after the cotillion." With no time to respond, Alex was escorted to the dance floor.

For the next few minutes, she gave special thanks to her maker that country dances were the rage in London this year — the cotillion involved multiple sets of paired partners, so she was able to, for the most part, avoid tedious conversation with Lord Waring. When, at the end of the dance, he suggested that they take a turn about the ballroom, she swallowed a quick *NO!* and instead replied, "That sounds lovely. However, I find that I am quite parched. Would you mind terribly escorting me to the refreshment rooms?"

Instead, eager to please, Waring offered to take her

directly to Ella and Vivi, who had somehow escaped their suitors and were deep in conversation on the sidelines of the ballroom. From there, he insisted, he would fetch her lemonade — and anything else she required — for fear she would find herself too parched from the walk all the way to the refreshments. Recognizing a boon when she saw one, Alex swallowed her snide response to his theory that an additional ten feet of walking would put her out of commission for the evening. Graciously accepting Lord Waring's offer, Alex refocused her attention on her friends and the man with whom they were conversing.

It was the same man she had noticed through the potted fern. He still had his back to her, but she was getting to know that side of him quite well. His shoulders were broader still than they had seemed when she was spying on him. They were certainly a defining characteristic, and she noted with appreciation the way his tailor had fitted his black jacket to them like a second skin. Taking in the cut of the garment drew her attention back to his hair, which she realized was a more golden shade of blond than she had first thought.

She mentally shook herself, growing irritated with her own idiocy. She'd spent most of her life around men and, from the looks of him, this one was no different from her brothers in age or station. Why was she being so silly? Who was he, anyway? How did he know Vivi and Ella?

As Alex and Waring drew closer, Vivi saw them and turned a brilliant smile in their direction. Taking his cue from

Vivi's distraction, the man turned and Alex skipped a step in surprise. She lost her grip on Waring's sleeve and, in an attempt to save herself from a devastatingly embarrassing moment of clumsiness, instead caught herself on the arm of the golden-haired, broad-shouldered object of her interest. Looking up through her lashes, she met his gaze — eyes she knew as well as her own — which just happened to be laughing down at her.

"Blackmoor." The name came out on a shocked *whoosh* of breath. *Blackmoor? Truly?* Blackmoor was the man she'd been noticing? Surely that couldn't be right. Could it? Looking up into his grey eyes, Alex could feel heat flooding her face. She pressed a cool, gloved hand to her face, willing the blush away. She *never* blushed. *What had gotten into her?* She pasted a smile on her face and looked at the others in the group. Vivi was attempting to manage a serene smile despite her clear desire to laugh, and Ella was looking at Alex with an odd expression, as though she were some creature to be studied in a laboratory.

Attempting to regain her composure, she looked up at Blackmoor and spoke, her voice sounding foreign even to her. "Lord Blackmoor. Good evening."

"Lady Alexandra, as always, the evening is made more entertaining by your arrival." He made certain that she was upright and stable before removing his arm. "Waring." He nodded in greeting to his old acquaintance.

"Good evening, Blackmoor, Lady Vivian, Lady Eleanor. You'll have to excuse me. If Lady Alexandra is well enough for me to leave, I have promised to fetch her some lemonade. May I bring some for you as well?"

Vivi responded, "In fact, Lord Waring, Lady Eleanor and I were about to take a turn about the room. We shall join you as far as the refreshment rooms, that is, if you can suffer our company."

Ever impressed with her friend's grace and tact, Alex watched, a trifle dumbfounded, as Vivi wove her tale for Lord Waring — ensuring that he could not refuse to walk with her and Ella without appearing the most boorish type of man. Of course, presented with Vivi in all her gentle graciousness, Alex would wager that Waring would forget *her* within moments of departing with his new charges. Vivi's skill at reshaping men's desires was uncanny, but Alex was too grateful for her friend's intervention with Waring to question it more than in passing. Instead, she simply offered a silent prayer of thanks for Lady Vivian Markwell and her unwavering talent.

So caught up in her friend's deftness, Alex forgot that she had been unceremoniously left with Blackmoor. *Almost* forgot, that is. Out of the corner of her eye, she saw him take a breath; he was about to speak. She steeled herself for what she was certain would be a teasing remark about her clumsiness and attempted a look of polite disinterest in preparation for his comment.

"Would you care to dance, Alex?"

Polite interest switched to confusion. That was not what she had been expecting. Before she could find words to respond, Blackmoor had led her onto the dance floor and wrapped her up in his arms for her first waltz of the evening. Her first waltz ever with a man who was not her brother. They were twirling across the room when she finally found her tongue.

"I would, indeed, care to dance, Lord Blackmoor," she said wryly. "How kind of you to ask. Would you like to see my dance card?"

Ignoring her sarcasm, he deftly avoided another couple and spun her out of their way. "You can't have expected me to let your first ball go by without dancing with you, Alex. Considering your obvious attempt to escape Waring, it seemed there was no time like the present. Don't you think?"

"I fail to see that I had much of a choice, frankly," she said with a smile. "But I suppose it could have been much worse."

"Oh? How?"

"You could have stepped on my gown — Waring did it twice."

He gazed down at her attire, letting a few moments go by before he spoke, his voice quieter, more thoughtful than usual. "Criminal. 'Tis a stunning gown."

Even Alex couldn't ignore the way his appreciative comment made her feel. Tempering the urge to preen, she smiled up at him. "Why, thank you, my lord. I'm rather fond of it myself."

He cleared his throat almost inaudibly and said, "You look beautiful, Alex. All grown up." Blackmoor's grey eyes darkened, narrowing on the garment in question, then rising to meet her gaze. The look in his eyes was one she'd never seen before, and it sent a tremor of excitement through her as she felt heat rising in her cheeks again.

He looked away, then back again, and the emotion she had seen there was gone, so quickly that she couldn't be certain it was ever there to begin with. She forced a smile, attempting to bring the conversation back to the realm of the comfortable. "Thank you, my lord."

"If I may speak frankly?"

"Certainly."

"I know you want to try out all your lessons, but take care with whom you test your skills. I noticed how Stanhope was looking at you earlier."

"Lord Stanhope was a charming partner." Alex met Blackmoor's eyes, daring him to disagree. "I'm certain I don't know to what you are referring."

"I think you know all too well to what I'm referring. Any man would have to be blind not to notice you. This dress is designed to lure a lion. I assure you that particular lion will bite."

"What are you saying?"

"Simply that I would prefer not to have to play protector tonight. I merely caution you to think twice before getting wrapped up with Stanhope, or any like him."

Alex's spine stiffened in response. Her tone turned frosty. "As usual, my lord, your caution — or shall I say interference? — is unnecessary. Need I remind you that I've been managing Freddie Stanhope since he was in short pants?"

His chuckle held no humor. "Take my advice, Alex. Your 'Freddie' is no longer in the schoolroom. And you're out of your league if you think you can, as you say, 'manage' him. Just because you wear a gown that marks you as all grown up doesn't mean you are prepared to take him on."

Alex's temper flared. "I require neither your advice, nor your opinion, my lord. I would thank you to remember that, besides the fact that you're not that much older than I am, I already have a father — and three brothers. I hardly need another overbearing male telling me what to do and with whom to do it."

"More like what *not* to do. And with whom *not* to do it."

She inhaled in a sharp intake of air, eyes narrowing, and made a move to leave him mid-waltz. To an outside observer, nothing changed about their movements — but Alex felt Blackmoor's arms turn to stone around her. He held her fast, and tight, and his voice lowered. "You will finish this waltz with me, Alexandra. I will not allow you the pleasure of giving me a set-down at your first ball."

Recognizing how damaging leaving him on the dance floor would have been to his reputation, not to mention her own, Alex remained in his arms, thoughts reeling. Why was she responding to him so strangely tonight? Ordinarily, she would have laughed off his concern. Clearly something was amiss. After all, hadn't she noticed the cut of his waistcoat, the width of his shoulders? In seventeen years, she had never noticed anything special about Gavin. And yet, even now, through her irritation and her anger, she was acutely aware of his hand on the small of her back, the heat of his gloved palm through the silk of her gown, the feel of his fingers resting against hers. What was wrong with her?

Alex looked up at him, searching his gaze for a hint of what he was really thinking. He was usually so unflappable, so calm, and yet — he had been tight with anger at the thought that Stanhope might have been interested in her. Was it possible he was experiencing the same mix of bizarre feelings that she was tonight? Could it be that he, too, had felt the tremor of emotion pass between them? Now his grey eyes were unreadable behind a mask of civility.

"I don't know what to say." She spoke quietly. "The excitement of the evening seems to have addled my brain a bit."

His gaze softened. "I shouldn't have taken such liberties. You are, of course, right. I am neither your father nor your brother. Let's not think of it again."

There was something about his comment that left Alex feeling even more unsettled. They'd always been as close as siblings; was he pulling away? She shook herself mentally. This new world was already turning her into a cabbagehead, and she'd only been a part of it for an evening. "That," she said, pushing her disquiet to the back of her mind, "sounds like an excellent idea."

He smiled and took a deep breath. "I forget, sometimes, that you aren't that little girl stuck up in a tree, Minx. It's hard not to jump in to save you whenever I think I should."

There was a pause before Alex could think of a retort. "Well, don't go shirking your duties as savior altogether." Her smile turned into a knowing grin. "After all . . . who else will save me from eager suitors with leaden feet?"

The couples around them turned to look as he laughed — entirely too loudly.

six

After the waltz, Blackmoor and Alex joined a waiting Vivi, Ella, and Will at the far end of the ballroom. The orchestra had paused in its performance, and Alex took a moment to drink in the sights and sounds of the ballroom — the experience of her first event of the season. The room was lit with thousands of candles placed in chandeliers high above the crowd of people. No one seemed bothered by the hot wax that dripped from the light fixtures; they were far too dazzled by the glorious satins and silks in every imaginable color that were illuminated around the room.

The roar of chatter was deafening — it made conversation nigh impossible if one wasn't within inches of one's partner — but over the crowd, Alex could pick out some unique sounds: Ella and Vivi's laughing chatter with Blackmoor and Will, the rustle of skirts as a gaggle of other young women brushed past her, the deep rumbling voices of a nearby group of men talking about a foxhunt planned for the coming week's end. Alex watched the hundreds of men and women making their way across the ballroom to the refreshment room and back again, stopping every few feet to speak to old acquaintances or to make new ones.

Tonight, London society was at its best: the women, dressed in gowns that could feed dozens of London's less fortunate, ready for another four months of gossip and jockeying for position; the men eager for another season to begin, keeping the women entertained and out of their orbit for a time. Alex was acutely aware of the elaborate game that played out around her as she surveyed the scene. In London, it really was about whom you were seen speaking with, especially at Almack's, and tonight offered a new set of chances to those with less title and less money to raise their own visibility by being spied in conversation with the most powerful members of the *ton*.

She shook her head, amazed at the arbitrary rules of the game as she watched the odious Duchess of Barrington, whose opinion — thanks to a very smart marriage match — mattered above most others in this world, regard a group of eager young hopefuls with devastating disinterest. With her searing ennui, the duchess was in stark relief to Alex's own parents, just as powerful in this room, who she noticed were graciously accepting the acquaintance of a young woman who certainly hadn't met a duke and duchess before tonight. The girl, Alex's age, blushed prettily and fell into a deep curtsy as the Duchess of Worthington spoke, and Alex smiled with pride as her mother introduced the newcomer to Nick, who, ever the gentleman, responded to the introduction with elegant ease.

It just goes to show, she thought to herself, throwing an

unnoticed glare in the direction of the Duchess of Barrington, *a title guarantees neither grace nor charm.*

Her reverie was cut short by the arrival of Penelope Grayson. Penelope's father, the Marquess of Haverford, was an old acquaintance of the Duke of Worthington, and the girls had spent much of their youth together as victims of that timeless parental blunder — the theory that, if adults enjoyed one another's company, their children must certainly do the same. And so she had been thrust into nurseries with Penelope for the duration of their joint childhood, forced to suffer her whining demands, her vapid dissertations on fashion and beauty, and her rather tiresome tendency toward bullying.

Alex could have forgotten all of Penelope's youthful transgressions if the other girl hadn't grown into a stunningly beautiful and spoiled woman, who never saw fit to alter her nasty habits. Alex sighed and exchanged a look with Vivi, who offered a generous smile in Penelope's direction. "Penelope! How lovely to see you."

Lady Penelope didn't spare a glance in Vivi's direction. She knew what, or rather *whom,* she was after, and she didn't waste time.

"Lord Blackmoor." Her voice was rich and smooth like caramel syrup. "I was afraid I might miss you in the crush, and I would have been devastated to miss our dance."

One of Alex's eyebrows kicked up at Penelope's blatant forwardness. She met Ella's eyes with surprise before returning her attention to the scene unfolding before them.

Blackmoor had taken Penelope's boldness in stride and, as the orchestra was beginning a new song, he extended his arm to his partner. "Lady Penelope, it would be my pleasure to partner you through the next quadrille. Shall we?"

And with that, they were off, into the throngs of revelers, leaving Alex speechless, staring after them. Almost speechless, that is. "Did you see that?!"

Vivi looked after Blackmoor and Penelope. "I will confess, she did seem a trifle presumptuous. And rather rude also. Was it me? Or did she completely ignore us?"

Ella spoke up: "'Twasn't you. She did, indeed, ignore us. But, in all honesty, Penelope has never cared much for us. I like to believe it's because our conversation is much too intellectual for her taste."

Alex snorted in a truly unladylike manner. "That's definitely it. But she's found her match in Blackmoor! Look at him! He's positively thrilled that she threw herself at him!" She watched as the couple in question spun away into the crowd, Blackmoor smiling down at some quip from Penelope. Rolling her eyes in disgust, she turned back to her friends.

"I really don't think anyone can blame us for wanting no part of the marriage mart if *she* is already the belle of the ball," Ella said. "My mother even had the audacity to ask me earlier if I didn't think I should have a gown made like hers! Lord deliver me from the London season!"

Vivi smiled. "It is enough to make one wish one could hide behind a potted fern for the entire evening, isn't it?"

Will cut in here, reminding the girls that he was with them. "I suppose I could deign to save at least one of you from another tedious dance partner. Lady Vivian? Shall we?" He held out a gloved hand to Vivi.

Smiling up at him in surprise at his use of her formal title, Vivi took his hand, teasing, "With pleasure, my lord. You will endeavor to keep me from dozing off, won't you?"

Will feigned solemnity. "I will try my hardest, my lady. Should you slumber, it shall be entirely my fault."

Ella and Alex laughed as the two disappeared into the dance. The girls chatted happily as they took a turn around the room, until they stumbled upon their fathers, deep in conversation with a man whom they had never met.

The Duke of Worthington noticed the girls weaving toward them and made the introductions. "My daughter, Alexandra, and Lady Eleanor Redburn, Lady Eleanor, may I introduce the Baron Montgrave?"

Alex followed Ella into a deep curtsy as the Frenchman bowed to them both with a charming, "*Enchantée*. It is always a treat for an old man to meet such beautiful young ladies."

Ella spoke first to the charismatic older man as he placed a kiss on her knuckles. "I am honored to meet you, my lord. May I ask how you came to be with us in London this season?"

"A stroke of very good luck, of course," the baron replied with a twinkle in his warm brown eyes. He continued in the glow of the girls' encouraging smiles, "The London season is as close as I dare get to Paris and its grandeur, my ladies. It has been many years since I have had a chance to enjoy myself at leisure. It is time for me to reemerge into the world I have so long missed."

Alex and Ella shared a knowing glance. It was clear that the baron was one of the many French nobles who had escaped France years earlier during the Revolution. With Napoleon imprisoned one year earlier on the island of Elba, off the coast of Italy, those escapees who had dispersed throughout England had begun reemerging in London, attempting to rebuild their lives in their new country as part of the *ton*. The baron, Alex and Ella had silently concluded, was one of these displaced nobles — an important one as well, if Alex's father was publicly chaperoning him into society.

Ella spoke again. "Certainly, my lord, we are happy that you have joined us . . . even more so in light of Bonaparte's recent escape and his deposition of King Louis."

Alex chimed in, "Absolutely. The knave may be rallying support across France, but he must not be allowed to continue to influence the lives of those he has already so terribly impacted."

Ella added, "Though I'm not certain that support is what he's rallying, what with instituting a draft and calling two million Frenchmen to war."

Alex nodded in agreement. "True. But with Wellington in charge, and so many nations banding together against Bonaparte's army, I feel confident that the rogue will meet his match soon enough." Turning back to the baron, she continued seamlessly, "Suffice to say that you are well met, my lord."

The frank political speech left the baron unable to conceal his surprise at the girls' impassioned patriotism and impressive knowledge of current events.

The Duke of Worthington, accustomed to his daughter, her friends, and their intellectual pursuits, interjected, "As you can see, Baron Montgrave, these particular young ladies tend toward an uncommonly more expansive view of the world than one might imagine at first glance." His words were laced with pride, and Alex gave thanks that it was one of their fathers who overheard the conversation — which would have sent either of their mothers into a swoon.

"A remarkable quality, to be sure," spoke the baron. "More young ladies could take their cues from you both!"

Alex said under her breath to her friend, "Perhaps the baron would consider providing lessons to the other gentlemen of the *ton*?"

The comment, followed by an irrepressible chuckle from Ella, was less private than Alex had intended, and the duke's eyes narrowed at his youngest child. "Alexandra, I feel certain that I don't need to speak with your mother about your candidness. Endeavor to keep me certain."

"Yes, Father." Alex recognized the gleam of pride deep in her father's green gaze and, despite his stern demeanor, knew she wasn't in too much trouble. She did know, however, that she should attempt to keep herself out of trouble with the duke and passed a quick glance to Ella, letting her friend know they should remove themselves from this particular conversation.

In unison, the girls dropped into deep curtsies and wished the baron adieu. The two clasped arms and skirted the edge of the packed ballroom, deciding to try to find Vivi again in the crush.

"What a fascinating character the baron is," Ella spoke hurriedly, in a distracted manner that Alex knew all too well.

"You're already putting him in your book, aren't you?" Alex teased. "Desperate for one of your journals?"

"Oh," Ella scoffed, "and you would rather be here, searching the crowd for someone . . . anyone . . . you enjoy the company of, rather than being at home doing something you love?"

Alex cocked her head and smiled at her friend. "Point taken." She scanned the crowd again. "I don't see Vivi anywhere . . . nor Will . . . there are too many people in this room to make anyone out in the crush." She turned toward the dance floor and strained to find Will's dark head over the tops of the now waltzing revelers. "You don't think they danced two in a row, do you?"

Ella shook her head. "No . . . Vivi wouldn't risk gossip like that, what with it being our first time out. . . ." She trailed off and Alex turned to her, curious to see what had stopped her train of thought. Ella's eyes were on a particular couple in the crowd, it seemed.

"What are you looking at? Or, rather, *whom* are you looking at?" She followed Ella's gaze, but twirling bodies blocked her view.

"It seems that Penelope doesn't consider two in a row a problem," Ella spoke so only Alex could hear. "She and Blackmoor are still dancing . . . and she looks like the cat that got the cream."

As if on cue, Alex's line of vision cleared, and she saw the couple in question. There was Gavin, holding the gorgeous Penelope in his arms. Their graceful movements only enhanced their image as a stunning couple: he, tall and golden-haired, she, petite and fair. Watching them, she could almost forget that Penelope was supremely unpleasant. *Could Gavin forget that, too?* Alex's brow creased as she considered that Penelope was likely an expert at Proper Conversation *and* Subtlety of the Dance. *He couldn't possibly think her a worthy candidate for courting, could he?*

". . . he *is* an earl." Alex was shaken from her thoughts by the end of Ella's statement.

"I beg your pardon?" Alex fibbed, "With the chatter and the music, I didn't hear."

"I said, no wonder she looks so proud of herself . . . he *is* an earl after all . . . and two dances this soon after his exiting mourning, newly titled . . ." She trailed off again.

She didn't have to finish her sentence. Alex understood perfectly. The gossips of the *ton* were likely already chattering about this; a newly minted earl and the daughter of a marquess dancing two dances in a row made for the most exciting kind of speculation — the kind that involved marriage.

"Of course, she *is* odious." Ella added, "Blackmoor must realize that . . . mustn't he?"

Alex turned away from the object of their conversation as other couples obscured her view once more, and spoke quietly, "One can only hope so."

Ignoring the unfamiliar gnawing that had begun in the pit of her stomach, she smiled a too-bright smile at her friend. "Lemonade?"

seven

No . . ."

Alex whined and pulled the coverlet up over her head, burrowing deeper into the warm cocoon of blankets and pillows to escape the brilliant sunlight that streamed into her bedchamber. "Eliza . . . I'm sleeping. Pull the curtains and go away . . . please?"

"That might work were it solely Eliza, Alexandra. But she brought reinforcements . . . and as your mother, I insist you rise. You're wasting the day away."

Alex pulled the covers down and opened one eye to peer above the fabric. She could see her mother standing in the sunlight, regarding the gardens below with a critical eye. Recognizing the expression on the duchess's face, she groaned and pushed the covers back, sitting up in bed. "Oh, no. You're going to assign me a task."

The duchess turned to face her daughter. "A task, indeed. But a task I think you'll find intriguing."

Alex cast a quizzical look at her mother and waited. A

smile broke across the duchess's face. "Dress. Then meet me to break your fast in the morning room."

Alex watched skeptically as her mother swept gracefully from the room without offering a single hint of what she wanted. For a brief moment, Alex considered ignoring the edict and going right back to sleep, but her curiosity — and her hunger — got the best of her. With an exaggerated sigh, she rose.

By the time she entered the morning room to meet her mother three quarters of an hour later, Alex's hunger had overcome all other emotions. She burst through the doors, already moving toward the sideboard where the morning meal had been set. She was several paces into the room before she became aware of her surroundings and slowed to a halt.

There were flowers. Everywhere. In every shade and shape imaginable, blossoms covered tabletops and bookshelves. There were posies perched on the duchess's writing desk, vases balanced on plant stands, and even three bouquets that had been placed on the marble floor in front of the room's fireplace. Turning in a slow circle, Alex took in the room before settling her gaze on the duchess, who, despite being seated as regally as any queen, was smiling quite foolishly.

"Good Lord," Alex spoke in amazement.

"Language, Alexandra. Ladies do not use that phrase. Your father and brothers have had too much influence on you."

"Mother, admit it's appropriate in this situation. You've cleaned out every hothouse in Britain!"

"Not I, daughter." The duchess did not move from her seat. "They. Every one of these blooms arrived with a card from a suitor."

Alex's eyebrows shot up. "Suitors of whom?"

"You know quite well that you took London by storm last night. Just as I expected you would."

A rumbling sound erupted from Alex's stomach and she was reminded of her hunger. Ignoring the smug expression that had taken over her mother's visage, she moved toward the sideboard and filled a plate with pastries and freshly sliced fruit while she took a deep breath and considered her next course of action.

"Mother, I cannot imagine what I could possibly have done to encourage the attentions of even a fraction of these 'suitors.' In fact, I went out of my way to avoid encouraging them."

She picked up a calling card from the blossoms that had been precariously perched between the breakfast trays and read the message. "Viscount St. John? He's got the intelligence of a goat. If this is an indication of the kind of suitors I've got simpering after me, it speaks to a significant problem with my perceived quality."

"Alexandra, there are some forty bouquets in this room alone, and I've had several posies sent to the upstairs parlor because of space constraints here. I feel confident that there are several notes from gentlemen who are not dull-witted." The duchess held up a stack of cards, which she had obviously collected prior to Alex's arrival. When she began to read them aloud, Alex collapsed onto a chaise nearby and grazed on her breakfast while commenting on the senders in question.

"Lord Denton. He's very well appointed, and a marquess."

"And doesn't fail to mention both the money and the title at any opportunity."

"Arrogance isn't a terrible trait in a male, Alexandra."

"It is when the male in question is a crashing bore as well."

The duchess sighed and flipped to a new card. "Simon, Lord St. Marks."

"Mother, I will not be matched with someone who is a half a foot shorter than me."

Another sigh from the duchess. "Lord Wentworth. He's first in line for a dukedom."

"So is Will; I wouldn't marry him either."

"What about me? Good God. Is it a funeral?" Alex was saved from her mother's quelling look by the arrival of Will, whose dry question earned *him* the irritated glance.

Alex popped a strawberry into her mouth and chewed thoroughly before speaking. "No, although that might be preferable to what it actually is." She spread her arms and indicated the flowers throughout the room. "These" — she paused for theatrical emphasis — "are all from my adoring fans. It seems I'm quite the rage."

"Well, there's no accounting for taste, Scamp." Humor laced Will's tone.

Alex threw her older brother a scowl and would have held it to increase the drama of the moment had she not been interrupted by the arrival of Lord Blackmoor. While most of London would have agreed that it was highly improper to pay a house visit before noon, Gavin was more family than guest, and his entry garnered no surprise. Smiling at the duchess and bowing low over her hand, he remarked wryly, "Well, it's a good thing I didn't arrive with flowers — they would have tipped this room's décor into the realm of the excessive."

The duchess returned his smile as Will and Alex laughed aloud. "Your presence is ever so much more a treat, my lord," Her Grace said, "although I will venture a guess that you're here for breakfast more than you are for a glimpse at Lady Alexandra."

Gavin went to the sideboard and began filling a plate for himself. "Indeed, it seems that the rest of London's male population has courting Alex well in hand, and so I find that breakfast is what's left to me." He cast a sidelong grin at Alex, who was sifting idly through calling cards, pretending not to be moved by his teasing.

And, in truth, it wasn't his teasing that did move her. That, she was used to. Instead, she was reminded of the previous evening and the whirlwind of confused emotions she had felt around him, Gavin, with whom this kind of verbal sparring was the status quo. By the light of day, she realized, the graceful, looming, discomfiting male was gone, and left was her old friend. His hair was still damp from his morning ablutions and, despite his impeccable waistcoat and breeches and the perfect knot in his cravat, he was back to being his relaxed and casual self.

It seemed that last night was an aberration and all those peculiar thoughts she had had were simply that — peculiar. And past. Thank goodness.

Returning from the food, plate in hand, Gavin paused just behind the chaise where Alex was ensconced. Looking over her shoulder at the cards in her hands, he spoke. "Of course, Lord Douglass sent you an invitation to ride this afternoon. He's up to his eyelids in gambling debt. You're not seriously considering accepting, are you?"

The manner in which he spoke, laced with superiority, crawled up Alex's spine, making her want to defy him even though she was well aware of the Viscount Douglass's shortcomings. Tamping the fiery response that sprang to her tongue, she offered a graceful shrug and flipped to the next card.

Blackmoor gave a snort of laughter. "Crane? He's an imbecile. You'd have him for breakfast."

Alex cast him a sidelong glance and remarked coolly, "Lord Blackmoor, I hadn't realized that you had taken such an interest in my suitors."

"I'm simply pointing out that all these flowers are for naught if the likes of Crane and Douglass are your options. There must be some men worthy of consideration in the group, no?"

As Alex opened her mouth to respond, she was interrupted by the duchess. "I must speak with Cook about the menu for the evening meal. Alexandra, you have at least fifteen invitations to ride along the Serpentine this afternoon. I expect you to accept one of them before I return."

At his sister's groan, Will laughed. "I wish I could stay and watch your torment, Alex, but I must be off to the War Office." Turning to Blackmoor, he offered a lopsided grin. "I assume you'll at least stay until you've finished breakfast? Keep track of anything worthy of teasing for me, will you?"

Blackmoor settled back into a nearby settee and extended his legs in front of him, crossing his ankles casually. "Indeed." Turning a friendly look on Alex, he offered, "Who is next on this unfathomably impressive list of marriageable males?"

Recognizing his sarcasm, Alex rolled her eyes in irritation. "Mother . . . don't leave me with him."

"Actually, I believe that Lord Blackmoor might be the perfect person to help you sort through these offers, Alexandra. He knows enough about the eligible men of the *ton* to be able to separate the scoundrels from the gems." Meeting the young man's eye, the duchess nodded in approval and offered a parting comment as she left the room with Will: "I shall approve the decision upon my return."

Left alone in the room with Gavin, Alex let out a sigh. "I fear I won't be able to find a way out of this. How did this even happen? I went out of my way to avoid attracting suitors last night."

Leaning back in his chair, Gavin leveled Alex with a serious look. "You've learned your first lesson, Minx. Men chase that which seems unattainable."

"No. What I learned was that men are gluttons for punishment. Why 'chase' me when they could catch any number of eligible young females from last evening?"

"Silly girl . . . because chasing you makes for more of a challenge — and more of a reward."

Alex offered an amused snort. "I assure you, my lord. Considering my feelings about being 'caught,' I would provide little, if any, reward."

While his body remained relaxed, his eyes narrowed on her and his voice deepened as he responded, "On the contrary, Alex. Your resistance to marriage would make the reward of successfully courting you that much sweeter. Turning your desire for spinsterhood into a desire for something else would be quite a coup for any man. Which is why all of these men" — he indicated the room with a lazy wave of his hand — "have thrown their hats in the ring."

Feeling slightly unnerved by Blackmoor's words, Alex stood and moved to the sideboard to pour herself a cup of tea. With her back to him, she spoke. "Surely not all men feel that way. After all, Penelope Grayson made her . . . availability . . .

rather plainly known last night, and you didn't seem to shy away from it."

"No, I didn't." The response was unapologetic.

"And I suppose you sent flowers to her house this morning, just as all these men did to me?"

"Actually, I didn't. But if I had, I can't see that it would matter. Why are you so interested, Alex?"

She turned from the sideboard, stirring her tea. "I find I'm rather fascinated by the whole ordeal, to be frank. Who knew one night at a ball could wreak such romantic havoc on so many men at one time?" Settling herself back on the settee, she resumed reading the stack of cards and invitations that had arrived that morning.

"Lord Fairfax thinks that my hair is the color of the eastern sky at dawn."

"Lord Fairfax is your father's age."

"Granted, but it's a flattering sentiment." At his harrumph, she continued, "Oh, my. The Marquess of Jonesborough requests I join him for a ride in his phaeton this afternoon; only he fears that my beauty will blind his horses." The end of the sentence was swallowed by Alex's own disbelieving giggle. "Surely he can't think I would take that seriously."

"Considering how seriously Jonesborough takes himself, I can't imagine how he would think otherwise."

Shuffling through several more cards quickly, Alex rolled her eyes to the ceiling and groaned, "What am I going to do? I actually must go riding with one of these dolts!" Leveling him with a glance, she queried with a sparkle in her eye, "You don't write such tripe to the women you hope to interest, do you?"

"I should hope not," he responded indignantly. "Good God, I have much more originality. These men clearly aren't thinking about how best they can interest you."

"What does that mean?"

"Quite simply, you're not the type to be wooed with poetry or false compliments."

"I'm not?" Now she was interested. "But I like poetry."

His reply brooked no rebuttal. "No, you don't. Not like this. They haven't got it right at all."

"Enlighten me, Lord Blackmoor, how should I be *wooed,* as you put it? I am intrigued by your obvious expertise."

He was quick to respond, "You're too vibrant for them. Too strong. You have a sharp mind and an exciting personality and an unexpected sense of humor. If these men were half the man you deserve, they would have already recognized all those things and they would be romancing you accordingly. They would be working to intrigue and amuse and inspire you — just as you do them. And they would know that only when they have won your mind will they even have a chance at winning your heart."

The room felt much warmer all of a sudden, and Alex resisted the urge to fan herself, trying to ignore the rapid increase in her pulse as color flooded her cheeks. In the silence that followed his impassioned speech, Gavin stood and walked over to her. A cocky grin spread across his face. "That's how I write to the women I hope to interest, Alex."

She attempted a cool response. "Perhaps . . ." Her voice caught and she cleared her throat, beginning anew. "Perhaps you should consider holding classes. I am acquainted with quite a few men who could do with some training. More than forty of them, it seems. Lord save me."

He chuckled as he removed the pile of calling cards from her hand and set them on a nearby table. Offering her a hand, he pulled her up to stand in front of him. "There's only one way to save you from them today."

"Oh?" The single syllable was all she could manage. Had he always been this broad? This tall? Had his eyes always been such a dark, smoky grey?

"Come riding with me."

eight

Alex sat tall in the high, two-seated carriage, one hand keeping her bonnet from flying off as the fleet-footed team of horses trotted down Park Lane toward Hyde Park. She smiled up at Blackmoor from underneath the wide-brimmed hat, green eyes flashing. "I certainly prefer riding with you, my lord."

"I thought you might."

"May I drive?"

"You think I'd consider handing over the reins of this remarkable equipage?" He replied with feigned superiority. For generations, the Earls of Blackmoor had prided themselves on having the most current and impressive modes of transportation. The most recent earl was no different, and the brand-new curricle in which they were riding was certain to be the envy of many.

"Indeed. I think you'd enjoy the experience of teaching me how."

"I've had this curricle for less than a week, Alex. You're not driving."

Alex replied with a comic pout, "I shall convince you otherwise, my lord. I warn you."

"Indeed? Well you are welcome to try, my lady."

He flashed a broad grin at her and called to his team as they turned into the park, offering a quick "Hold on!" to Alex. The carriage tilted slightly, and she grabbed the seat beneath her, yelping as they slowed to a crawl, waiting to take a place in the mass of people walking and riding along the Serpentine that afternoon. Turning a lazy smile on her, he inquired, "All right?"

"Fine, now that I'm not in danger of toppling out of the curricle!" She cast him a sidelong glance and caught his snicker. "You meant to terrify me!"

"Never!" he defended himself, the portrait of innocence. "I suggested you hold on, did I not?"

Exasperated, she rolled her eyes, turning to look around them. The ride along Rotten Row in Hyde Park at this, *the fashionable hour,* was one of the most revered traditions in London aristocracy. It was a chance to see and be seen, to display one's position in society, and, more than anything else, to witness — and perpetuate — the latest gossip of the *ton*. The path was packed with members of the *beau monde,* in open-air carriages, on horseback, walking along the sandy path, men with their walking sticks, women with their silk bonnets and pale linen parasols. Alex smiled brightly at the Countess of Shrewsbury, as the older woman tipped her head and reached out a hand to greet her.

"Lady Alexandra, Lord Blackmoor," the countess said politely as Blackmoor tipped his hat. "'Tis a fine afternoon for a ride, is it not?"

"Oh, indeed, my lady," Alex replied, "and such a pleasure to find you here!" She lowered her voice, adding in a near-whisper, "I wasn't sure what I would discover!"

The countess, ever the portrait of propriety, replied with all decorum, "I'm certain Blackmoor will protect you from anything overly unusual, my dear."

Alex looked at her companion and tilted her head, pretending to consider the statement before turning back to the countess. "I suppose he'll have to do."

The cheek of the statement in such a public locale surprised the older woman, who met Blackmoor's laughing eyes and shook her head slightly and spoke with disdain, "Young people . . . so different from the way we were in my day."

Alex immediately dipped her head in chagrin. "I beg your pardon, my lady."

The countess nodded curtly in farewell to both of them and moved off to greet the next acquaintance she found on the path, leaving Alex to turn a concerned look on Blackmoor. "Well, that came off rather poorly, it seems."

Blackmoor tried to hide his humor, somewhat unsuccessfully. "You shouldn't allow her opinion to dictate your behavior."

Alex winced. "Lady Shrewsbury is not incorrect. I should endeavor to be more ladylike and less . . . well . . . not. More like her."

"Lady Shrewsbury" — he said the name as if he had just received a whiff of a not altogether pleasant scent — "has always been the portrait of stiffness and staidness. You should endeavor to be nothing like her."

"Her opinion about my . . . candor . . . is shared by many of our parents' set."

"Nonsense," he said, tipping his hat to the Marquess of Houghton, who was riding alongside the eldest daughter of Viscount Grosvenor. "Your candidness is charming and not at all off-putting. Our parents' friends adore you. You are . . . lively."

"Lively." Alex tested the word on her tongue. "That makes me sound like an unpredictable racing horse." A broad grin spread across Blackmoor's face and Alex resisted the urge to hit him. That *would* have been unpredictable. "Do you think me horselike, my lord?"

Realizing the threat to his personage, Blackmoor wiped the smile from his face and replied, "Not at all. I said I think you charming."

"A fine start."

"And I appreciate your exuberance." His eyes glittered with barely contained laughter.

"Like that of a child." Hers sparkled with irritation.

"And, of course, you are entertaining."

"Excellent. Like the aforementioned child's toy."

He couldn't hide a chuckle. "Not at all. You are a far better companion than any of the toys I had as a child."

"Oh, I am most flattered."

"You should be. I had some tremendous toys."

Eyes wide, she turned on him, catching his laughing gaze. "Oh! You are incorrigible! Between you and my brothers, it's no wonder I can't manage to be more of a delicate flower!"

Blackmoor stopped in the midst of acknowledging the Viscountess of Hawksmore, who, accompanied by her enormous black poodle, walked past. He turned back to Alex and answered with one eyebrow raised, "I beg your pardon? A delicate flower?"

Alex sat back in the curricle, quoting in a singsong voice, *"A young lady should be as a delicate flower; a fragile bud, with care, will blossom by the hour."*

Blackmoor's eyes widened. "Where on earth did you hear that rubbish?"

"My governess."

"I do not traditionally speak ill of women, but your governess is a cabbagehead." Alex laughed as Blackmoor continued in horror, "What a ridiculous sentiment. No one could actually take it seriously. It *rhymes,* for goodness sake."

She leaned out to take the hand of Lady Redding, greeting her as she rode past on a magnificent grey. Turning back to Blackmoor, she said, "Of course, it rhymes. It's supposed to be easily remembered."

"It should be forgotten. Promptly."

"Oh, and I imagine you're going to tell me that it is incorrect? That men don't want wives whom they can mold into the bloom of their choice? That we are not merely bulbs to be gardened by our husbands?"

"The flower metaphor is insulting in any number of ways. Primarily to our intelligence. I beg you to cease using it."

"Fine. But the point remains. Men refuse to consider the possibility that women have their own opinions, their own character. And women . . . well, we are as much to blame. We allow you to believe that we simply wait to be guided by your superior intellect and sense of right. You saw the letters I received this morning, Blackmoor. They want me because I am rich. Or perhaps because I am young. Or attractive enough. But do you truly believe that those men will continue to court me when they see that I joke and tease with my brothers? When they find that I am far more at home in the stables than in the sewing room? When they discover that I read the newspaper and enjoy discussing politics?"

"I think that if they don't want all those things, you're better off without them."

Alex rolled her eyes. "That's not the issue. I'm better off without the lot of you. Perhaps I would consider being married to someone who didn't mind all my 'unladylike' qualities . . . but I'm safe from the institution either way. The fact is, no man wants a woman who is his intellectual equal."

"Your generalizations wound me," he said wryly as he tipped his hat to the Duke of Nottingham, who raised his walking stick in response.

"They shouldn't. You can't be expected to feel differently from the rest of your sex."

"I most certainly feel differently."

Alex snorted in disbelief.

"You do not think me honest?"

"I think you believe that you are being honest. It's simply that I saw you last night."

"Last night?"

"Indeed. Penelope Grayson captured your interest. You've admitted as much. And I can only imagine she did it by being a delicate flower. Because I have serious doubts about her being your intellectual equal."

The words came flooding out of her mouth before she had thought about just how insulting they would be, to both Penelope and to Gavin. Feeling color flood her cheeks, she bit the inside of her cheek, not knowing how to escape from the mess she had so effortlessly created. Instead, she sat quietly, waiting for him to speak, periodically lifting one gloved hand in greeting to one of the hundreds of people who seemed, suddenly, to be crowding around them.

It really wasn't her business, how Blackmoor felt about Penelope. *So why did the idea that he enjoyed her company bother her so very much?* She pushed the niggling voice to the back of her mind and tried to convince herself that her outburst was only borne of concerned friendship. After all, she didn't want Blackmoor making a decision he could very well regret.

She was his friend. She was concerned. Hence, concerned friendship.

She wished he would say something.

The statement had been offensive, certainly. Well, more toward Penelope than to Blackmoor. She hadn't questioned *his* intelligence. *No, I simply questioned the intelligence of the woman he was courting.* She started at the thought. He wasn't *courting* her, was he? He couldn't be. If he were, he wouldn't have had the time to take Alex riding today. He certainly wouldn't have taken her here, to Rotten Row, where they were certain to be seen by anyone and everyone. Of course, no one here would actually believe that she and Blackmoor were a couple. She didn't even have a chaperone with her, for goodness sake. It was clear that they were more like siblings than anything else. All the more reason for her to have expressed her distaste for Penelope. *Quite.* She'd done the right thing. Even if it smarted a bit.

How was it that men could remain so stoically quiet when they wanted?

She stole a glance at him out of the corner of her eye. He was focused on the traffic around them, his jaw set firmly as he wielded the reins of the pair of lovely tan geldings pulling along the curricle. Gone was the teasing humor that had characterized their afternoon. He was not happy, this much was clear. What remained to be seen was just how unhappy he was.

The silence was chipping away at her sanity. Truly.

And then, just when she thought he would never speak, he did.

"You do Penelope a discredit."

Of all the things he could have said, this was not the one she had wanted to hear. Guilt began to gnaw at her. "I beg your pardon?"

"You have not witnessed my interactions with Penelope. You have no grasp of her intellect and no understanding of our conversations. Have you?"

"I —" He held up a hand to stop her from speaking.

"Nay, Alexandra. No excuses. Have you any understanding of my relationship with Penelope?"

"No."

"Indeed. You have judged it — and her, I might add — wrongly. Were she here, you would owe her an apology."

Alex flushed, embarrassed, and blinked back the tears that had sprung to her eyes in response to his scolding. He was impassioned and filled with intense affront — all for Penelope's honor. She had no doubt that, were she anyone else, he would have delivered a scathing set-down. Instead, his tone revealed not anger with her opinions but disappointment in her voicing them. All at once, she was aware of his position, not as her friend but as a well-bred gentleman, defending a woman's honor. And, for a fleeting moment, she couldn't help but envy Penelope just a little. *How would it feel to have Blackmoor defend her?*

"That said," he pressed on, deliberately ignoring her embarrassment, "you are right about most men. We are, of course, initially drawn to the immediate. To beauty, wealth, youth, what have you. Each of us has our own weakness. But without the rest — the intelligence, the wit, the humor — our attraction is short-lived. At least, mine is. And I am not alone. Of that I am certain."

He had moved past her criticism of Penelope deftly, without allowing for discussion, arguing his side of the debate with cool reason, conceding where necessary, and concluding with an unflappable, quiet certainty.

It was as though her insult had never been uttered. Of course, it had been, and she was going to have to apologize. She grimaced at the thought. She *hated* apologizing. She took a deep breath. "My apologies. I never meant to imply that Penelope's intellect was inferior."

He smiled, reaching out to tap her on her chin, "Of course you did, Minx. However, I appreciate that it has never been easy for you to apologize, and so I will accept this one without argument." She blushed, chastised, as his eyes narrowed on a point over her shoulder. "Besides, I am not overly fond of certain members of *your* legion of suitors."

Confused, Alex turned her head to follow his gaze and broke into a broad smile when she saw Lord Stanhope seated high on a beautiful black gelding riding next to the carriage. Stanhope tipped his hat and offered a greeting. "Lord Blackmoor, this is a stunning curricle. I should like one just like it for myself!" Turning to Alex, his voice dropped. "And you are doubly lucky — for you have found the only companion worthy of such transport. Lady Alexandra, as ever, it is a pleasure to see you." He allowed himself a lazy perusal of her attire before continuing, "You are particularly lovely this afternoon . . . that color only makes you more beautiful."

Alex looked down at the dark blue riding habit she had donned for her outing, appreciating the rich texture of the fabric and the deep color against her bright skin, and she smiled warmly into Stanhope's glittering brown eyes. Taking in the cut of his dark coat, the perfect knot in his cravat, the tilt of his gleaming black hat, she replied, "Why, thank you, my lord. And you look rather dashing yourself!"

He leaned over with a conspiratorial, flirty whisper: "I took extra care in preparing for this outing, Lady Alexandra. One never knows when one might run into a lady of extraordinary beauty."

She laughed at his bald statement and replied with a shake of her head, "You're incorrigible!"

He joined her in her laughter and turned his attention to Blackmoor. "Your companion seems to think I'm rather more than incorrigible, my lady."

"Indeed," agreed Blackmoor, darkly, "it's not the first word I would use to describe you, Stanhope."

"Come now," Stanhope teased, "you've always enjoyed my exploits in the past, old chap." He turned back to Alex with a wide smile. "After all, what's wrong with a little bit of flirting between friends?"

Alex cut in before Blackmoor could speak, "There's

nothing at all wrong with it, Freddie. It's my fault that Blackmoor is in such an ill humor. I'm afraid I've landed him there."

Stanhope responded with feigned shock, "Surely not! You couldn't possibly bring ill humor. Shall I tell you why?"

"Please do!" Alex was beginning to really enjoy herself.

Stanhope leaned close. "Too pretty."

Blackmoor rolled his eyes in obvious irritation as Alex's laugh tinkled around them. "Stanhope, don't you have somewhere else to be? Perhaps someone else to ply with your charm and wit?"

His rudeness was undeniable, and Alex felt compelled to speak. "I rather enjoy Lord Stanhope's charm and wit. I find it quite refreshing, honestly."

Stanhope's face broke into a devastatingly handsome grin. "Well said, my lady. However, Lord Blackmoor did win your company this afternoon, and I should hate to take any more of your attention. That said, may I have your permission to call on you on Sunday for a similar excursion?" Reaching for her hand and waggling his eyebrows, he added, "I shall endeavor to be all propriety."

She couldn't control the giggle that escaped her at his silliness and she placed her hand in his, watching as he effortlessly bowed over it despite their awkward positions. "I should like that very much, my lord. Sunday it is."

Stanhope's "Capital" was lost as Blackmoor urged the curricle forward and Alex's hand was wrenched from the other man's grasp. She leaned out the side of the carriage to wave good-bye to her friend, then turned back to her companion. "That wasn't very nice. Freddie didn't even get a chance to say his farewells."

"Didn't he? I thought he did that while quite improperly asking you to spend Sunday afternoon with him *while* you were in the company of another gentleman."

"For goodness sake, Blackmoor, I don't know why it bothers you so much. After all, it's not as though you and I are *actually* on an outing."

He turned a surprised look on her and waved a hand to indicate their surroundings. "No? How is this not an outing?"

"You know very well what I mean. Certainly we are on an outing. But not in the way that most of these other couples are 'on an outing.' There, look there." She pointed to a couple walking toward them on the other side of the Row, the eldest son of the Marquess of Budleigh and the youngest daughter of the Earl of Exeter. The young woman was looking at her companion with a look of starry-eyed adoration, and he appeared to be returning her attentions. "They are courting and, to look at them, they might well be the first match of the season. A good one, too," she added, distracted for a moment by the twosome.

He spoke, shaking her from her reverie. "How does this relate to Stanhope's impropriety?"

"There was nothing improper about Stanhope's behavior, and you know it. You and I look nothing like those two. And everyone who sees us — especially Stanhope, who has been friends with us both for years — knows we're just out for a ride. Not *out* for *a ride.*"

He looked at her, shaking his head in confusion. "Women truly are strange and unknowable creatures."

She smiled at him, color high on her cheeks. "Indeed. But your kind would not like us quite so much if we were all transparency."

After a few moments of thought, he nodded. "That much is true, Alex. That much is true." They rode along in silence for a few minutes before he pressed, "So, are you . . . intrigued . . . by Stanhope?"

"Intrigued by him?"

"Indeed. Do you find him . . ." he paused.

"Intriguing?" she teased.

He sent her an exasperated look.

"Lord Stanhope is a good friend and an even better companion. He is entertaining and interesting and intelligent and full of energy. I can think of few others with whom I would like to spend an afternoon. However, you know my opinion of marriage and all of its trappings. I'm not interested in it. Not with Freddie, nor with anyone else. And he knows that as well as anyone, I should think."

"I rather imagine that he's not looking for marriage either," Blackmoor replied drily.

"What does that mean?"

"Simply that men like Stanhope are not the marrying kind. At the risk of repeating our conversation from last night and engaging in an additional verbal battle, I caution you. I know Stanhope. He's rarely after something respectable. Which leaves your good reputation in the balance."

"I shan't repeat our argument, Blackmoor. I will simply remind you that Stanhope and I are friends. We have been for years. Just as you have been, I might remind you. Yes, he's a rake. Yes, he prides himself on his dastardly reputation. But you and I both know that he's more bark than bite, and that he is approximately as likely as you are to do damage to either me or my character." Her tone turned teasing. "If you're allowed to defend Penelope's honor, do I not deserve the same chance to defend Freddie?"

The noncommittal grunt he released was the closest he would come to admitting that Alex was right in this case, but when she heard it she knew she had won. For now.

Allowing a few moments to pass, she turned and asked impishly, "Tell me, my lord, in all seriousness, when will I get a chance to drive this gig?"

He laughed before responding, "In all seriousness, my lady, not any time in the near future."

nine

"Your mother allowed you to forgo an outing that would have brought you closer to marriage to go riding with Blackmoor?" Ella's eyes were enormous in their amazement.

One side of Alex's mouth turned up. "Indeed. When she asked me who I'd chosen, Gavin stepped in and convinced her it was all for the best because we would see a number of the men in question on our ride, and I could make 'an informed decision by the light of day as to who I would consider a potential husband.' She agreed without protest. It really was quite marvelous. What about you two? How did you fare on the morning after?" Alex looked from Ella to Vivi as they walked across Hyde Park meadow searching for the perfect spot to picnic in the midday sun.

Vivi spoke first. "I received callers all afternoon, which was as uninspiring as one would imagine, considering that both of my aunts swooped in to chaperone the entire event." Alex and Ella groaned in sympathy as Vivi went on. "Individually, they're tolerable, but as a pair, they're completely insufferable. They simpered over every eligible male who entered the house with a complete disregard for personality or motive. It appears all they're hoping for is a heartbeat. I've never been happier to see my father as I was when he came home and ended the whole fiasco."

"So you didn't receive a visit from The One, I'm guessing?" Ella asked drily.

Vivi laughed and shook her head. "I certainly hope not!" Pointing to a sunny rise in the meadow nearby, perfectly situated under an enormous oak, she suggested, "I think that looks like the perfect spot for a picnic."

Alex agreed, "And it's in a line of sight to the entrance to the park, which means Nick and Kit will find us easily."

The girls continued chatting happily as two footmen spread a large square of linen on the warm green grass and set stakes at its corners to anchor it in the spring breeze. One set a large wicker basket that he had carried from the carriage on the edge of the square, stood, and spoke. "My ladies, your picnic is ready."

Vivi turned with a smile. "Thank you, George. And you, John. This is lovely. There's no need for you to stand on ceremony . . . please, enjoy this wonderful day." With short bows to the girls, the two footmen moved several yards off to join the girls' ladies' maids, who were acting as chaperones for the afternoon. The servants opened a second basket of food and began their own afternoon luncheon.

The girls had just settled down and started unpacking the picnic basket when they heard a loud noise from across the meadow and saw Nick and Kit running toward them with no regard for decorum. Alex shook her head, watching them. "Boys. A shilling says that Nick challenged Kit to a race."

Ella looked up from her task and grinned. "Kit will win, as always."

"And Nick will pout, as always." Vivi looked out across the meadow in the direction from which the boys had come. "It looks like someone else came with them . . ." She squinted in the sunlight to make out the figure. "Is that Lord Stanhope?"

Alex shielded her eyes in the midmorning sun and attempted to make out the features on the young man in the distance. "It certainly is Stanhope. . . . I had better be careful," she said, her tone laced with sarcasm. "Blackmoor thinks I'm in danger of spending too much time with him."

Ella settled onto the blanket and smoothed her skirts before beginning to unpack the luncheon from the basket. "Yet another double standard. Rakes are too dangerous as companions to women, but when there are other men nearby, they're perfectly acceptable . . . as long as they have a title."

Vivi looked at her friend thoughtfully. "I think perhaps Stanhope is a rake willing to be reformed."

"If you're suggesting what I think you're suggesting" — Alex stared wide-eyed at her friend — "your brain is obviously addled."

"Think what you will." Vivi smiled smugly. "I wager I'll be proven right before the afternoon is through."

A smart retort was left on the tip of Alex's tongue as Kit flew up the rise and nearly crashed into the massive oak. Turning quickly, he leaned back against the tree with his arms crossed and made a show of looking bored as Nick tore up behind him.

"Oh, Nick, you're here at last. We were just wondering what had happened to you."

Nick glared at his brother while he caught his breath. "I'll get you next time — I didn't eat much of a breakfast today."

"Is that your excuse for all the other times you've lost to him in a footrace?" Alex said teasingly. "Really, Nick . . . I should think you'd have learned your lesson by now. He's faster than you."

Kit smirked at his brother. "See? Even our baby sister knows it."

Taking a glass of lemonade from Ella, Alex continued, "However, given the choice between speed and intelligence, I'd say you made away with the better part of that deal." Everyone laughed at Kit's narrowed eyes and, with a smile, Alex extended a plate of roasted quail to him as a peace offering.

"Did you bring Lord Stanhope with you?" asked Alex. "Or is it coincidence that he's heading in this direction?"

Nick shook his head. "Stanhope called on us this morning at Worthington House. After some conversation, he decided to join us."

Vivi looked straight at Alex and queried innocently, "Oh? He just stopped by Worthington House this morning? By chance?" Alex shot her friend a quelling look. Vivi popped a grape in her mouth and smiled around it. After swallowing, she continued, not looking away from her friend, "How interesting."

Stanhope heard the tail end of the conversation and spoke as he climbed the last few feet of the rise to the picnic blanket. "I hope you don't mind my intrusion, my ladies." Bowing low, he granted the girls one of his trademark lopsided grins, letting his gaze linger on Alex. "When I heard such a trio would be here, I couldn't resist tagging along."

"By all means, Lord Stanhope, there is plenty to be shared, including this lovely spot." Ella spoke from her perch on the corner of the blanket. She had extracted her journal and begun sketching the scenery that lay before them.

"Indeed." The tenor of Stanhope's voice deepened and he winked exaggeratedly at Alex, who couldn't contain her laughter at his obvious flirting. In return, he offered her another broad grin, and seated himself on the blanket, leaning back against the trunk of the oak and accepting an oat cake from a basket proffered by Vivi, who was struggling to keep her smug look unnoticed.

Alex rolled her eyes at her friend and turned so that Vivi wasn't in her direct line of sight. "Lord Stanhope, I seem to recall Will saying that you have a talent for art. Is that still the case?"

Stanhope shook his head. "To be honest, Lady Stafford,

it's been years since I've had a hand in artistry of any kind. I'm sorry to disappoint." Redirecting his gaze to Ella, he continued, "But Lady Eleanor, I see that you are quite the accomplished artist. Would you be willing to show us the contents of your sketchbook?"

Ella looked up from her work, appearing not a little like a doe caught unawares by a hunter. After clearing her throat daintily, something that her friends knew she did to gain time to think of a proper response, she seemed to realize that Stanhope was not the type of person to take no for an answer. Add to that Nick's encouraging, "Lady Eleanor is too modest — she has a remarkable eye for charcoal drawings," and she knew she couldn't escape.

Flipping to the front of her sketchbook, Ella quickly turned the pages, past landscapes and still life drawings, saying, "It's all quite boring, actually. . . ."

When she reached a page in the book that held a stunning portrait of Alex, Stanhope spoke quietly, "That's not at all boring." Vivi coughed into her hand; Alex shot her an exasperated glance.

"May I?" He reached for the sketchbook, which Ella turned over reluctantly.

Looking down at the drawing, Stanhope spoke, his voice thick with appreciation. "It's a remarkable likeness, Lady Eleanor. You've captured movement and life here — something that is virtually impossible for most who try their hand at being artists." Smiling at Ella, he continued, "Now I understand why I rarely see you without paper and pencil."

He continued to flip through the sketchbook, pointing out places where Ella had drawn a perfect line, or shaded a figure just so. The two were soon deep in conversation about Ella's art, and his compliments were so heartfelt that Alex had no doubt that Freddie Stanhope was far less of a rake than he let on.

Even Nick and Kit were distracted from their discussion of the new curricle that had just passed the group; they appeared slightly dumbfounded at the earnestness of their friend. Alex couldn't resist saying, "You see? It wouldn't hurt the two of you to take some interest in something other than horses, hunting, and cards. Perhaps you should consider taking up a pursuit or two which are slightly more cultured?"

Vivi spoke up, laughing at Alex, "At the risk of betraying our friendship, Alex, it's not as though you've been consumed by artistic tendencies yourself."

Alex smiled broadly. "On the contrary . . . I'm just not good at them, so I leave them to you and Ella. Instead, I endeavor to be an excellent *champion* of the arts. I think I'm quite a success at that."

Stanhope looked up from his appreciation of Ella's work and smiled back at her. "Champions are certainly as important as the artists themselves, Lady Alexandra."

She laughed. "Thank you, Lord Stanhope, you're very kind, although I'll admit I'm not sure I believe you." Her response brought a rich laugh from him, reminding her of how much she had always enjoyed his company.

He moved closer, replying with a gleam in his rich brown eyes, "Then I shall have to attempt to convince you."

Vivi cleared her throat delicately and made a production of speaking brightly to Ella across the picnic, "Ella, you should try your hand at drawing a collection of figures . . . perhaps Nick and Kit and I should be your subjects this afternoon?" With a graceful movement, she settled herself nearer the Worthington brothers, conveniently upwind of Alex and Lord Stanhope, and produced a deck of cards. "It's not the most masculine of games, my lords, but may I tempt you into a round of whist?"

And, with that, Vivi had redirected everyone's attention away from Alex and Stanhope, who were now left alone on their patch of linen. Nick noticed and said with a mock threat in his voice, "I've got my eye on you, Stanhope. . . . Remember, you flirt with my only sister."

Stanhope nodded at Nick with feigned seriousness and replied, "I wouldn't dare be inappropriate, Lord Farrow."

His use of Nick's seldom used title amused the group, and he turned a wide grin on Alex as laughter floated across the green.

"Your reputation is quite impressive, my lord," Alex spoke quietly, referencing Nick's jest, her tone half teasing. "I confess, growing up with you, I wouldn't have expected it."

"I could play as though I do not understand your inference, my lady, but that would be a silly pretense. I assume you're referring to my notoriety as a rake? You shouldn't believe everything you hear gossiped about in ballrooms."

"Oh, no need to worry, my lord. I don't."

"No?"

"Not remotely. Considering my memories of you from our shared childhood, I find it quite difficult to believe you a danger either to me or to my reputation."

He chuckled and replied quietly, "Be careful, my lady. There's a fine line between complimenting a gentleman and wounding his ego."

Impishly, she smiled up at him. "My apologies, Lord Stanhope. Of course, I meant that I don't believe you pose a threat to either my reputation or to me *at this particular moment*. I would certainly think twice before allowing you the chance to escort me somewhere where your notorious wickedness could be unleashed, however."

With a loud laugh that caused the other four members of their party to look over, he flashed her an admiring glance. "Much better, and exactly what I imagine the elderly ladies of the *ton* would want you to think. After all, if the rumors are to be believed, I eat young ladies fresh on the marriage mart for breakfast."

"Ah, well, then, I am safe from you. I am not 'on the marriage mart.'"

"Oh, you aren't?" His reply was laced with interest.

She shook her head with a smile, "No. I'm not. I'm not interested in marriage."

One of his eyebrows cocked. "You're not?"

"No. When you were seventeen, were you thinking about marriage?"

His response was filled with humor. "Certainly not."

"Aha!" She pointed at him with emphasis. "You see? That answer proves my point! You think it's completely unfathomable that a boy of seventeen even think about marriage!"

"Yes. I do."

"So why should I be thinking about it?"

"An excellent question."

His frank response surprised her and she pulled back to assess him. "You really mean that."

"To be sure. I've never understood the expectation that women and men should adhere to different rules and protocols when it comes to courtship and marriage. I say, stay unattached as long as you like. From the marriages I've witnessed in the course of my life, the institution isn't quite what it's cracked up to be anyway." Leaning closer, he wriggled his eyebrows in mock villainy and continued, "I shouldn't like to see you married off too soon, anyway, my lady."

The extreme flirtation inspired a burst of laughter from Alex, which forced Stanhope to chuckle himself and to offer, "Well, what did you expect? I have a reputation to keep up!"

Alex's eyes twinkled with humor, and she grinned broadly. "Why, Frederick, Lord Stanhope. You're a fraud!"

He leaned close to her ear and spoke in a voice too quiet to be overheard by their neighbors, "Shhh. Don't let that get around. 'Twill ruin me."

So thoroughly had Alex been enjoying their banter that she hadn't noticed the approach of two newcomers to their idyllic afternoon. Looking up from Lord Stanhope, she noticed that they had arrived just as she had burst into laughter, and her humor died in her throat. There, standing at the edge of the linen square, gazing down with expressions that could only be described as, respectively, bored uninterest and supreme aggravation, were Penelope Grayson and Gavin, Lord Blackmoor.

From his place on the linen blanket, Lord Stanhope, curious about Alex's sudden change in demeanor, followed the direction of her gaze and, as proper etiquette demanded, immediately stood to greet Penelope and Blackmoor, along with the already standing Nick and Kit. "Lady Penelope, as always, it is a pleasure to see you. You've only made this pleasant afternoon more lovely."

One of Alex's eyebrows shot up.

"Thank you, my lord. I admit that I was skeptical about a walk in the park. I prefer to ride, but the day is bright and sunny, if on the cool side. I hope I do not catch a chill."

At this, Alex rolled her eyes, only to be caught by Blackmoor, whose gaze sharpened. Pretending not to notice,

Alex smoothed her skirts and looked over at Ella, who had stopped sketching to send an *Is she serious?* look in Alex's direction.

"You must join us!" Nick exclaimed. "What luck that we would meet!" With a resigned sigh, Alex stood to move closer to Ella — secretly afraid that the expanse of linen that had been unoccupied would be filled with the odious Penelope, and Alex would be forced to ruin a perfectly charming afternoon by interacting with the unpleasant young woman.

Before she could move, however, Blackmoor intercepted her, speaking quietly while bowing low over her hand. "Lady Alexandra, I trust that you don't object to our company for the afternoon. I would hate to ruin your outing." Their gazes met and Alex noted the warning in his grey eyes; she knew he was daring her to say something negative about his arrival with Penelope, and she stiffened, wishing she could wipe the expression from his face without causing a scene that would be discussed in London ballrooms for years. Of course, she didn't. In a feat of good manners that rivaled those of Queen Charlotte herself, Alex plastered a smile on her lips and spoke brightly, albeit through her teeth, "Certainly not, my lord. I cannot think of two more welcome additions to our little gathering." Removing her hand forcefully from his grasp, she continued, "I think I shall take a walk — I do so enjoy them . . . especially in the cool air." Her remark, designed to underscore the ridiculousness of his companion, hit home and his eyes narrowed at her boldness.

Vivi, who had overheard their conversation, stood and offered, "I should like to join you, Alex. I would benefit from a turn about the green."

Ella spoke from her perch on the blanket, "I shall come, too!"

And with that, the three were off, walking down their little hill and onto the greensward. Alex set the pace, her long legs eating up the ground as she marched away from the group, Ella and Vivi rushing to catch up.

"It's utterly remarkable how a perfectly pleasant afternoon can be ruined by the arrival of one unpleasant person."

Vivi spoke drily, "Are we talking about Penelope? Or Blackmoor?"

"If we keep going at this pace," said Ella, "I'm not going to be talking much at all . . . I'll need all the breath I have just to keep from swooning for lack of air."

Alex slowed her strides. "We're talking about both! Though, to be fair, she's *always* unpleasant. What befuddles me is that he seems to be becoming unpleasant himself . . . as he becomes more and more enamored of her!"

"With all due respect, Alex, you seem slightly more than befuddled. You seem . . ." Vivi paused, searching for the word.

"Furious," Ella supplied frankly.

"I'm not furious," Alex said in frustration, "but besides not understanding what he sees in her . . . I simply find it unbelievable that he would think he could speak to me as if I were a child! It makes me . . ." She stopped, at a loss for words.

"Furious?" Ella offered.

Alex threw her a glare. "Irritated."

"Blackmoor seems just as chivalrous as always to me," said Vivi. "Although, considering his prior warnings to you about Stanhope, it wouldn't surprise me if he were slightly unnerved by the portrait the two of you were making."

"It would serve him right!" Then, forgetting her ire momentarily, Alex turned to Vivi. "What portrait? We were simply enjoying our afternoon. Stanhope has been a perfect gentleman."

"That may well be the case, Alex, but the two of you did appear rather . . ." Vivi let her sentence trail off.

"Cozy." This, again, from Ella.

"Must you finish all her sentences?" Alex gave Ella an exasperated look.

Ella smiled brightly. "It's a particular skill."

"Stanhope and I were not 'cozy.' We were having a perfectly harmless conversation until Blackmoor appeared with that awful . . ."

"Penelope." In the pause that followed her addition, Ella looked innocently at Alex, a twinkle in her cornflower-blue eyes.

Unable to be angry with her friend, Alex chuckled and wagged a finger in warning. "Ella. You tread on thin ice."

“Ah, but you must admit, my ability to exasperate is part of my charm.”

“You have charm?”

Vivi answered with laughter in her voice, “A very small amount. If you blink, you might miss it.”

“Oh!” Ella cried out in mock offense, and the three laughed together.

Alex smiled and continued, “I suppose I shouldn’t let them mar an otherwise lovely day. I shall rise above it.”

Vivi nodded. “Very generous of you.”

“Thank you. I rather thought so.”

Ella spoke, squinting at a figure approaching them. “Is that Baron Montgrave? It is! Vivi, you have to meet him. He’s got some fascinating tales — you’re going to just adore him.”

“Well, considering your eagerness to reacquaint yourself with him . . . I find I am quite eager myself.” Vivi looked toward the tall Frenchman and continued, “If what you both say of the baron is true, he’s bound to be the most interesting part of the afternoon.”

Alex spoke under her breath as the baron drew near, “That’s not saying much, considering the recent less than scintillating addition of Penelope to the afternoon.”

Ella turned back at Alex’s sarcasm. “As your friend, I feel I must tell you that you’re becoming obsessed.”

“I am not obsessed! I simply —”

“Baron Montgrave!” Ella spoke cheerfully as the Frenchman reached them. “What a pleasure to see you!

You've rescued us from an afternoon filled with repetitive conversation!"

Standing slightly behind her friend, Alex poked Ella in the back none too lightly and over her quiet "Ow!" pasted a smile on her face to rival her friend's. "Indeed, my lord, you are well met."

Bowing deeply, the baron returned the girls' smiles. "Surely it is you who have rescued me, my ladies. Fortune appears to have smiled upon me to have provided me with such elegant company."

Alex turned to Vivi. "My lord, may I introduce our dear friend Lady Vivian Markwell? Lady Vivian, I present the Baron Montgrave."

"*Enchantée.*" The baron bowed low over Vivian's hand. "I know your father well and have heard him speak of you with great pride. It is an honor to meet you finally."

Vivi fell into a deep curtsy and met the baron's warm gaze. "It is a pleasure to make your acquaintance, my lord. What brings you to this meadow by the Serpentine today?"

"One can never have too many afternoon walks in the beautiful weather. That is something I learned in the country and I am loathe to forget it now in the bustle of the city."

Alex smiled. "Well said, Baron. I imagine that, after a lifetime in France, you must find us rather soggy."

With a chuckle, the baron nodded in agreement as Ella spoke. "We were taking advantage of this lovely weather ourselves, as it happens. Would you care to join our little party, my lord?" She extended her hand to indicate the cluster of young people up on the knoll.

Following her gaze, the baron shook his head to decline gracefully. "Thank you, no, my ladies. I fear I would ruin such a youthful outing."

"Nonsense!" Alex's unladylike outburst drew startled looks from all three of her companions. Looking at her friends, she lowered her voice defensively, "Well, it is."

"What Lady Alexandra means to say, my lord," Vivi offered, unable to hide a wide, amused grin, "is that you are more than welcome at our little gathering; we would very much enjoy your company."

Laughter came to Alex's eye and she interjected, "Isn't that what I said?"

The baron laughed again and spoke warmly, "Certainly, my lady, that is what I heard." Offering an arm, he continued, "May I escort you back to your party, although I regret I will not join you?"

Alex took the aging Frenchman's arm and spoke in a conspiratorial tone, "Thank you, my lord — both for the escort and for your failure to mention my bad behavior. I assure you, my parents have done their best and all discernible flaws are entirely my own."

"And I assure you, Lady Alexandra, I have seen none of these flaws that you speak of. Surely, they do not exist."

Alex laughed. "My family — particularly my brothers — would disagree with you on that point, Baron." She lowered her voice to a conspiratorial whisper. "No matter what you say, you are a welcome addition to our little world — mine especially."

"I shall happily defend you to your brothers, Lady Alexandra. Being a brother myself, I am sure I speak their language well. There are four, are there not?"

Alex shook her head with a quick laugh. "Thankfully, no. I've only three brothers — three too many, it seems some days."

"Of course . . . I do not know why I thought there were four."

"You are not alone. It sometimes feels that way. Lord Blackmoor and they are thick as thieves, which explains his constant presence and the confusion about the number of Stafford siblings."

The baron stilled, looking at Alex quizzically. "Lord Blackmoor, you say — friends with your brothers?"

"That is correct."

"Ah, that is interesting."

"Is it? After seventeen years of their combined company, good sir, I'm afraid I find it rather more tiresome than interesting."

He chuckled good-naturedly at her response and continued, more seriously, "If I may, how is the new, young earl faring with the loss of his father?"

It was a common enough question, one that Alex had heard a number of times. She answered without thinking,

"Well enough, I think. He does not speak of it much, and he seems to have — matured — if that makes sense. Our families have always been very close and I was well aware of how important his relationship with his father was to Lord Blackmoor." Alex's voice had softened and her gaze, of its own accord, had moved to Gavin up on the knoll, smiling at something Kit was saying. She couldn't help thinking that even his smile was subdued in comparison to that of a year ago. "I am filled with sorrow for the pain he must feel."

She trailed off, realizing that Ella and Vivi were both looking at her with surprised expressions. She was sharing too much with this little-known companion — too much about Blackmoor, but more importantly, too much of her own emotions. Young English ladies were not supposed to have such opinions and thoughts. They were not supposed to speak so freely. Looking at the Frenchman, Alex couldn't help but notice his obvious discomfort with the situation — he was looking slightly desperate to escape.

With an inner sigh, Alex changed tack, a wry smile on her face. "I fear, my lord, you are too easy to speak with. I should not share so much of my thinking. I must be boring you."

"Not at all, my lady." The Frenchman looked distractedly into the distance, lost in thought. "The elder earl was a fine man — a great hero. I'm sorry to hear of his loss."

"You are not alone. He was much revered by those who knew him well."

"May I ask . . . ?" The question hung in the air between them, the normally poised baron seeming uncertain of the proper etiquette in this particular situation.

Alex took pity on him and did not wait for him to finish his query. She knew what he was asking. With a tiny nod, she spoke. "It was an accident — the earl was thrown from his horse at the Blackmoor estate. He fell to his death." Without thinking, she continued, "One almost cannot believe that it was an accident." She waved a hand in dismissal at his surprised look. "It's silly, of course. The earl had few, if any, enemies."

Alex couldn't help but notice that the old man had gone white as a sheet. "Baron, are you all right?" She looked back with alarm toward Vivi and Ella.

"I am quite well, yes, my lady. Unfortunately, the hour grows late, and I must regretfully take my leave." Bowing low to the trio of girls, he made quick work of his farewell and hurried off, as though he couldn't get away fast enough.

His abrupt decision to depart underscored his obvious discomfort with Alex's frank conversation. She watched his speedy exit across the greensward, feeling slightly sorry for herself and, with a sigh, turned back toward the little group on the hill.

Hearing Penelope's giggles and the boys' laughter, she had a sudden desire to be far away from there, far away from that place that required so much effort, so much thought. She found herself exhausted by the entire charade of this first week in society. She had always known it would be a struggle to be the perfect company — to say all the proper things without appearing too opinionated, too frank, too much herself — but now, watching her friends and her brothers laugh and joke together, all so seamlessly integrated into their roles as members of London society, she couldn't help but wonder if there was something wrong with her.

She watched as Blackmoor leaned in to say something just out of earshot to Penelope, and felt a flash of irritation as she responded with a well-practiced demure smile and shy dip of her head. *Ugh.* Yes. Alex had definitely had enough of society for today.

She caught Stanhope's eye and, gallant as ever, he stood and moved toward her. "Are you unwell, Lady Alexandra?"

She couldn't stop herself from looking past his broad shoulders, from meeting Blackmoor's unreadable gaze as he looked up from his cards, distracted for a moment. A warning flashed ever so briefly in his grey eyes — gone so quickly that Alex might have imagined it.

She ignored it anyway and replied, "Not at all, my lord. Just a slight headache. I think I shall return home, and by tonight, I should be right as rain. Would you mind very much escorting me to Worthington House? I wouldn't like to ruin the afternoon for everyone else."

ten

Fear was foul company. Especially at night.

He prowled his darkened apartments, playing his actions over and over in his mind, desperately attempting to find some misstep that, when rectified, would bring him closer to the answers for which he was searching. He had to find out what the new earl knew.

His lip curled in an unconscious sneer as he paced the floor. He now knew from multiple sources that the young pup remained unconvinced that his father's death was an accident, and that Blackmoor continued to search for evidence of foul play. He was unconcerned about information that the boy might find in the public record about that cold January day. It was easy enough, after all, to bribe a local constable or two. Instead, he worried that young Blackmoor's search would turn up information uncovered by the former earl . . . information that would reveal his part in the villainy. Information that would indict him not simply for murder — but for treason as well.

Turning to a looking glass, he stared at his reflection, noting the paleness of his skin, the sunken state of his eyes. It had been an eternity since he had slept through the night, unplagued by the demons that haunted him in the darkness. He had been able to take a small pleasure in Blackmoor's death . . . but now, as this suffocating blackness surrounded him, he found little comfort. He was becoming consumed by fear from all sides — fear of the powerful men to whom he answered, who were losing their patience with each passing day, who would soon be unwilling to hear his excuses and would take their revenge by any means necessary . . . including blood.

He swore fiercely and, with force borne of frustration, lifted a candelabra from a nearby table and hurled it at his reflection, embracing the sound of shattering glass — enjoying the way he looked in the fractured mirror. He saw himself repeated in each shard and, for the first time in months, felt as though he were not alone.

Events beyond his control were taking place across the Continent. Napoleon was pressing north and war was again imminent. Time was running out. If he didn't find answers for his powerful partners, he would lose everything for which he had worked. He was left with little choice — not that he was saddened by what he knew he must do next. He could not let another Earl of Blackmoor ruin his well-laid plans. No, he must prevent that at all costs, by any means necessary. If the young earl knew anything, he would soon share it . . . or pay the price.

He smiled wickedly into the broken mirror, then spoke aloud.

"Let's not fool ourselves. The brat will pay the price no matter what he knows."

"It's hard to believe my hair can do this!" Alex was unable to keep the wonder from her voice as she craned her neck to see the back of her head in the candlelit mirror of her bedchamber. "Of course," she continued drily, "it's hard to believe that much about this picture is the product of nature."

It was the evening of the first Worthington House dinner of the season — an affair renowned by those lucky enough to receive an invitation, and Alex's first formal dinner of the season. For some reason, tonight's festivities made the thought of eating the evening meal in the home she'd known all her life somewhat unnerving. Her reflection did little to change that.

Wrapped in another of Madame Fernaud's masterpieces, this time a pale pink silk that fell in luxurious waves to matching silk slippers, Alex had just been released from Eliza's highly skilled hands, her hair now twisted and tucked and pinned and curled in an intricate design that left her long neck exposed in one of the most fashionable styles of the season.

Alex couldn't help but feel that all this elaborate pampering was rather unnecessary — especially considering she'd known most of those who planned to be in attendance for the great majority of her lifetime — but she'd already learned in this short season to pick her battles with her mother. And this was not one into which she was willing to enter.

A knock on her bedchamber door snapped her from her thoughts. She called out for her visitor to enter, and smiled brilliantly when she saw her father reflected in the mirror. Standing, she turned toward him, dropped into an exaggerated curtsy, and, smiling broadly, said, "Your Grace. I trust I pass inspection?"

He chuckled at her use of the ducal address and offered her a hand to lift her from her position. Tilting his head, he answered in a voice rich with humor. "Far be it from me to answer that particular question. I wouldn't dare risk removing that opinion from the purview of the duchess. You know that." Lowering his voice to a conspiratorial whisper, he continued, "Suffice to say, my lady, that I believe you are the most beautiful of my offspring."

Alex burst into laughter and leaned up to kiss her father's cheek. "Well said . . . ever the diplomat. Although I rather think it shouldn't be that difficult to be the most beautiful when compared to the hulking brutes you call sons."

"Not diplomacy at all, daughter. You look lovely. And, sadly, very grown up. When did you get so tall?"

Alex was just a few inches from her father's height, and she smiled at the question. "Strong Stafford blood, of course, Father. Are you certain we're not descended from the Vikings?"

"Looking at the four of you, one does wonder. But then there is I, the diminutive duke . . . pathetically small and not at all Norse." He spoke with exaggerated self-pity to gain a laugh from his daughter, then changed the subject. "Are you ready for your entrance at your first Worthington House dinner?

Wrinkling her nose, Alex replied, "I'm afraid as ready as ever. I'm surprised you came to fetch me instead of Mother. I would have thought she'd want to appraise my appearance."

"Your mother is busy making last-minute changes to the seating arrangements to ensure complete perfection."

He paused as Alex rolled her eyes. "And, as the Duke of Worthington, it falls to me to escort the most beautiful young lady at the gathering to the festivities."

Alex smiled. "Ah, you forget, Father, that I am a graduate of an obscene number of hours of instruction in Proper Conversation, which includes the voluminous rules and regulations regarding dinners and escorts. I know you lie. Your job, as the host, is to escort the highest-ranking lady to the festivities." She queried innocently, "Perhaps you would like for me to arrange a refresher course for you?"

"Ah, but *you* forget, daughter. The best part of being a duke is that one can change the rules at one's whim . . . and no one dares disagree."

"An excellent benefit."

"I've always thought so. Shall we go?" He offered an arm for his daughter, then stopped as she took hold of it. "Wait. I've forgotten something."

From his coat pocket, he removed a long string of jewels and held it up for Alex to see. She gasped and looked at her father incredulously. "Grandmother's sapphires?" She couldn't help herself from reaching for the stunning strand of pink sapphires. "But, Father . . . they were so much a part of her . . . they're virtually iconic. I don't think . . ."

"Nonsense. Your grandmother was headstrong and brilliant and took the *ton* by storm. I'm told she spent her first season breaking a score of hearts and boldly inserting her opinion where it wasn't desired. Frankly, you remind me entirely of her, and she would be as proud of you tonight as I am. She'd want you to make your debut at a Worthington salon in these. Of that, I am certain." And then, with the regal tone perfected by years of expecting all within earshot to do the ducal bidding, he ordered, "Turn around."

She did, and soon felt the cool weight of the necklace that had been so integral a part of her grandmother. Turning toward the mirror, she caught a glimpse of someone she barely recognized. *Was that really she?* The duke nodded firmly at the reflection. "Now you're ready to make your appearance as the Stafford you are."

There was something about the moment that struck deep at the core of her, something that filled her heart with equal parts nervousness and pride — nervousness at the responsibility she had not just to her father or her mother, but to a line of remarkable, honorable men and women who could be traced back to the earliest days of Britain, and pride that she had such a noble line to call her own. Taking her father's arm, she made a silent vow to try her best to make them proud.

There was a reason why an invitation to a Worthington House dinner was one of the most highly coveted of the season. They had been hosted for years, in a tradition that had been handed down from duchess to duchess for generations. On these evenings, the enormous dining table at Worthington House was filled with the most impressively titled members of London society, as well as with those deemed most interesting. This, of course, infuriated any who held an ancient title or an obscenely large estate and were left off the invitation list . . . all the while making the invitation itself one that was not to be declined.

Over centuries, the dinners had been attended by some of the most well-known and well-respected people in history, from playwrights and poets to politicians and royalty and everyone in between. Family lore spoke of one such dinner that had hosted William Shakespeare and Queen Elizabeth — legend had it that it was on this particular evening that the Queen had commissioned a play from Shakespeare for the royal Twelfth Night festivities, resulting in one of the playwright's most famous comedies. The proof? The then Duke and Duchess of Worthington were Sebastian and Olivia, coincidentally the names of two of the play's main characters, who fall deeply in love.

Alex had heard the story countless times and never entirely believed it, finding it a little too outlandish for her taste, but tonight she was coming close to changing her opinion. Looking around her, she saw that this evening her mother had outdone herself. In a far corner, the Duke of Sunderland, revered for his ability to raise the best racing horses in England, was being introduced to Marcus Sinew, the common-born publisher of the *Times,* who was rumored to be one of the smartest and most charming businessmen in all of England. By contrast, the Duchess of Sunderland, a powerful voice in the movement to stop child labor, was receiving a young member of Parliament who was expected to become prime minister in his sure-to-be-impressive future.

Everywhere she turned, amidst impeccably mannered servants laden with refreshments, people with vastly different but fascinating skills were deep in conversation — laughing, chattering, and enjoying themselves. There was no inane flirting nor boring discussion of fashion or livestock. No, these were the thinkers and doers of London society. Her mother had achieved what few other hostesses could boast — frank, exciting, honest conversation with fascinating company, and Alex was relieved by how comfortable she felt in the room.

She took a tiny sip of her champagne and soaked in the atmosphere. Across the room, she saw Ella in a heated conversation with Will and Vivi's father, the Marquess of Langford. She smiled at the clear admiration on the men's faces, realizing that the trio must be talking politics . . . and Ella was clearly holding her own.

A rumbling from her stomach interrupted her thoughts. Attempting to be subtle, Alex looked toward the ancient clock at the end of the room and wondered when dinner might begin.

"Hungry?"

A blush rose on her cheeks as she turned to meet Blackmoor's amused gaze. "You caught me. I'm famished — but you mustn't tell my mother. Ladies aren't supposed to have physical needs. Or, at least, they're not supposed to express them."

"I see. Well, then, I shall endeavor to keep your mind off the one at hand."

She gazed at him, taking notice of his handsome frame. He was wearing a stunning coat, a deep midnight blue so dark it was almost black. The crisp white of his shirt and cravat brought out the bronze of his skin and the blue-grey of his eyes — so serious and adult. But deep in his eyes, beneath his hardened exterior, she saw a hint of the same boy who'd been her savior her whole life. She let out a tiny sigh. Frankly, it was exhausting to argue with him — she rather missed him. The challenge of the season, combined with the demons she was sure he was fighting, had gotten the better of them both.

She was about to say something alluding to that when he spoke, his tone clear and earnest. "We seem to have started off this season on the wrong foot."

She was flooded with relief that he shared her sentiments. "Exactly my thoughts, my lord." Their gazes locked, clear green and rich grey, and Alex felt warmth rising in her cheeks at the honesty of the moment. Theirs was a friendship which — until recently — had never been strained, had never been complicated; it had always been filled with fun and humor and silliness. She still hadn't a thorough grasp on how or why it seemed to be undergoing such an oddly emotional change. Did he understand?

"I am thrilled we are in accord. Shall we swear a truce?"

Clearly he was less concerned about their changing relationship than she was, and now certainly wasn't the time to discuss it anyway. Falling back on the comfort of humor, Alex cocked her head, pretending to consider the proposition seriously. He laughed, attracting attention from the other guests, and whispered, "Minx."

Alex rewarded him with a grin and all was forgiven — her rudeness to Penelope, his arrogance, their mutual distractions over the past several weeks. They shared a moment filled with silent pleasure, a moment lasting just long enough to once again raise the color on Alex's cheeks.

The dinner chimes rang, interrupting their private moment, and Alex, despite years of training in the proper method of being escorted to dinner was suddenly lost . . . a stranger in her own home. She watched as those around them paired off — highest-ranking men with their highest-ranked female counterparts — and she felt panic begin to rise in her chest as she realized she had no idea where her place was in this moment. Who was to escort her into dinner?

Her father was escorting the Dowager Duchess of Lockwood into the dining hall; he was followed by her mother, escorted by the Duke of Sunderland. She watched as Vivi and Ella both took the arms of their escorts — no help there, as the gentlemen in question were Will and Nick. She couldn't be accompanied to dinner by Kit — he was her brother. It was like watching an elaborate dance to which she had forgotten the steps — she knew she should have given more attention to her governess's droning.

Her mother was going to have her hide. Perhaps she could beg off and cry headache — that would solve the whole problem.

Lost in her own mental hysterics, Alex had forgotten Blackmoor, standing at her side. Turning, she saw his calm smile — he was clearly amused by her panic. He waited for her to realize what he'd known all along . . . that he, as an unrelated earl, was a perfectly proper escort for the daughter of a duke.

With a sigh of relief, she took the arm he offered, whispering, "That was cruel. I thought you declared a truce?"

As they made their way to dinner, he replied, "On the contrary. I *offered* a truce. You did not accept."

"Mere words, sir."

"That may be. But this is London in season — words are paramount."

She chuckled. "Either way, I must thank you — you seem to be ever saving me from getting myself into trouble."

With an exaggerated sigh, he replied, "It's a task I resigned myself to long ago, Alex."

She couldn't help but think of the first time he'd saved her. "Lucky for you, you don't have to catch me jumping from trees anymore. I daresay your more recent missions have been rather more easy."

"I wouldn't be so certain," he spoke enigmatically.

She didn't have a chance to ask him what he meant, because they had arrived in the dining hall and were immediately swept up in the energy of the conversation and the extraordinary food.

Alex found herself seated at the far end of the table, to the left of the Marquess of Langford, sure to be a fascinating dinner companion. It didn't hurt that he was the father of one of her closest friends, which served to put her at ease. She sent a silent offering of thanks to her mother for the seating arrangement. On her left was Mr. Sinew, whom she almost immediately decided she liked — the newspaper publisher was clearly intelligent and unpretentious, a welcome change to most members of the *ton*.

Across the table was Lady Charlotte Twizzleton, a brilliant woman who, at the age of six and twenty, was considered very much "on the shelf" and who very much didn't seem to care. Instead, she had traveled the world, attended salons with the greatest minds of the era, and spent her days talking with whomever she chose about whatever she chose.

Alex had always found Lady Charlotte a particular inspiration and she was pleased to note that, while the duchess was clearly obsessed with seeing her only daughter married off without delay, it didn't seem to have diminished her admiration for such a freethinking young woman . . . or else why seat Alex near such a risky influence?

Vivi and Ella were seated farther away, a fact that Alex noted with slight disappointment, but she threw herself into the vibrant conversation, which ran a gamut of fascinating topics, from art to politics to the ever-present war. Her excitement and interest in the discussion were soon joined by the remarkable realization that these particular gentlemen seemed actually to listen to the opinions of the women around them! What was this strange new world that her parents had been hiding from her?

Turning, Alex looked down the table at her mother, who was holding court at the end of the room. She watched with fascination as the duchess said something witty, garnering a round of laughter from her companions. She caught Alex's eye over the feast laid out between them, and with a slow nod of acknowledgment, she shared a knowing look with her youngest child, as if to say, *Your mother isn't all she seems, is she?*

Alex felt admiration burst in her chest. For all her frustrating qualities, her mother certainly was a remarkable hostess. For the second time that night, she felt very proud to be a Stafford . . . and very honored to have received an invitation to this particular gathering.

eleven

After dinner, the guests adjourned to the music room, where the conversation continued, and they were able to mingle with each other. Despite her intense enjoyment of her dinner companions, Alex was particularly happy to be able to ensconce herself in a corner of the room with Vivi and Ella — whom she'd missed during the meal.

"I've heard about these dinners for years." Vivi spoke in a hushed voice but was unable to keep the excitement from her tone. "But I never imagined they would be so . . ."

"Different from every other event we've ever attended or been prepared for?" Alex finished for her friend. "I know! Imagine how you would feel if the dinner were hosted by *your* parents. I'm barely able to recognize them! How was your company?"

Vivi replied, "I was seated with Lucian Sewell, Blackmoor's uncle, and the dowager duchess. He was quiet but charming, and she was positively outrageous! You wouldn't believe the things she's willing to say!"

Looking across the room, Alex watched as the aged character in question swatted Ella's father with the tip of her ever-present walking stick. She pointed out the interaction to the other girls and said, "Oh . . . I think we can imagine."

Ella laughed at her father's indignation. "I hope you didn't upset her, Vivi — I wouldn't like to be on the receiving end of that stick."

"I *have* been on the end of that stick," Alex said. "It's as pointy as you'd imagine. But it doesn't compare to the scolding you receive as part of your punishment for perceived slights."

She hunched over and raised the pitch of her voice, mimicking the old woman — sending the other two girls into gales of laughter at her eerily accurate impression. The laughter drew the attention of the rest of the room and an oddly knowing look from the Dowager Duchess of Lockwood herself.

"Uh-oh . . ." Alex gave her friends a sheepish look, making them both snicker. "I've a feeling I've been caught."

A masculine voice interrupted them. "You've definitely been caught — I've received that look one or two times myself. Prepare yourself for a deafening set-down the next time she's got you in earshot."

She turned to Blackmoor. "She'll have to catch me first."

"Don't let the cane fool you. She's decidedly fleet-footed when she wants to be." Then Blackmoor spoke to the trio. "I've been sent by the duchess and countess to separate the three of you. Your mothers evidently don't trust you to stay out of trouble."

Vivi chuckled. "Unfortunately, they appear to be right. And not alone. My father is looking equally concerned — I seem to be caught as well." She continued, "I suppose I'm going to have to go make amends. Would anyone like to join me?"

Ella grinned. "I'll come. After all, your father is far less likely to give us a scolding than my mother is at the moment."

Left alone, Alex turned to Blackmoor and with mock accusation, "Well, you certainly ruined that fun, my lord."

With a short bow, he responded, "It's a particular gift of mine. Would a turn about the room provide you with any entertainment?"

She took the offered arm and answered casually, "I suppose that if I have to take a turn about the room with someone, you're better than most."

"Your ability to flatter is absolutely mind-reeling, Lady Alexandra."

"It's a particular gift of mine, my lord."

He laughed at her use of his own words. "I noticed you were having a good time at dinner. You seemed to be participating in a very exciting conversation."

"I was lucky to be seated with fascinating company. If a little surprised by the entire experience."

"Surprised?"

"I suppose I never imagined my parents to be so different as hosts from how they are as parents. It's silly, really. I mean, of course, they have lives beyond their children."

His voice grew serious. "It's not silly, Alex. It's never easy to discover your parents are more than they seem."

Alex sensed they were talking about something more than the evening at hand. Noticing they had come upon the entrance to the terrace that overlooked the back gardens, she recognized the possibility for a private conversation and said, "I find I am a little warm. Do you mind escorting me outside?"

He gave her a slightly surprised look but nodded in agreement, and they moved through the open glass doors into the cool London night.

They were not alone on the balcony, however, for they found themselves interrupting the Baron Montgrave and Lucian Sewell, who were deep in conversation.

"There is nothing to do." Lucian spoke quietly.

"There is everything!" the baron replied, his voice louder, more excited.

That was all they overheard before the men became aware of their presence and Blackmoor spoke, "Apologies, Uncle. Baron. We did not mean to interrupt." He made a move to turn Alex away from the conversation and return inside, when his uncle spoke.

"No need for apologies. The baron and I were just talking about the war" — he turned toward his nephew with a half smile — "and frankly, you've saved me from some embarrassment."

"I was merely discussing the remarkable part your uncle has played in the war, Lord Blackmoor," the baron added without looking away from Sewell.

Lucian tipped his head in a manner Alex recognized as affected humility. "Baron Montgrave exaggerates. I am hardly the hero he makes me out to be."

"Not so. I assume your uncle has kept silent about his actions over the last few years, Lord Blackmoor. I can only hope that someday you will ask him to enlighten you about his . . . exploits."

Lucian shook his head and met the eyes of the baron, Alex noticed. His next words were directed at the Frenchman. "My nephew need not hear of my past, Baron. It is just that. The past." Offering a short bow to Alex, he continued, "Lady Alexandra, a pleasure as always. I think I shall return inside."

With that, Sewell took his leave, the baron quick on his heels, leaving Blackmoor and Alex on the terrace with the cool night breeze around them.

Alex had the distinct feeling that the conversation they had witnessed had been weightier than it seemed . . . although she couldn't quite discern why she felt so. Shaking off her thoughts, she looked for a way to lighten the moment for Blackmoor, who seemed lost in his own reverie.

"Well. They certainly were an unconventional pair."

Looking off into the darkened garden, Gavin murmured his agreement. "My uncle seems to collect companions who don't quite fit him." Distractedly, he continued, "As I was saying . . . it's not uncommon to discover that your elders are somewhat different from how they seem. My uncle Lucian exemplifies that point."

"Your time together has not changed that?"

Blackmoor gave a little laugh. "Not in the slightest. He is as much a mystery now as he was when I was a boy — only now . . ." He trailed off.

Alex meant to let the silence hang until he was ready to say more. Truly, she did. But, unfortunately, she couldn't help herself. "Now?"

He stayed quiet, and she thought he might ignore her question — so far away he was from this moment, this night. Just when she was about to change the subject, he spoke quietly. "Now he is the only link I have to my father. And, much as I try, I can't seem to find any of my father in him. And I wouldn't be surprised if he said the very same thing of me."

"Why do you say that?" she blurted out before she could stop herself. Once the question was spoken, she qualified it almost immediately. "Not seeing your father in him — I understand that — they are markedly different men, to be sure. But why do you say that he must do the same?"

He turned to look at her and she was surprised by the troubled expression in his eyes, dark grey in the dim light.

"I never had the chance to learn to be like him." This time, she stayed quiet, watching his throat work, his eyes darken, as he attempted to find words that would make sense. "He died so early. So much sooner than I had ever — At night, when I am home in that blasted house, all I can think is that I should have been more attentive. I should have paid him more mind."

The words were tumbling from his lips, and Alex desperately wanted to console him. "You couldn't have known . . ."

"I know that. I just wish I'd . . . I just wish I'd been more. Better." He took a deep breath, pausing long enough to make her wonder if he was going to speak again. Just when she thought she was going to have to break the silence, to reassure him, he spoke in a whisper, "I wish I'd been a better son."

Her response was instant. "You were a wonderful son. You *are* a wonderful son. He believed that. I know that as well as I know my own name."

"You don't know that."

"I do."

"How could you?"

He looked at her, really looked at her, for the first time since they'd come out to the terrace, and she was surprised by how much a man he appeared in the darkness. The light shadowed his face, harshening the angles of his straight nose, his strong jaw. His eyes glittered with something unnamed and Alex didn't know if it was a trick of the light, but she couldn't look away from him.

Instead, she reached out, placing her hand on the warm smooth fabric of his jacket where it hugged his arm, not knowing what to say to make this whole situation well again. She settled for a gentle and impassioned, “I have spent much of my life with fathers and sons. I know a good match when I see one. He loved you, Gavin. He was proud of you. And there is so much of him in you — so much of his strength, his humor, his character.”

Her touch seemed to pull him out of his daze, and he looked down at her slim, white hand, placing his own on hers before recapturing her gaze. One half of his mouth quirked in an attempt at a smile, and he spoke. “That’s the first time you’ve called me Gavin since the season began.” His breath exhaled on a little laugh. “I thought perhaps you’d forgotten my given name.”

She tried to ignore the feelings coursing through her at his touch as she replied, “I’m just trying to get used to your being an earl. I have to keep reminding myself.”

“You’re not alone. I find I have to remind *myself* most days. And I assure you, I’d much prefer not to be Blackmoor.” His voice quieted. “What I wouldn’t give to be Gavin again.”

Alex searched for the right words. “I cannot imagine how difficult this must be for you.” She paused, then pushed on. “In my opinion, I think you make an excellent earl . . . I always knew you would. And, more than that, I’m certain your father is very proud, wherever he is.”

He turned his head to look at her, but remained silent.

An emotion she couldn't define flashed in his eyes — something she'd never seen in them before. She continued, "And, even though you may not recognize him now, Gavin is still there. Still as strong as ever."

His eyes darkened as he straightened and faced her. He moved his arm underneath her hand, twisting it and lacing her fingers through his own. She was keenly aware of the heat of his skin on hers, the intensity in his gaze. The moment stretched out between them and Alex had the feeling that something she did not fully understand was happening. She met his eyes and he stepped closer to her, leaving little room between them. As he looked down at her, a lock of his hair fell across his forehead. Her fingers itched to push it back from his face.

"You really believe that?"

"Every word."

Her breath caught as he raised his free hand to her face, tipping it upward toward the light. The touch sent a strange feeling through her, something she'd never felt before this moment.

When he spoke, she could hear the surprise in his voice. "You make me want to believe it." He was mere inches from her and their gazes were locked together.

And all of a sudden, she knew. He was going to kiss her. And she wanted him to. More than she could have imagined. Her breath caught as his gaze moved from her eyes to her lips and her whole body tensed as she watched him move closer.

His lips were so close to her own that she could feel the light touch of his breath on her skin. Her eyes fluttered closed and she waited on tenterhooks . . . all her senses screaming, *He's going to kiss you!*

Only, he didn't.

Instead, just as Alex was sure she was feeling the beginnings of her first kiss, she heard his soft curse. Her eyes flew open as he jumped back from her, loosing her hand. She found herself rather dizzy from his quick movement and the instant loss of his warmth.

"We cannot do this."

"We cannot?" The words came out soft and bewildered.

"No!" He stopped and raked his fingers through his hair, taking a deep breath, looking anywhere but at her. She had no idea what to say or how to act — after all, it's not every day one of your dearest friends nearly kisses you. So she stayed quiet.

He cleared his throat and spoke. "We are as good as family." And that was that. "I should escort you back inside."

She willed her voice to remain steady and was never so thankful as when her response came out sounding as though she experienced this particular situation most every day. "Of course. I shouldn't like to miss any of the festivities."

She ignored his offered arm and brushed past him toward the bright lights of the drawing room, leaving him to follow behind.

twelve

"It's all Alex's fault. If it weren't for her, we would be able to carry on as we always have without Mother making us do her bidding." Kit looked across the table at Will, who nodded his head firmly in agreement and dealt the next hand of *vingt-et-un*, the card game they were playing.

Nick looked down at his cards with an air of superiority. "At least I have a legitimate reason to miss the Salisbury Ball. Mother can't deny me the trip back to Oxford that's been planned for weeks. The two of you are on your own!"

He flipped his cards, showing them with a confident flourish, and grimaced when he saw that he'd lost roundly to all three of the others.

Blackmoor, who occupied the fourth seat at the table, commented, "I should say that rather takes the sting off, doesn't it, Kit? Will?"

The boys all laughed and continued their conversation as Will collected his winnings from the center of the table and began to shuffle the cards for another hand. Kit spoke next.

"She can't force us to go to the ball. We're grown men, for Lord's sake!"

Will cocked an eyebrow at his younger brother. "You don't think she can force us? We are speaking of the same mother, correct? Small frame, enormous will?"

Kit sighed and leaned back in his chair, leveling his older brother with a stare. "How are we going to escape?"

"We're not," said Will. "This is one of those balls that we can't avoid — Nicola Salisbury has been a friend of Alex's for years. She's not going to miss this for anything."

Nick spoke up. "That may be true, but I really am beginning to think that Alex is no more interested in attending the Salisbury Ball than we are. She's been rather more difficult than usual in the last few days, don't you think?"

Kit replied distractedly, "No, not that I've noticed."

Blackmoor cut in, his question appearing to all as casual curiosity. "Has she told you that something is bothering her?"

Nick shook his head, waving his hand dismissively. "No, not in so many words. She simply seems to have developed more of a disdain for events of the season. She hasn't been eager to attend much in the last week."

Will snorted. "Alex has never been very keen on events of the season. I wouldn't worry about her. As I said, Nicola is a friend. She'll want to go. One of us has to chaperone her. And, since I'm older and of a higher rank, I get to decide who that will be. Care to hazard a guess, Kit?" His green eyes twinkled with laughter.

"Bollocks!" This from Kit, who was not about to accept this particular decision without a fight. "It can't be me!"

"Why not?"

Kit paused, clearly searching for a viable excuse to avoid the ball in question. His eyes lit up with excitement when he'd hit on the right thing. "The hunting party I've an invitation to is just as viable a location to meet an eligible young lady as any, I daresay. I shall simply tell Mother that." He looked veritably triumphant.

Will groaned, knowing his mother well enough to see that she would take Kit's statement to mean that there was a particular eligible young lady to whom he was referring. "Well played, Brother."

Kit nodded his head in acceptance of the compliment and Will sighed, slowly shuffling the cards, deep in thought as he attempted to devise an excellent excuse to escape from brotherly duties.

Blackmoor, who had been rather silent for the duration of the conversation, cleared his throat, softly interrupting his friends' thoughts.

"I happen to be attending the ball. I daresay I could chaperone her."

Will's eyes lit up at his friend's words. "Truly?" At Blackmoor's nod, he continued, "Brilliant! Everyone thinks of you as one of her brothers anyway . . . you practically are, for goodness sake!"

Blackmoor cleared his throat again. "Indeed."

Attempting to contain his excitement at his narrow escape, Will tried for a serious, concerned look at his friend. That particular visage did not come easily. "Are you sure, Blackmoor? I can't think of anything worse than an evening of watching over Alex as she attracts legions of milksop fans."

Blackmoor laughed shortly and replied, "Neither can I." After a pause during which he realized that he needed to say more to his friends, he continued, "But I'm attending anyway, so . . . it simply seems the logical solution."

"Capital! I knew there was a reason we kept you around, chap!"

Nick shook his head in amazement at his older brother. "It's simply incredible, the luck you have. If that had been me, I'd have somehow ended up having to escort her, Vivi, and Ella for the rest of the season!"

A clock in the hallway of Blackmoor House rang loudly, announcing the arrival of six o'clock. All three Staffords started.

Will threw his cards down and stood. "That's our cue, lads. Mother wants us home for dinner this evening to discuss the plans for the Worthington Ball."

Nick sighed and rose, then spoke with exasperation in his voice. "You'd think there was nothing more important in all of the British Empire than the season. Lord save us from idle mothers."

"Don't suppose you'd care to join us, Blackmoor?" This from Kit. "After all, you seem quite adept at limiting our involvement in all things season-related."

"I imagine I've done enough for you this particular evening," he said. "A night discussing a ball with your mother as well? I think not."

Will clapped Gavin on the shoulder. "Well said, Blackmoor. We shall let you escape this time — but only because you are such a very good friend."

With that, the three brothers took their leave and Blackmoor found himself alone once more in his study in the dwindling light.

He swore roundly, cursing himself for making the unintelligent — nay, idiotic — offer to escort Alex to the Salisbury Ball. What had he been thinking?

"Clearly not much," he spoke aloud to the room at large.

There was nothing about this situation that could go right. It was bad enough that he'd come dangerously close to compromising Alex's honor with her entire family standing mere feet away — but now he was offering to chaperone her? Alone?

"She's as good as your sister!" Again, he spoke aloud, his voice laced with self-disgust.

Except she wasn't his sister, and he knew that. The emotions he'd felt on the balcony the previous week were far from brotherly. *Very far from brotherly.* Which was why he'd been making every effort to avoid her for the past week. *Eight days.* Not that he'd noticed. Well, he had noticed. But only because they were friends. *Just friends.* And it was to stay that way. The Stafford family had done too much for him, too much for his family, for him to throw it all away and go off kissing Alex. *They trusted him.* And he would not betray that trust. Besides, Alex probably hadn't given that event on the balcony a second thought. *They were only friends.*

"Right, then. That's that."

He paused, then shook his head. He really did need to stop talking to himself.

Alex stood outside the door to the Worthington House sitting room and took a deep breath, gathering her courage before she entered. She knew Blackmoor was on the other side of the door, waiting to escort her to the Salisbury Ball as though nothing had happened between them — as though she hadn't made a fool of herself and thought he was going to kiss her, then stormed off to sulk for the rest of the evening. Or week. Or two.

She had been attempting to remain calm all day, promising herself that she would ignore the fact that he'd practically vanished from existence for the last two weeks. *Sixteen days.* Not that she was counting. She had told herself all afternoon that everything was perfectly normal rather than supremely awkward, that this evening was something she'd been looking forward to, rather than immensely dreading, and that she had never thought of Gavin in any way except as a very dear, very sweet friend. She'd chosen *dear* and *sweet* because they were words she used for children, puppies, and the elderly.

Of course, thinking of Gavin as a puppy hadn't quite settled her ire. To the contrary, as she'd dressed, she'd grown more and more irritated. Irritated with him for being the only person willing to escort her to the ball this evening . . . irritated with her brothers for missing this particular event . . . and irritated with Nicola Salisbury, who'd been her friend since her days in the nursery, for having a mother who would host a ball at all.

"Well, I might as well get this over with," she spoke aloud to the foyer. "It's only a carriage ride, after all . . . after which I shall ignore him for the rest of the evening." Taking a deep breath, squaring her shoulders, and pasting an entirely too bright smile on her face, she turned the handle of the enormous mahogany door and swung it open.

"Good evening, Lord Blackmoor." The words came out a touch too loudly, but she ignored that fact and pressed on. "I trust the evening finds you well?"

Blackmoor turned from where he stood at the window and his eyes widened almost imperceptibly at the picture Alex made, bathed in the brilliant light of the hallway behind her. He swallowed, and Alex took no small amount of pleasure in the fact that he looked as though his mouth had filled with sawdust in just a few brief seconds. She did not let on that she noticed. Or that she knew precisely why he seemed so uncomfortable.

While she had dressed, she had made the decision to take revenge on Blackmoor the only way a young lady in her first season could without making a scene — by donning a ball gown designed to send men into fits.

Madame Fernaud and her mother had created this particular gown in the most current style of the season. The color was a deep, smoky violet — one of her favorites, which showed off her coloring beautifully. The cut was *en vogue*; the dramatically low neckline would have sent her father into conniptions, her brothers as well for that matter — so tonight, when they were all absent and she was being nursemaided by Blackmoor, provided the perfect evening to wear it.

She didn't pretend that there wasn't another reason she had decided to wear this particular gown on this particular evening. Blackmoor was standing in this room, looking equal parts irritated and stunned. *He* couldn't object — as much as she was certain he wanted to. She looked gorgeous in this dress. If she caused a stir tonight, it would be his to deal with and that would serve him right. And they both knew it.

She smiled brilliantly as she noticed he was looking anywhere but directly at her. *Coward,* she thought to herself. *I'll show you to almost kiss me, then disappear for a fortnight.* He swallowed visibly and her grin grew even broader.

"Shall we go, my lord? I should hate to miss the first waltz."

Her words spurred him to action. And he moved gracefully across the room, offering her his arm. "Of course. We couldn't possibly miss the first waltz."

Was there a hint of sarcasm in his tone?

Crossing the foyer, Gavin reminded himself of his pledge to remain aloof this evening and attempted a suitably brotherly, "You look lovely, of course, Alex, but don't you think that gown a touch revealing?"

"I hadn't noticed, my lord."

One of Gavin's golden eyebrows rose at her statement — which he knew was a bald lie. Recognizing a conversation that would best be avoided, Gavin emitted a deep, noncommittal sound from the back of his throat, and with that, they were off.

In the carriage, the two sat silently in an unspoken agreement not to address the previous weeks' events. This was fine with Alex, who, in spite of being thoroughly satisfied with the fact that she had unsettled Blackmoor by wearing a wonderfully revealing dress, remained largely embarrassed by the entire course of events at the Worthington dinner and would prefer they were never addressed again.

She'd just stood there, wavering in the dark, waiting for him to kiss her! Oh! What a fool she must have looked — she'd be surprised if Gavin hadn't gone laughing to her brothers! Oooh . . . she could just imagine his response: *Someone has to get that chit married off!*

Yes, the entire experience was mortifying. She could feel her face flushing now just thinking about it. With a silent prayer of thanks for the dark carriage, she willed her blush away — he clearly wasn't thinking about the dinner . . . so she wouldn't think about it either. Even if it killed her.

Clearing her throat, she forced out, "Thank you for escorting me tonight."

"Of course, Alex. No need to thank me. I was planning to attend, and I know how much you would have hated to miss Nicola's ball."

"That's my reason, yes. But why are you here?"

Gavin leaned back on the seat and stretched out his long legs in front of him. "The most common reason of all, I imagine."

She cocked her head. "Which is?"

"Mothers. And their infernal quest to have their sons matched."

She smiled. Her first authentic one since the beginning of the evening. "Yours as well?"

"Of course. And, because she is in mourning this season, she has little else to do besides dream up places for me to go to meet my future wife. If you ask me, the mourning requirements for widows with children of a marriageable age should be severely limited."

"So why attend the balls at all? She's in the North Country, for goodness sake. She can't force you."

"First, you seem to forget my mother's ability to wield the sword of guilt. She's desperate for news of the season, so I feel obligated to provide it.

"More than that," he continued, "she's now hounding me to step into my duties as earl and, while I feel certain that if she were here every day I could roundly ignore her, the fact that she is absent leads me to at least humor her. Well, that in addition to the fact that I'm certain she's got an army of spies larger than the War Office and I'm afraid of her wrath."

Alex dipped her head respectfully. "A good son. Truly."

"Mmmmm." His reply was noncommittal. "Of course, there is a reason that doesn't have to do with my mother."

Alex's eyebrows rose with her curiosity as the carriage slowed to a halt.

"I couldn't very well let you attend a ball unescorted." The words were still hanging in the air as the door to the carriage opened and Gavin stepped down onto the gravel walkway leading to Salisbury House, turning back to offer his hand to help her descend from the vehicle.

As she did, she spoke with a tone laced with humor. "That would have, indeed, been a risk. Imagine the trouble in which I could find myself without you to watch over me." She paused, pretending to consider the trouble in question, and with an exaggerated sigh, pointed out, "Your overwhelming desire to save me is rather unaccommodating, my lord." She felt a flood of pleasure at his rich laughter and allowed herself to be escorted inside.

Inside, they were announced at the entrance to the ball and greeted by Lord and Lady Salisbury, an odd pair not simply because they were polar opposites — Lord Salisbury tall and reedlike with a somewhat unremarkable personality and his lady a rather small, rotund woman who was, quite possibly, the cheeriest soul in the *ton* — but also because they were thoroughly and publicly smitten with each other, even after six children, all of whom were completely embarrassed by their parents.

"My dears!" spoke Lady Salisbury in her typically excited fashion as she kissed Alex on both cheeks. "We are delighted to host you as always! Nicola has been waiting for you, Alex! But you will have to wait to see her! You have arrived just in time! The first waltz is starting now! You mustn't miss it!"

And with a quick greeting for Lord Salisbury, they were swept up in a wave of people moving toward the dance floor. Lady Salisbury had been right — the music began immediately.

"Have you ever noticed," Blackmoor offered, "that Lady Salisbury speaks not in sentences but in exclamations?"

Alex caught her giggle and turned an impish gaze on him. "My lord! Whatever do you mean?!"

His rich laughter swirled around them. "If I am damned for noting such a thing about such a kind woman, you are surely joining me for imitating her."

The two relaxed and danced in companionable silence. Sneaking a glance up at Gavin, she attempted to discover some sign that the previous weeks' events had rattled him at all. She couldn't and, in that moment, whirling across the ballroom, she realized that she'd been silly to think that Gavin, this Gavin, whom she'd known all her life, might have given a second thought to her in any way other than as a very dear friend.

She sighed with twin relief and disappointment — relief because they wouldn't have to talk about the incident and could go on as though it had never happened, and disappointment for the very same reasons.

The latter emotion frightened her slightly and led her to take leave of his company after the waltz to seek out Nicola Salisbury, whom she found without much difficulty, deep in conversation with Ella and Vivi, across the room.

Nicola had always been a welcome addition to their trio — a wickedly funny person who was always willing to say something outlandish. A Salisbury, Nicola's pedigree and immense wealth required the rest of London society to tolerate her unique personality. Not that she cared a whit. She was one of the few people Alex knew who did and said whatever she liked and truly didn't care what others thought of her — a rare quality in a member of the *ton* — and Alex had always quite liked her.

Making her way toward the threesome, Alex couldn't help but smile. None of her friends had any interest in the fact that they were virtually surrounded by eligible young men, all attempting to look calm and confident but managing only to look desperate for the attention of the three young women.

She shook her head with something close to pity for the poor young pups. None of them would garner more than a polite smile from her friends tonight — of that, she was quite certain.

Arriving at the spot where they were, Alex adopted her best stage whisper and said, "You lot really ought to keep moving — you're attracting a crowd."

With equal starts, the threesome looked up and scanned their surroundings, prompting their admirers to smile, sweep into elaborate bows, and generally make fools of themselves.

Nicola rolled her eyes quite publicly and leaned in to hug Alex. "Ridiculous. Do they really think fawning is going to help their common cause? And hello to you, Lady Alexandra." She spoke the title exaggeratedly, holding Alex at arm's length to study her. "This color is incredible on you. The neckline, too. My God — if they were interested in us . . . they're quite beside themselves now! I think Waring is in need of smelling salts. Did I see you come in with Blackmoor? He has his work as escort cut out for him this evening!"

Alex laughed at the exaggerated compliments as Vivi spoke. "Good Lord! How did there come to be so many of them? Which one of us do you suppose they're here for?"

"I'm not certain they've crafted much of an opinion on that front, to be honest," Alex said with a smile. "I should think that if any one of you showed the smallest amount of interest, any one of them would come running."

"Dear God, don't do that, then!" Nicola replied with mock alarm.

"What interesting creatures." Ella spoke with such an undertone of scientific research that the rest of the girls couldn't help their laughter.

Looking over Alex's shoulder, Vivi lowered her voice and spoke just loudly enough for the group to hear. "Careful, Alex, here comes someone whom I daresay knows exactly 'which one' he's here for."

Before Alex could turn to see who Vivi was speaking of, she heard the rich, amused tenor of Freddie Stanhope's voice. "You four shouldn't be over here all by yourselves. The sharks are circling."

With genuine pleasure, Alex smiled up at her friend. "We were just noticing that ourselves, my lord. You are certainly well met."

"Indeed," Nicola boldly added, "unless you are circling as well, my lord?"

Freddie put his hand to his chest in mock hurt. "Certainly not, my lady. You wound me to suggest such a thing." He added a distinctly lewd waggle of his eyebrows, sending the girls into giggles.

In a conspiratorial whisper, he continued, "Shall I escort you beauties elsewhere and away from these young pups?"

Ella replied with amusement, "I'm not certain they wouldn't follow, but your plan seems as good as any."

Freddie leaned toward Ella. "I wouldn't be concerned. Not one of them appears to be committed to proper wooing — if they were worth their salt, I would have had to throw elbows to get so close to the four of you."

"Intriguing," spoke Alex. "So now that you have laid claim to us — someone will have to throw elbows to intercede?"

Freddie turned a wickedly handsome smile on her. "Lady Alexandra, I'm not the kind of man to lay claim to four women at once — I'm merely offering my protection to all of you. For now" — he paused, pretending to consider a vital question — "I shall simply fill your dance cards."

He proceeded to do just that, ending with Alex. As he looked down at the little card dangling from her wrist, he shook his head in mock disappointment. "Why, Alexandra Stafford — it can't be possible you have the next waltz free. Unless . . . you were saving it for a dashing suitor?"

"Indeed, my lord, I was." Alex cocked her head and considered him. "But I suppose you'll do."

And, with that, he whisked her into his arms and onto the dance floor. He didn't waste any time before flirting wickedly. "You're the most beautiful woman in the room, Alex."

She smiled up at him. "And you are the greatest bounder in the room, Freddie."

"True. Yet you can't help but enjoy my company. Admit it."

"I never said I didn't enjoy it . . . but I'm told it's risky. Ella and Vivi think you've got me in your sights."

"And if they were right?" His voice was deeper than usual, and she imagined this was exactly the tone he'd practiced to send young women into fits.

She scoffed. "Save it, Stanhope. If you thought even for a minute that I might possibly fall for you, you'd run. Far. And fast."

"Too true, my brilliant, perceptive friend. Too true."

"Someday, Freddie . . . someday, some young lady is going to set you on your ear. And you won't be able to resist her."

"Never."

"And, with such pompous self-confidence, it's a certainty."

"I shall shamelessly flirt with you and drive her away."

"This isn't shameless flirting already?"

"Not at all! I'm just getting started." They swirled under the twinkling lights as Alex's laughter drifted across the dance floor and he continued casually, "But, my lady, you seem to have an altogether different admirer who can't take his eyes off you. And, at this particular moment, he doesn't appear at all pleased that you are enjoying yourself in my arms." She started to look to see to whom he was referring, when he stopped her quickly. "Don't look, kitten. Then he'll know we're discussing him."

"Who?"

"You mean you don't know? You haven't noticed him watching you all evening? All season?"

"Freddie, WHO?"

"Blackmoor, of course."

"You're touched." Alex laughed, shaking her head. "He's not been watching me all season, and if he *has* been watching me tonight, it's only because he feels obligated to. He's my chaperone for the evening."

Freddie laughed shortly. "Really? Your *chaperone*? It seems to me that your family are the ones who are touched, Alex. They're practically feeding you to the lion."

"You don't know what you're talking about, Freddie. Blackmoor has no interest in me other than pseudobrotherly admiration."

"Oh? I've two sisters myself, if you'll remember, Alex. And I've never looked at one of them quite the way he's looking at you right now."

It took all of Alex's strength not to look. "Which is how, precisely?"

"As though he doesn't know if he wants to kiss you or kill you."

She gasped, a blush coming to her cheeks. "Freddie!"

"Don't shoot the messenger, sweet."

"You're sorely mistaken."

"Perhaps." The music came to a crescendo and they whirled to a halt, Freddie bowing low over her hand and lingering a touch longer than was entirely proper. He winked up at her and whispered, "Let's find out, shall we?" Then, louder and with a rakish grin, "Shall we find the exit to the garden, my lady? I daresay we both could use some . . . air."

"I don't think that will be at all necessary, Stanhope." The statement cut through the air like a knife, and Alex felt her stomach drop with the realization that Blackmoor was standing immediately behind her. She looked up at Freddie, wide-eyed, not quite knowing what to do.

He spoke with an air of bored dismissal. "Blackmoor, what a surprise. What is it you want?"

Blackmoor's tone brooked no refusal, but was surprisingly hushed, only loud enough for the three of them to hear. "I want you to stay away from Lady Alexandra, Stanhope. She is most definitely not in need of a walk in the gardens with the likes of you."

"I suppose you would be a better companion?" Freddie drawled. Alex could sense that this conversation was not going to end well but had a nagging suspicion that Freddie was quite enjoying himself.

"Most certainly. I'm practically her brother." Freddie gave a short laugh at this, which made Blackmoor even more angry. "More importantly," he continued, "I'm her escort this evening, and I say where she goes and who she goes with. And she is most certainly not going anywhere with you."

"I beg your pardon?" Alex spoke, keeping her voice hushed, but pulling herself up to her full height and stepping between the two men. Her face flushed with indignation as she leveled Blackmoor with a dark look. "What did you just say?" He looked down at her mutely as she pressed on. "I'm almost certain that you implied . . . nay . . . dictated . . . that you have some kind of control over my behavior."

He opened his mouth to speak, but she cut him off. "I think it best you say no more, my lord, lest you embarrass yourself further. Let me be clear. Last I was aware, you were neither my husband nor my father nor my king. Therefore, any control you may imagine you hold over me is just that — imaginary." She continued, her anger making her voice waver, "If I want to take a walk in the gardens with Stanhope, or with anyone else for that matter, that is entirely my business. I will thank you to stay out of my affairs. Or need I remind you that it is not *Stanhope* whom I've had to be wary of on balconies recently?"

Her whispered question dropped between them, and Blackmoor's face turned to stone. She saw fury flash before he offered her a short bow and turned away, only to be swallowed up almost immediately by the crush of people who remained unaware of the scene that had just occurred.

Fists clenched in fury, Alex watched him go.

"Well . . ." drawled Stanhope once he disappeared, "that was certainly more illuminating than I had expected it would be."

"Oh, shut up, Freddie."

"My lips are sealed, kitten . . . but may I make a small suggestion? Two, actually."

"As if I could stop you?"

"First, I wouldn't necessarily mention that part about balconies so freely and in such close company. It's not exactly a flattering picture of Blackmoor . . . and could be damaging to your reputation."

"Thank you, Freddie." Her voice was laced with sarcasm. "I hadn't realized that."

"Sarcasm doesn't become you, sweet." He pressed on. "Second . . . I'd imagine Blackmoor will be rather . . . put out . . . that you brought that up in front of me."

"More than put out," she replied. "Livid."

"A choice word."

"So what's your second suggestion?"

"Tread lightly."

"That's it? That's the best advice you can give me?"

"All right, tread *very* lightly."

thirteen

Alex did walk in the gardens that evening — alone.

She snuck out not long after the debacle with Blackmoor, shaking with fury. She was furious with him for being so boorish, furious with herself for being so quick to rise, and furious with Freddie for seeming to understand everything that was happening — when she didn't even *know* what was happening at any given moment.

She trudged up the garden path, feeling more miserable by the moment as she moved farther from the house.

She really shouldn't have mentioned the balcony in front of Stanhope. Not that she was worried that he would tell anyone — despite Blackmoor's opinion of him, Alex knew Freddie had a strong sense of right and it simply wouldn't cross his mind to do or say anything that would impugn her honor.

No, she shouldn't have said anything about the balcony because she should have known it would insult and offend Blackmoor. He hated to be caught unawares, prided himself on being able to predict the trajectory of a conversation, and she'd ambushed him — not only because she'd said it in front of Stanhope, but because she'd said it at all — breaking their clear unspoken agreement never to discuss it again.

Perhaps *that* was what bothered her so much . . . the fact that he was thoroughly prepared to forever ignore the fact that for one fleeting moment, they might have been more than friends. Not that she wanted that. *Or did she?* No! Certainly not. And even if she did, she most certainly did not want to marry, which meant she couldn't very well go kissing him on balconies. Or anywhere else for that matter.

Of course, she did wish they'd kissed that one time. She was very curious about this part of the whole dilemma. And now it was all she thought about when she thought about him. She sighed. "Oh, Alexandra. How have you become such a complete ninny?"

The whispered question hung in the air — no answer springing immediately to mind. She sighed again heavily and took a seat on one of the marble benches that were distributed about the Salisbury gardens. She pulled her slippered feet up beneath her gown, wrapping her arms about her knees.

She could hear the faint sounds of the ball in the distance, laughter and chatter intermingled with the notes of a country dance, and she wondered if Vivi and Ella were dancing, and with whom. The quiet sounds were matched by the dim light spilling across the gardens and allowing her to just barely see in the darkness. She rested her chin on her knees and closed her eyes, wondering how long she would be able to stay outside the ball before someone realized she was missing and came looking for her. She was going to have to make her way back at some point and seek out someone to escort her home — if she knew one thing, she knew she would not ask Blackmoor to perform the task.

She heard a rustle behind her and she stood nervously, knowing that she could find herself in rather a lot of trouble in the event she were discovered by a single gentleman. She peered into the darkness beyond as a female figure appeared, rushing up the garden path and muttering to herself. Squinting, Alex recognized Ella — clearly wrapped up in her own thoughts and not looking where she was going.

"What are you doing out here all alone?" Alex didn't hide the surprise in her tone as she stepped into her friend's path.

The question caught Ella unaware and, with an extraordinarily loud shriek, she jumped into the air, terrified. The sight was so comical that Alex doubled over with welcome laughter.

When she straightened again, Ella was holding her hand to her chest, waiting for her heart to stop racing. She said sternly, "That wasn't as amusing as you seem to think."

Alex smirked at her friend. "That's because you were on the wrong end of the hilarity. You are incredibly well met, Ella."

"What are you doing out here?" Ella had recovered and was back to her inquisitive self.

"I asked you that first, if you'll recall."

"Vaguely. That happened just as you took a dozen years off my life?"

"Just then, yes."

"I rather think that you should tell me first. Considering you terrified me and then laughed at me."

"It's a ridiculous and somewhat lengthy story that makes me appear alternately unpleasant and irrational. I'd rather not discuss it at this particular moment."

Ella cocked her head. "That sounds like a *very* interesting story. I will allow you to postpone sharing it only because I have a very interesting story of my own."

"And this is why I adore you. Not only do you spare me embarrassment, you do it in the most entertaining of ways."

"'Tis true."

Alex resumed her seat on the bench and patted the space next to her. "Join me, friend. I welcome your allegedly interesting story."

Ella seated herself beside Alex and began, "I was avoiding the next dance on my card —"

"With whom?"

"Lord Grabeham."

"Aah . . . Grabhands." Alex nodded with an air of understanding.

"Quite." Ella pressed on, "So I escaped to the balcony, where I saw Baron Montgrave slipping off into the garden —"

"Oh, Ella. Your obsession really is becoming rather worrisome."

"It's not an obsession! Which you would understand if you would let me finish a sentence."

"If that isn't the pot calling the kettle black, I don't know what is, but" — Alex offered an exaggerated magnanimous gesture — "please, go on."

Ella tipped her head. "Thank you. Where was I?"

"While I'm not entirely sure, I think you might have been traipsing off into the darkness with a man who is thrice your age."

"Shh! First, there was no traipsing involved. I followed him. At a discreet distance."

"I beg your pardon?!"

"And second, keep your voice down! If someone overheard, it could ruin me!"

"All right!" Alex whispered. "What would *possess* you to follow him —"

"At a discreet distance," Ella cut in.

"Fine, at a discreet distance — into a deserted garden?"

"Well, it doesn't seem that it was *entirely* deserted," Ella pointed out, "but we will come to that particular truth later, I assure you. I don't *know* why I did it . . . curiosity, boredom, whatever. It is really irrelevant now, really. The point is, I did."

"And?"

"And . . . I think . . ." Ella's voice lowered to a whisper that Alex could barely hear. "I think I overheard something I shouldn't have."

"Like what?" The two had their heads bowed so closely together that they were almost touching.

"I'm not entirely sure. The baron met with another gentleman in the garden, but I couldn't make out the other person or the conversation very clearly — they were speaking very quietly, and I had just the smallest inkling that they were discussing something . . ."

Alex waited as Ella paused for drama. Ella adored dramatic emphasis.

"Nefarious."

Ella's whisper barely made any sound at all, and Alex couldn't help the half smile that played at the corner of her mouth. "Nefarious?"

Ella nodded once, curtly. "Yes. Nefarious."

"All right, Ella." Alex's tone was designed to humor her friend as she sat back on the bench. "What 'nefarious' thing do you think you overheard?"

"Again, I can't be certain of that part of it," Ella was quick to respond, "but there are a few things I *am* certain of." She began ticking off her fingers as she spoke. "First, he was most definitely meeting someone at a time that had been predetermined in a place that had been prearranged. He went straight to the spot without dawdling."

"All right, but that means little, you understand."

Ignoring Alex, she pressed on. "Second, the person he met was not dressed in formal attire. I had the distinct impression that the other man was not a guest of the Salisburys. *And* . . . they greeted each other in French!"

"That is odd, considering the baron is French," Alex said drily.

Ella gave her a quelling look. "Third, the conversation was laced with obscurity. They were discussing 'the problem,' and 'the situation.' At one point, the other gentleman said something about 'the situation being resolved this evening without delay.'"

Alex opened her mouth to speak, only to be stopped by Ella's raised hand and dramatic flourish. "*And* . . . if all of that weren't enough . . . I could swear I heard the baron refer to *un voleur.*"

"A thief? Are you certain?"

"Not entirely . . . but that could have been it! Who speaks in such a manner? Spies, if you ask me."

Alex laughed aloud before saying, "Few people speak that way, I'll grant you. But we still have little indication that the baron is anything more than a kind, if slightly eccentric, old man. We certainly have no indication that he is a spy, for goodness sake. Vivi's father and Blackmoor's uncle both know him and find him to be a welcome addition to their circles, so I see no reason to surmise that he's a villain of the first water. Would you like to hear my theory on the matter?"

"Most certainly," Ella replied eagerly.

"You've been thinking about your novel too much . . .

and your imagination has become overactive." This was said with a grin.

"That may be the case," Ella agreed in a tone that suggested she'd not thought of that possibility.

"*May* be? You think that sweet old man is out to topple the Crown."

"Quite." Ella cleared her throat. "But it *was* an odd occurrence."

"Certainly. But I highly doubt it was an issue of national security. How did it end?"

"Calmly. They shook hands and parted ways. I waited five minutes or so and made my way back — and found you!" Her tone turned excited and curious. "What are *you* doing out here, Alexandra Stafford?"

"Not terribly much," Alex spoke casually. "Taking in the evening air, pondering life's mysteries, selling state secrets to the French . . ."

Ella chuckled. "A common occurrence this evening, it seems." She paused for a moment, waiting for Alex to speak. When she didn't, Ella spoke again. "Are you going to tell me?"

"I'd rather hoped not to."

Ella nodded thoughtfully. "Are you all right?"

"Yes. Just nursing a slight case of embarrassment and irritation."

"Ah. So you shall be fine."

"Indeed."

The two sat in companionable silence borne of years of friendship, each allowing the other's presence to calm her. Alex took a deep breath and looked up at the starlit sky, wondering if she and Ella would be missed if they stayed out here for the rest of the evening.

Sadly, they would be. Not looking away from the sky, Alex spoke. "We should make our way back."

"I suppose so."

They stood and fluffed their skirts, then crossed the lush gardens to the ballroom. As they ascended the steps to the open doors, where several couples were standing in the fresh air, Ella spoke a touch louder than usual, "It was a lovely walk we took, don't you agree?"

Alex smiled at her friend. "Most calming indeed. Thank you very much for thinking of it." She nodded at Lord Denton, who bowed as they passed, clearly hearing their conversation.

"Think nothing of it," Ella offered with a grin as they stepped over the threshold and into the ballroom.

The two had paused just barely, attempting to get their bearings, when the hairs on the back of Alex's neck rose. She knew before looking that Blackmoor was standing nearby.

There he was, an appropriate distance from her, a combination of boredom and anger in his eyes. She had a feeling the boredom was affected, but she was quite certain that the anger was entirely real. Ella glanced over and noticed him with a smile, offering a quick, "Good evening, Lord Blackmoor," before remarking to Alex, "I see Vivi by the refreshment table. . . . I'm going to join her. I shall see you inside?"

"Yes." Alex's response was lost in the crowd as Ella pushed through. She sighed and muttered to herself, "You know, for someone so observant, Ella, you can be rather oblivious when you want to be." She turned back to Blackmoor and spoke up, "If you are here to scold me, I assure you it's unnecessary."

"I'm here to tell you that I'm leaving. If you would care for transport home, you should say your good-byes." His voice was cool and distant.

She briefly considered refusing him and asking the Marquess of Langford to bring her home, but she knew that would make Blackmoor even more irritated, and she wasn't in the mood to push him any further.

"Very well, my lord" — she made her voice as cool as his own — "I shall only be a few minutes."

The two rode home in stony silence, neither interested in forgiving or forgetting the events of the evening. When the carriage arrived at Worthington House, Blackmoor, ever the gentleman, exited the carriage to help Alex down from the vehicle. Once on solid ground, Alex offered a quiet, "Thank you, my lord."

He did not respond, except to offer a short bow, at which point she turned and entered the house, closing the door behind her and not waiting to see if he returned to the carriage or not. She thanked the night footman who had been waiting for her return home, and relieved him of his duties so that he could find his bed. Just as she'd done that, her mother's voice spilled into the foyer from the library. "Alexandra? Is that you?" And, with a sigh, Alex went to find her.

"Indeed, 'tis I, the princess returned from the ball," she quipped as she threw herself into a leather chair, kicked off her slippers, tucked her feet up under her, and began unbuttoning her elbow-length gloves.

Her mother and father were seated in identical chairs in a ritual she had witnessed hundreds of times before. When one of the children was out of the house and expected back late, they would stay awake and keep each other company as they waited for the child who was due home. Her father would nurse a glass of scotch while her mother read, but they always ended up chatting. Alex had fallen asleep on the floor of the library to the sound of their discussions countless times as she was growing up. As difficult as her evening had been, it comforted her to join them.

Her father spoke first, his rich voice gently questioning, "That doesn't sound like the response of a young lady home from a thoroughly amusing evening."

"Was the ball not enjoyable, my love?" This from her mother.

"The ball itself was lovely," Alex shared, peeling one long sheath of satin down her wrist and off her hand, draping it across the arm of the chair. "Nicola was gorgeous and entertaining as ever, and Lord and Lady Salisbury were . . . well,

Lord and Lady Salisbury." The last drew a smile from both her parents.

"If that's the case, why are you so subdued?" her father queried, teasing. "Did some oaf step on your toes during a quadrille?"

Alex offered him a half smile she didn't quite feel. "I wish that were the case. No, if you must know, Blackmoor and I had a falling-out."

"Whatever about?" asked the duchess.

Sighing, Alex focused entirely on her glove as she tugged each satin finger from her hand. "Well, everything was fine until I danced with someone of whom he did not approve."

"Who?" The duke perked up.

Yanking the glove from her hand, she waved it in frustration. "Freddie Stanhope! Thoroughly innocuous Freddie Stanhope."

"I thought Stanhope and Blackmoor were friends?" The duchess looked to Alex's father for confirmation. He didn't speak as Alex continued.

"So did I, until this season. Will, Nick, and Kit seem to enjoy Freddie's company as much as ever, but Blackmoor thinks him a rogue and not to be trusted around females. Especially me. Which is ridiculous, considering Freddie and I have been friends for ages."

"It is rather strange. I've always rather liked young Stanhope," said the duchess.

This elicited a laugh from His Grace. "I imagine that's exactly why Gavin thinks the way he does. For generations women have 'rather liked' the Stanhope men." Turning back to Alex, he asked, "Has young Stanhope been inappropriate in your presence?"

"Never," Alex spoke vehemently. "To the contrary, Freddie's been a capital friend — certainly a bit of a rake — but harmless. After all, I've known him for years and he's very close with Nick. We just have fun together and Blackmoor seems out to ruin anything that seems to entertain me. He takes his role as surrogate brother too seriously, and tonight he overstepped his bounds, leaving me a touch —"

She stopped and returned to working the fabric of her skirts. Her voice quieted as she finished her sentence on a whispered, "— incensed."

The duke laughed at the sheepish way she spoke her final word, but her mother did not seem so amused. "Oh, Alexandra," she spoke knowingly, "what did you do?"

"Nothing!" Alex's face and tone were the combination of perfect defensiveness. "He started it by implying that he was my keeper . . . as though I were some animal! He doesn't trust me to know what's best for myself or how to care for myself, and so I told him *exactly* what I thought!"

"Intriguing," spoke the duke, his tone laced with amusement. "In private, I hope."

"Well — you see — that's the problem."

Alex felt a blush rising as her father laughed out loud and her mother gasped, "Alexandra Stafford!" The duchess spoke to her husband sharply. "This is because you are too lenient with her." Turning back to Alex, she queried, "Where did you 'tell him *exactly* what you thought'?"

The answer sped out, "On the ballroom floor . . . but no one heard!"

"Alexandra!" her mother cried.

"No one?" This from the duke.

"Well, no one except Freddie."

When her father spoke next, he did so with a tone of humor. "I'd lay odds that, considering Blackmoor's opinion of Stanhope, he hardly thinks of him as 'no one.'"

"Quite," Her Grace added. "Yes, well, that would explain why you and Gavin had a falling-out."

Alex was about to again defend herself when the sound of Harquist clearing his throat interrupted her. Alex turned in surprise, as Harquist rarely had much to say this late in the evening. The old man spoke quickly, "My lord and ladies, Lord Blackmoor is here and requests an audience."

Alex turned a stunned look on her mother and father, who looked surprised and curious respectively. She spoke in an urgent whisper. "Father, don't accept him, please? I can't have another moment of his overbearing attitude this evening."

"I most certainly will accept him, Alexandra," replied the Duke. "You'll have to suffer through. Send him in, Harquist, thank you."

Alex sent a pleading look at her mother, who made no move to rescue her youngest child and only daughter. Alex wondered if she had enough time to escape the room before Blackmoor arrived.

"My lord," Gavin spoke as he crossed the threshold, "forgive me for calling at such a late hour."

Drat. No escape, Alex thought to herself as she patently avoided looking at him.

"It's never too late an hour for you, Gavin." Alex's father stood. "You look like the Devil. What's happened to you?"

Alex couldn't help but look up at Gavin upon hearing the tone in her father's voice. He did indeed look the worse for wear. His face was flushed and he was breathing heavily, as though he'd run all the way over. Was it possible he'd come to apologize? One of her eyebrows rose in curiosity as he opened his mouth to speak.

"I never would have bothered you had it not been a matter of particular import. You see —" Alex leaned forward. Could it be that he was going to confess his actions at the Worthington House dinner? What could he possibly be here for in the middle of the night?

"It's Blackmoor House. I've been robbed."

fourteen

He stalked his rooms, furious.

This night had been essential to his plans. He'd convinced his partners that they should give him one more chance — one more day to discover what they were desperate to find. He'd promised that he would find the documents they now knew the deceased earl had possessed. He'd sworn he could complete this — the smallest of tasks. For he knew that if anyone else found the information before him, his would be the first neck placed in the hangman's noose.

And he had failed.

He'd not given the study as thorough an inspection as he'd wanted. He'd started . . . he'd emptied the desk and searched the cupboards. He'd just begun to examine the bookshelves when he saw the carriage lanterns in the drive of Worthington House and realized that his time had run out.

If only the brat hadn't come home early from the ball. If only he'd stayed out with the rest of the shallow, debauched members of the ton, *celebrating in excess, as though there were nothing in the world to worry about. What could have happened to force him to come home hours before he was expected? Maybe the Worthington twit had taken ill . . . leaving*

Blackmoor little more to do than escort her home. What good manners. He sneered at the thought.

And then, in an instant, he was struck with an undeniable sense of calm. The solution was clear, as though there had never been any doubt.

Without information, there was no way he could be caught, and the boy was the only person convinced there was more to the earl's death than appeared at first glance. The boy was the problem — always had been. The Earl of Blackmoor was all that was left between him and his safety. His freedom. Without him, no one would care to search for answers about the happenings on the Essex estate. No one would care to discover the truth about the earl's death.

The solution was clear.

He already had Blackmoor blood on his hands. What was a little more?

Several hours later, Alex was still in the library with her mother, only now they were waiting for the return of her father from Blackmoor House, where he'd gone immediately following Blackmoor's startling announcement.

Blackmoor's words were still hanging in the air when the duke had leapt into action, asking Harquist to wake the footmen to take messages to the Bow Street Runners, the private investigators who kept the peace in London, and to the Marquess of Langford, who was one of the best investigators in Britain. Once the messengers were dispatched, the duke and young earl returned to Blackmoor House to assess the situation. His Grace had said little, except to tell his wife and daughter that they should not wait for him to return before retiring to their beds.

Of course, the Stafford women had no intention of taking to their bedchambers before they knew what exactly had transpired that evening at Blackmoor House and what was going to be done to find the criminal who had robbed Gavin.

Alex had alternately attempted to read, to embroider, and to catch up on her correspondence to cousins on the Continent, to no avail. Instead, now she found herself awake at quarter past three in the morning, listening to the sound of her mother's breathing as the duchess napped in her chair.

The waiting gave her plenty of time to reflect on her behavior at the ball, at the Worthington dinner, and in the two weeks that separated the events, as well as on her own feelings for Blackmoor, which she was terrified to admit.

The more she thought about him, the more she worried — not about the burglary, which was unfortunate, to be sure, but would be addressed by Bow Street and her father. No, she worried about the fact that they were so clearly growing apart; she worried that they seemed to have a markedly different relationship now from what they'd ever had before; and she worried that she'd ruined whatever relationship they might have by losing her temper in front of Freddie. She simply hadn't been herself since they'd nearly kissed.

They *had* nearly kissed, hadn't they?

Torturing herself, she replayed the scene on the Worthington House balcony over and over in her mind, each time wondering if she'd been mad to think that he was actually going to kiss her. Perhaps all this emotion was for naught. Perhaps she'd misread the situation — after all, it was not a situation in which she commonly found herself. Perhaps they *hadn't* been close to kissing. Perhaps it was all in her head. She hadn't really wanted to kiss him anyway.

Of course she had.

Yes, she had wanted the kiss. She still did. No, she wanted more than that. She wanted him to want her back. When on earth had that happened? She sighed, dismayed by the fact that the season had made most things in her life unpleasantly complicated.

The clock in the hallway chimed half past three, marking two hours since her father and Gavin had left the house to meet the runner. Alex looked up at the ceiling, wondering how much longer she would have to wait before her father came home with news.

She had just decided to send a footman over to Blackmoor House to check on the status of the evening when she heard the front door open and her father's rich tenor. "It's no trouble at all, Gavin. You know that. Your mother would have our heads if we didn't offer you a roof tonight, of all nights. More important, the duchess wouldn't stand for anything else. This I know."

Alex stood and walked to the door of the library to find the duke and Blackmoor handing their topcoats and walking sticks to Harquist, who had stayed awake to await his master. "Thank you, Harquist. Please have a chamber made for Lord Blackmoor, and then that will be all, my good man. You have outdone yourself this evening," the duke said warmly.

Blackmoor chimed in, "Indeed, Harquist. Thank you for all your help."

"My lords, it was my pleasure," spoke the old man. "Lord Blackmoor, the crimson chamber already awaits you. Her Grace expected you would join us this evening." With a short bow he took his leave.

The duke offered Blackmoor a weary smile. "You see? You are quite welcome here tonight, my boy." Turning, he noticed Alex. "Still awake, moppet?"

She nodded seriously. "Of course. Mother and I stayed awake to make certain that everything was set to right." With a nod over her shoulder she corrected herself. "Well, Mother and I stayed *downstairs* to make certain that everything was set to right. Awake is another matter."

As if on cue, the duchess emerged from the library to wrap Blackmoor in an enveloping hug as she said, "I know you're an earl now, Gavin, but even earls need some mothering now and then."

Gavin's arms caught the duchess in a firm hold as he hugged her back and said, "Indeed, they do."

The duchess pulled back and placed a kiss on each of Blackmoor's cheeks. "You will stay with us tonight." It was not a question.

"Yes, thank you, Your Grace."

The duchess waved away the thanks. "The crimson room is already prepared. Alexandra will remind you of the way."

Gavin nodded. "Thank you, Your Grace."

"Nonsense. We shall see you at breakfast." Turning to Alex, she spoke regally, "Alexandra, I should think Gavin has had enough excitement for one evening. Endeavor not to add to it."

A blush rose high on Alex's cheeks as she accepted her mother's kiss. "Yes, Mother."

"Good night."

And, with that, the duke and duchess took their leave of Alex and Blackmoor, and climbed the stairs to their bedchambers.

Shaking herself out of her trance following her parents' departure, Alex turned and re-entered the library to put out the candles and prepare a light to guide them to the upper floors of the house. The task kept her from thinking too seriously about the fact that she was, once again, alone with Blackmoor. She turned from her task, candle in hand, to find him leaning against the doorjamb, rubbing the back of his neck and watching her intently.

Alex spoke quickly, eager to fill the air. "My lord, is all well?"

He offered her a brief, tired smile. "As well as can be expected, I imagine. I confess, I am happy to be here tonight."

"We are happy to host you. I imagine things will look better in the morning . . . or at least brighter."

"One can certainly hope."

"Neither my mother nor I would have stood for your being alone at Blackmoor House this evening."

Gavin smiled wearily. "The two of you are an irresistible force. I shan't put up a fight."

In the pause that followed, Alex searched for a safe topic — one that would offset her nervousness about being alone with him. "Was much taken in the burglary?"

He shook his head quickly. "No. In fact, nothing that I could discern. It seems that the intruder was interrupted. I'm left with all my possessions, but quite a mess to clean up."

"You mean the intruder was in the house when you arrived home?" The idea sent a chill down Alex's spine.

"I imagine so." Seeing the alarm on Alex's face, Gavin stepped toward her. "But I did not see him. So all is well."

"Aside from the fact that you could have been killed, you mean . . . and all because of me!"

"Because of you?" His confusion was obvious in his tone.

"Of course! If we hadn't quarreled . . ." She trailed off.

"If we hadn't quarreled, I wouldn't have surprised the intruder and I could well be missing valuable items from

Blackmoor House. As it is, I've lost only the time it takes to set the study to right."

"Still . . ." She paused, then spoke, looking down at her feet. "I'm sorry."

"There's no need for you to apologize."

"There is. I'm not just sorry about the burglary — although I am sorry about that. I'm sorry about this evening, and about Freddie, and for making you so very angry, and . . . for everything." By the end of the sentence, her voice was barely a whisper.

"Alex."

She couldn't look up at him.

"Alexandra. Look at me."

With a sigh, she did, meeting his gaze as he spoke firmly. "You don't have to apologize for any of that. I incited you . . . I know that now as much as I knew it then. I'm sorry that I was boorish. I should have checked my behavior long before it came to our arguing in the middle of a ball." He reached out and took the candle from her hands, setting it on a nearby table before taking her hands in his. "*I'm* the one who should be apologizing. I don't know what got into me about Freddie. I've always quite liked him. But this season . . . seeing him flirting with you . . . it's been . . . difficult to watch. And I *know* my behavior has been reprehensible."

"You have to stop thinking of me as your sister, Gavin."

He offered her a half smile. "That seems to be the singular problem." Confusion clouded her emerald eyes as he continued,

"You see, I *haven't* been thinking of you as my sister. In fact, the way I've been thinking when it comes to you is the very *opposite* of brotherly."

The words hung in the air and Alex's eyes widened as understanding dawned.

He offered a self-deprecating smile. "I see you take my meaning." He let go of her hands and ran his fingers through his hair as though he didn't know what to do with them. "You needn't worry. I'm not going to act on my feelings."

"Why?" Alex asked the question without thinking.

"If only I knew why. It began at the start of the season, and at first I chalked it up to my missing you while I was in mourning. Which I did. But instead of the feelings dissipating as I spent time in your company" — he slashed a hand through the air in frustration — "they only seemed to grow stronger."

Alex looked up at him, meeting his frustrated grey eyes. "Not why are you feeling the way you are, Gavin. Why aren't you going to act on those feelings?"

He froze. Neither of them moved, each afraid to take the next step. The first step.

The moment stretched out into what seemed like an eternity and Alex began to feel awkward, as though she had said the wrong thing. "I — I'm sorry. I — I don't know what prompted me to ask such a thing." She started to take a step backward.

"No." The word was soft, but brooked no refusal. She went still as he continued, "There are a dozen reasons why I shouldn't act on them." He lifted his hands to cradle her face between them. "A hundred reasons why I should turn around and walk out of this room." He leaned down until he was a hairbreadth away from her. "But I'm through listening to them." And, with that, he kissed her.

The instant she felt his lips touch hers, feather soft, Alex couldn't stop herself from returning the kiss, from reveling in it. His lips were warm and firm, and the feeling of them so wonderful that all thought escaped her. This was it, her first kiss — and with such an unexpected person in such an unexpected place at such an unexpected time. But it was perfect . . . and she never wanted it to end. She wanted to stand here forever, basking in the glow of this perfect moment — the feel of his hands on her cheeks, the warmth of his body, the sound of his breathing, the way her head was spinning.

Of course, it did end. Too soon. But, when it was over, he placed his forehead against her own, closed his eyes, and took a deep breath, as though steadying himself before letting her go.

"I've been waiting to do that for weeks," he said with surprise in his voice. "I'm rather shocked that it happened."

She smiled shyly. "No more shocked than I, I imagine."

"So you don't want to stomp on my foot and run from the room?"

"Not at all. I rather enjoyed the whole experience."

He chuckled. "I'm happy to hear that."

She blushed at his laugh and looked down at the floor, wondering what the proper etiquette was for this particular situation. Fast on the heels of that question came the realization that there was absolutely no code of conduct to follow, as their behavior had been highly improper. *What happened now?*

The question floated through her mind just as the clock in the hallway struck four. She met Gavin's gaze with a startled one of her own.

He responded by picking up the candle from where he'd set it earlier and telling her, "I think it's time to take to our beds, Lady Alexandra. This has been a particularly full evening."

She hid the disappointment from her reply. "Most certainly. You must be exhausted."

He raised an eyebrow at her statement and turned toward the door, "On the contrary, I seem to have an excess of energy now, thanks to you."

She blushed again, thankful for the dim light. *What had gotten into her?*

He waited for her to pass through the doorway into the foyer before following her with the light. At the foot of the stairs, just before Alex began her ascent, he spoke quietly, "Hold." She looked back at him curiously as he whispered, "I didn't accept the chance to properly escort you home tonight, Alex. At least let me offer you a proper companion now."

He held out his hand, and she took it. They climbed the stairs in silence.

Much later, when Alex was lying in bed, unable to sleep for the pounding of her heart, she imagined she could still feel the warmth of his palm pressed against her own.

Her first kiss. With *Gavin.* The words tumbled over and over in her head as she replayed the moment, the sound of their breathing, the movement of his hands, the way the firelight caught the gold in his hair as it fell across his forehead when he leaned down to her.

She sighed and whispered his name in the darkness of her bedchamber before turning onto her side and looking out the window at the moonlit treetops beyond. She felt the energy of the evening coursing through her, keeping her from sleep. Her mind was racing; there was so much to think about — so much that had changed. Gavin would never be just a friend again. She would never think of him as a brother again. He would always be the first man she'd kissed.

Now she understood what everyone meant when they talked about romance . . . *this feeling* had launched the thousand ships of the Trojan War, *this feeling* had sent Guinevere into the arms of Lancelot, *this feeling* had driven Fitzwilliam Darcy to confess his love for Elizabeth Bennett. She giggled in the darkness at her silliness, giddy with excitement. She'd scoffed at it for years . . . she'd never believed that this kind of wonderful, rapturous romance could exist beyond legend. And yet, that evening, in Gavin's arms, she'd had a taste of it.

Clutching her pillow to her face, she screamed in excitement, then rolled onto her back with a sigh, imagining Gavin sleeping just a few rooms away. She wondered what tomorrow would bring.

fifteen

"So let me see if I fully understand . . . ." Ella was sitting on Alex's bed, watching as Eliza carefully curled a long strand of Alex's hair and arranged it atop her head. "Blackmoor arrived home earlier than usual and surprised the intruder, leaving him to run off without actually removing anything from Blackmoor House?"

"Yes. That's precisely what we think happened."

The three girls were in Alex's bedchamber, preparing for the long-awaited Worthington Ball. While, traditionally, they all would have dressed at home and arrived separately, they had agreed that, tonight, they would dress together. Eliza, whom they all adored, had agreed to share her genius for hair and *maquillage* with them that evening, so Vivi and Ella had arrived, gowns in tow, for tea and were now waiting patiently for her to finish with Alex's hair and move on to them.

Alex didn't fool herself into thinking that she hadn't had an ulterior motive for inviting them this evening, as it had been several days since her kiss with Blackmoor and, while she had seen him a handful of times, the experience had not been repeated. It wasn't that he'd been standoffish. On the contrary, everything with Blackmoor seemed to be restored to the way it had been for years. He arrived at Worthington House for tea, or supper, or dinner, jested with her brothers, chatted with her parents, and was generally his usual charming self.

But not a mention of the kiss! No attempt to repeat it! No reference to it whatsoever, which both frustrated and confused her, leaving her wondering if she was imagining the kiss meant more than it did — after all, Blackmoor had had a particularly difficult time of it that evening, and perhaps the kiss had been a strange occurrence. She'd been running this possibility over and over in her mind and, finally, had decided it was time to tell her friends. She was tired of her stomach twisting every time he entered the room or she heard his voice, irritated by how surly she was beginning to feel about the whole situation, and she needed a dose of objectivity to regain her sanity.

Of course, she hadn't told them yet. She wasn't quite sure how one announced to one's friends and one's maid that she'd been kissed. The whole experience made her feel rather like a fish out of water. The idea of simply blurting it out in the middle of conversation was distasteful — she didn't want to make a scene, especially if it wasn't an event of import. So, instead, she had told them about the burglary at Blackmoor House, which allowed her to shore up the courage to tell them the rest.

Vivi spoke from her place on the settee on the opposite side of Alex's dressing table. "My father said the house was thoroughly ransacked. Did you see?"

"No. Though Gavin said that the damage was mostly confined to the study. He seems to think that the intruder wasn't simply looking for something of value. He was looking for something specific."

"My father said the same," Vivi agreed, "but it seems that no one knows what, exactly, someone would be looking for there . . . so no one can be sure if the item in question was indeed taken."

"Perhaps it was something that belonged to the former earl?" Ella surmised.

"Perhaps. But wouldn't Gavin know if there was something of importance that his father possessed?" Alex wondered as Eliza fussed over another curl.

"It's possible." Ella ran her hand back and forth over the coverlet. "But the earl's death was such a surprise, maybe not."

"Well, what is most important at this point is that Blackmoor is safe. Between my father and Bow Street, someone will get to the bottom of it." Vivi stood and walked to stand behind Eliza, watching her work as she asked Alex. "Did he sleep at Blackmoor House that night?"

Alex shook her head, garnering a stern look from Eliza as the maid tugged on a curl a touch too firmly. "No. My mother never would have stood for that. He came here after the investigators left."

"Poor Blackmoor, it must have been a difficult night for him." Vivi speculated. "Were you able to talk much when he arrived here? Or was it too late to do so?"

"No, my mother and I waited for him."

Vivi nodded, recognizing that, of course, Alex and the duchess would have waited. "How was he?"

"He was . . ." Alex paused, looking at her reflection in the mirror, pretending to be caught up in Eliza's work as she realized that now was the appropriate time to tell her friends exactly what had happened. "Fine . . . tired and certainly overwhelmed, but we . . ." She took a deep breath, then lost her courage. "We stayed up for a time and talked and he seemed to be in fairly good spirits."

"Did he say anything more about the state of the robbery? Suggest any suspects? Mention any clues?"

Vivi laughed at Ella's line of questioning as Alex watched Eliza insert the final pin into her hair. She smiled up at her maid and thanked her, announcing "There's no one on the island of Britain who is more of a genius with hair than you are, Eliza."

She turned the spot at the dressing table over to Vivi and moved to her wardrobe to retrieve the chemise that she would be wearing under her ball gown that evening. As she did so, Ella prodded again, flopping back on the bed. "Well? Did he?"

Taking another deep breath, Alex answered, "No. He failed to mention any of those things. I rather think he was too busy kissing me."

There was a moment of silence as the words hung in the air of the chamber, and then three gasps erupted in the room, followed by an "Ow!" from Vivi as Eliza accidentally yanked on a strand of her hair.

Alex couldn't help the nervous giggle that escaped from her as she looked from one face to the next. Vivi's shock had quickly turned to excitement; Eliza was the portrait of surprise; and Ella looked thoroughly dumbfounded.

Ella spoke first. "I beg your pardon?"

"He DID? And you haven't TOLD us?" This from Vivi, who had twisted around in her chair and had waved off Eliza.

Which suited Eliza, it seemed, for she couldn't hold back a starry-eyed "Oh! Lady Alexandra!"

Alex sat in a nearby chair, embarrassed by all the attention, and said, "Yes. He did. I didn't tell you because it's not really something that one feels entirely comfortable speaking aloud." Looking at Eliza, she continued, "I wouldn't get too excited, Eliza. I've been given no indication that it will happen again."

Vivi and Ella pounced on that. "What?"

"Why not?" from Eliza.

Alex shook her head and looked up at the ceiling. "Because he's ignoring the whole event!"

Ever the pragmatist, Ella asked, "What do you mean he's ignoring you? I thought you said you'd seen him since?"

"I didn't say he was ignoring *me*. I said he was ignoring *it*. I have seen him. He's been here, talked with me, shared meals with my whole family." She looked at her slippered foot, draped over the arm of her chair. "He just hasn't . . . mentioned . . . or even appeared to remember . . . the kiss."

"How is that possible?" Vivi asked. "Surely, he must be at least more . . . attentive? Than before?" She looked to Eliza for support. The maid nodded eagerly.

Alex let out a frustrated breath. "Oh, he's being the perfect gentleman. Charming, entertaining — entirely Gavin. It's not as though he's avoiding me. It's as though it never happened. Which I suppose is better than last time."

Ella and Vivi met each other's gaze. Ella said, "I beg your pardon. Again? Last time?"

"There was a LAST TIME?" Vivi queried excitedly.

"Oh, Lady Alexandra!" This, again, from Eliza.

"Hold." Alex slashed a hand through the air, leveling a gaze at Eliza, then Vivi. "Don't go off into some fantasy world. This is not as rose-colored as you seem to think," she continued grumpily. "If you keep looking at me, we're never going to be ready for the ball tonight."

"Who can think about a ball at a time like this?" Vivi interjected, even as she turned to face the mirror again, offering Eliza her back. "You simply cannot expect that we wouldn't be more interested in this conversation than in something as trivial as hair." The maid nodded agreeably but lifted the hair iron nevertheless.

Ella spoke up, "Excellent attempt at evasion, Alex, but you failed to answer the question. There was a 'last time'?"

"Not exactly," Alex mumbled.

"How, exactly, then?"

"You'd make an excellent Bow Street Runner yourself, Ella," Alex said grouchily, ignoring her friend's nod of thanks. "All right. The evening of the Worthington House dinner, Gavin and I were on the balcony, talking, and I *thought* he *might* kiss me. But he didn't. And then he summarily avoided me for a fortnight."

"Ah . . . so *that's* what put you in such a vicious mood for days later," Ella pointed out.

"I was *not* in a vicious mood!" Alex looked over her shoulder for support from Vivi only to catch her and Eliza sharing a wry look in the dressing table mirror. "Traitors. All of you."

Vivi smiled, careful not to move her head. "Go on."

"There isn't much more to say. The other night, after the robbery at Blackmoor House, we found ourselves alone in the library and . . . he kissed me."

"Oh! Lady Alexandra!" Eliza exclaimed yet again, causing Alex to wonder if her maid had lost control of her linguistic faculties.

"How very excellent!" exclaimed Vivi.

"Well, I thought so, too . . . but now . . . I'm not so certain it was of any import whatsoever."

"Nonsense. Kissing is most important. I repeat, how very excellent!"

"Your hopeless romanticism isn't helping this situation, Vivi. I assure you this is nothing to be sighed over. This is real. And if we'd been caught, I'd have been ruined. Technically, I'm ruined anyway."

"Nonsense," said Ella, "everyone knows that you're not *truly* ruined unless you get caught in the act. I defy you to show me one female who goes to the altar without kissing her betrothed."

"Ruined! How exciting! How romantic!" Vivi waxed rhapsodic. Ella and Alex looked at her as though she'd grown a second head.

"NOT exciting, Vivi. Decidedly NOT romantic," Alex protested. "Romantic is being kissed, then wooed. Or wooed, then kissed. I assure you there has been no wooing!"

Vivi continued starry-eyed and lost to the excitement. "He KISSED you! BLACKMOOR KISSED YOU!"

Ella interjected, "And the entire house shall know she's ruined if you continue at that volume, Vivian. Not that you are, Alex."

"Thank you," Alex said.

Vivi lowered her voice. "I am sorry. I simply got carried away."

"It is all right. I knew before I told you that you were likely to react like we were all caught up in some kind of gothic novel," Alex offered with a sigh.

She continued, hearing the sadness in her own voice, "While I am certainly in no position to understand what *should* occur now, I feel certain that being ignored is not it!"

"To be fair, it doesn't seem that he is ignoring you," Ella pointed out, ever the pragmatist.

"You'll understand if that doesn't enhance my mood," Alex said shortly, then exhaled in frustration. "This is *exactly* why I *promised* myself I would not husband hunt this season. I swore an oath to stay above the fray! The entire male species is unintelligible!"

"Indeed," said Ella, speculating aloud, "this *is* an odd turn of events. And *I* thought he was courting Penelope." The words were out of her mouth before she could stop them.

"You did?" Alex looked up in surprise.

"Ella!" Vivi admonished. "That is most certainly *not* what Alex needs to hear at this particular moment."

"Well, it is clearly an incorrect conclusion," said Ella, defensively. "I mean, if he were, he wouldn't have kissed Alex!"

"Why did you think he was courting Penelope?" Alex cut straight to the point.

"No reason, really, except that at most gatherings we've all attended, Penelope has been . . . in rather close proximity to him." Seeing the disappointment on Alex's face, she added quickly, "But it's probably me imagining things. I do that, remember?"

Vivi jumped in quickly to agree, "Yes. You do. It is far more likely that Penelope has been close to him because she's like a creeping ivy — lovely, but damaging. Blackmoor kissed *you,* Alex, which clearly means that *you're* the person in whom he is interested. He wouldn't have done it if he were angling for Penelope Grayson. I'm certain he's of better stock than that."

"With the exception of his recent behavior toward you," Ella added.

"Ella!" Vivi's tone was amazed. "It would do you well to stop speaking until you have something helpful to say. There are times when your inability to distinguish between what is appropriate and inappropriate astounds me."

"Well, that would make his ignoring the whole event more understandable," Alex said with more calm than she felt. "After all, he had a particularly difficult evening and was most certainly on edge. He's always felt comfortable with me, so perhaps the kiss just . . . happened."

"Alex" — Vivi was matter-of-fact — "kisses don't just *happen.*"

"We don't know that. We've never been kissed."

"I think that's exactly her point, Alex," Ella offered.

Alex shook her head. "But how could we even speculate on this? We've only been out for two months!"

"We can speculate on this because we know that if we were caught kissing, we'd be forced into marriage," Ella replied, "and, since most people we know have not been forced into marriage, we can assume they don't go around kissing everyone in the vicinity." She offered Vivi a smug look. "You see? I can be helpful."

"Oh, please," Alex pressed on. "I've been kissed once and almost kissed once in the span of three weeks, and I haven't been caught. It can't be *that* out of the ordinary. Maybe he's kissing Penelope, too."

"Ugh." Ella could not hide her disgust at this idea. "I do not want that picture in my head."

"You're the one who sent her down this path!" Vivi stood, Eliza having finished arranging her hair in long, gorgeous dark curls. "You deserve to be disgusted. I have no sympathy for you." Turning to Alex as Ella slid onto the bench in front of the dressing table for her turn, Vivi said earnestly, "I don't know much about kissing or about courting, Alex, but I do know that Blackmoor has always adored you. Always."

"Then why is he ignoring me? Why hasn't he mentioned it? Why hasn't he tried to kiss me again?" She gasped, covering her mouth. "What if I was *terrible* at it?"

"You weren't," Vivi said.

"Certainly not," Ella agreed.

"Oh, how do you know?" Alex said, now enveloped in self-doubt. "Maybe I did it all wrong!"

"This might be a good time to discuss the kiss in question," Ella offered. "What was it like?"

"I thought it was wonderful! I wanted to do it again, immediately! But what if it was awful and I just didn't know it?!"

"That simply cannot be the case!" Vivi shook her head in earnest.

"Indeed," Eliza broke her silence, "if it made you want to do it again, and soon, 'twas a good kiss."

"For me . . . but what about for him?"

"He had to have enjoyed it, Alex," Ella said.

Alex's frantic frustration bubbled over. "Then why isn't he interested in me? Why doesn't he want to do it again? Maybe he *does* want Penelope!" Her voice became small. "Why doesn't he want *me*?"

"Alex," Ella asked curiously, "are you saying . . . Do *you* want *him*?"

Alex thought carefully about Ella's question. Did she want Gavin? "Well . . . the kiss was quite lovely."

"Of course, it was," Vivi said, "but . . . what about the man himself? Could you love him?"

Love? Gavin? She looked at the other three girls, each staring back at her as though she were about to reveal some history-altering secret. It was too much to think about, really. "I . . . I don't know. I've always thought of him as a brother. But recently . . . everything has changed. He kissed me and I *wanted* him to and it . . . everything feels different. But I don't know what to think. Maybe nothing is different to him. Maybe it didn't mean anything to him."

Vivi walked over to Alex, then took her shoulders in hand and spoke with firm conviction, "I may not know much about this kissing business, Alex, but I do know that Gavin would never do anything to hurt you. Including kissing you if he didn't mean it at least a little."

Alex offered Vivi a half smile. "You're right, but what if that's the problem? What if he means it only a little?"

Vivi went quiet for a long time before her face brightened in a conspiratorial smile. "Well, then, we'll just have to make sure he ends up meaning it a great deal."

sixteen

"I don't think I've ever seen so many people in one room! My God! The entire *ton* must be here!" Vivi exclaimed, unable to tear her gaze from the sea of people below.

Vivi, Ella, and Alex stood on the upper level of Worthington House, looking down on the ballroom. They were shielded in an alcove on the second floor as they considered the mass of people who were here for the Worthington Ball. Each year, the duke and duchess hosted the grandest and most legendary ball of the season. No one who received an invitation missed the opportunity to attend.

Alex commented acerbically, "I think my mother may very well have invited the entire *ton*."

She was watching the lady in question as she greeted the never-ending stream of guests pouring into the enormous ballroom. The room sat empty much of the year until mid-April, when its curtains were opened and the dustcloths were removed from its furniture for a thorough inspection in preparation for this night. Then, for weeks, servants shined the dozens of crystal chandeliers, polished the expansive oak and mahogany floor with beeswax, and washed the floor-to-ceiling windows to ensure that everything would be perfect for this evening.

And perfect it was. Thousands of candles were lit in the enormous candelabras hanging from the ceiling and standing around the room, giving the entire space a magical, golden glow. The orchestra was placed at the top of the room, farthest away from the entrance, obscured by shrubbery that had been brought into the room specifically to create the illusion of invisibility. Off the main chamber, directly underneath the girls, were multiple antechambers, each outfitted for a different purpose: a refreshment room complete with a spread of lemonade, wine, biscuits, and coffee; a supper room that would be opened midway through the ball; a card room for elderly guests to rest and play whist while keeping out a watchful eye for any juicy gossip; a men's smoking room; and a ladies' salon, offering a space to which ladies could escape in the case of damage to their elaborate gowns. Her mother had thought of everything, and that attention to detail was what set this event apart from the others of the season.

"It is quite a stunning sight," Ella pointed out. "How many people do you think are here?"

Alex replied distractedly, "Between five and six hundred, I think." She took a deep breath, as if preparing for battle, and turned to her friends. "Although there are three less than there should be, I venture to say. While I'd much rather stay up here and watch the whole event from afar, I have a feeling that someone will come looking for us if we don't make an appearance soon."

"Agreed." Vivi looked at her friends and added, "And what a stunning appearance we shall make!"

She was right, of course. With the help of the remarkable Eliza, the three had dressed and applied their cosmetics to perfection. They were attired in gowns that had been made by Madame Fernaud for this particular event. Alex imagined they made a stunning trio. Vivi wore a gorgeous gold damask silk with a high Empire waist and fitted sleeves that accentuated her dark features and her already long, reedlike form. The color was certain to be the envy of every woman present, because it was such a difficult color to wear and yet it seemed as if it were created specifically for Vivian.

Ella, in contrast, was wearing a pale pink georgette with a wide, plunging neckline that both highlighted her lovely hourglass figure and underscored Madame Fernaud's distinct nod to her own French heritage. The pink fabric, the color of the palest of seashells, moved like gossamer and perfectly complemented Ella's fair coloring — which was already the envy of every female member of the peerage.

Alex's gown rounded out the trio, an ice-blue satin shot through with silver thread that shimmered in the light as though it were made of droplets of water just on the verge of freezing. It was a dress to be marveled at — her mother had ensured as much, claiming that the Worthington Ball was precisely where she expected Alex to ensnare her future husband. At the time, Alex had been too deeply engrossed in her third reading of *Pride and Prejudice* to care at all about the dress, but now, as she was thinking about impressing Blackmoor, she wanted to kiss her mother for making such remarkable decisions regarding the construction of the beautiful garment.

As they descended the center stairway of Worthington House, noticing clusters of guests turning to watch their entrance, Vivi turned to her friends with a brilliant smile and spoke through her teeth, "I simply do not understand the appeal of the turban. Lady Barrington looks as if a feather pillow has attached itself to her head."

Unable to miss the headwear in question, Alex adopted the same method of conversation and replied, "Indeed. Although considering the enormous peacock feather protruding from the thing, it appears as though there may be some kind of exotic bird trapped under there."

"Should we attempt a rescue?" Ella asked casually, sending all three girls into bright laughter.

As they reached the ground floor, Alex leaned toward Ella and spoke just loudly enough for her friend to hear, "Do try not to let your overactive imagination whisk you into the gardens tonight."

Ella flashed a bright smile and replied teasingly, "Certainly not! Although I was thinking that the strange conversation I overheard the other night might well have had something to do with the excitement with Blackmoor." She paused, then continued with a laugh, "Well . . . the *earlier* excitement with Blackmoor, at least."

Alex laughed again. "No such thing as a coincidence in your mind, is there?"

"Never. Coincidence eliminates the entertainment of speculation!"

"Indeed."

And, with that, they were caught up in the swirl of the evening. They entered the ballroom just minutes before the first dance, a minuet, began and they were enveloped by a crowd of young aristocrats all angling for a place on their dance cards. Alex found herself in the dance with Lord St. Marks, a sweet but small marquess whom she'd always quite liked. She was finding the dance quite enjoyable, until she noticed Blackmoor over the top of her partner's head. He was having a wonderful time, smiling and laughing with the lady in his arms — who happened to be Penelope Grayson. Alex was overcome by a flash of jealousy. *How could he be dancing with her after he kissed me?*

"She's got the nature of an asp," Alex muttered to herself.

"I beg your pardon, my lady?"

She looked down at St. Marks with a smile and said, "Uh . . . I am reading Shakespeare's *Antony and Cleopatra,* my lord, and I cannot seem to shake the horrid vision of the queen's death. Death by asp. Quite dreadful, you know."

From the look of obvious confusion on St. Marks's face, she was certain he'd never had such an odd conversation during a ball before and, had she been in any other frame of mind, she would have found a great deal of humor in his drawn-out "Rather," clearly the only response he could conjure.

They had turned in such a manner that Alex was no longer able to see Penelope and Blackmoor without craning her neck indelicately, so, instead, she simply counted steps until the dance was over. Two hundred and forty-three steps, to be exact. St. Marks promenaded her the customary halfway around the perimeter of the room and bowed his farewell — a farewell she rather thought he was looking forward to — and Alex went searching for someone to entertain her and distract her from her own preoccupations.

In less than a half a minute, she came face-to-face with Blackmoor himself, all crisp cravat and broad shoulders and bright smile, and Alex's mood grew darker. *How could he be enjoying himself to such an impressive degree?*

"Lady Alexandra," he said, offering her a devastating smile and a short bow.

"Lord Blackmoor," she said, unable to keep a tinge of churlishness from her tone, "I thought you were with Penelope."

"I was," he answered amiably, "but she met up with some friends and I decided to make my rounds. Are your brothers here?" He looked out at the crowd, searching for the Stafford boys.

Irrationally, she wanted to stomp on his foot. Instead, she said sarcastically, "I'm certain they are, considering this is their ancestral home."

"Ah, well, I expect they'll turn up." He lifted her gloved hand and took the ribboned pencil there in hand. Looking down at her dance card, a lock of blond hair fell across his forehead as he observed, "I see you have the next waltz free. May I?"

Distracted by his hair, her overwhelming desire to push it back from his forehead, and his clear, questioning gaze, she forgot to remain aloof. "Yes, of course." She watched as he slashed *Blackmoor* across the card, noticing the strength of his script before shaking herself and silently admonishing her inner lunatic.

"Shall we?" He offered her an arm and escorted her to the center of the crowded ballroom just in time for the waltz to begin. When it did, she felt immediately and unexplainably disoriented, uncertain of whether the feeling sprang from the spinning steps of the dance or the fact that she was keenly aware of the heat of his palm even through the twin fabrics of their gloves. She couldn't stop herself from focusing on that heat, on the weight of his other hand on the small of her back, on the way his hair curled over the edge of his formal jacket, on the space where the angle of his jaw met the sleek line of his neck. She wondered if that skin was as soft as it looked. Shaking her head in a desperate attempt to ignore the feelings she was having, she closed her eyes and let him guide her in swaying circles, willing herself to think of him not as the man who had kissed her a week ago, but as the man who had infuriated her more often than not of late. She inhaled deeply.

He smells simply wonderful.

She disgusted herself. Truly. *Stop being such a ninny, Alexandra!*

"Are you feeling all right, Alex?" His question was quiet, as to only be heard by her, and when she opened her eyes, she saw the concern in his grey gaze.

She spoke quickly, stringing her words together without pause, "Yes, I'm fine, I'm sorry, I just, I suppose I'm a little overexcited with the ball and the anticipation of the evening."

"Oh?" The word was slow and accompanied by a raised eyebrow.

"Yes." She scrambled for an explanation. "Ella and Vivi were here all afternoon and I think we drank too much tea." She almost groaned aloud. *I drank too much tea?* The answer sounded inane even to her.

"Too much tea." One side of his mouth twitched up.

She wanted an end to this conversation. "Indeed. I'm feeling rather peaked, actually. Perhaps we could just stay silent?"

"Certainly." *Was that humor in his voice?*

"Excellent."

It seemed like a millennium for Alex before the dance ended and she was able to step away from him, allowing him to walk her the expected distance. Only he didn't stop halfway around the ballroom. On the contrary, he escorted her straight out of the room, toward the doors that had been left open onto the gardens that Worthington House shared with Blackmoor House.

She tugged on her hand, attempting to remove it from his arm. He wouldn't allow it. "Where are we going?"

"You were feeling peaked. I thought, perhaps, you might like some fresh air."

"I find that I'm feeling much better. I wouldn't like to catch a chill."

"Oh, I don't think there's a chance of that." She detected a hint of humor in his voice again.

They arrived on the balcony, which was deserted of others, and he released her. "Now, would you care to tell me what has you so distressed?"

"I told you —"

"Yes. You did. Tea." He smiled. "You're a terrible liar in a pinch, Minx."

"It's not a lie!"

"No?" He crossed his arms and leaned back against the marble banister edging the balcony.

"No!" she exclaimed. He looked at her. Waiting. "All right! Yes! It's a lie. If you must know, I'm rather . . . nervous around you."

"Really? I hadn't noticed."

She offered him a quelling look. "Stop looking so amused."

To give him his due, he did stop. "Very well. Why are you nervous?"

She couldn't help but look at him as though his brain were addled. "You honestly cannot imagine why?"

He did not respond, but waited for her to continue. She gripped the cool marble banister and looked out into the darkened garden. What should she say? In her mind it was not only obvious why she was nervous — but expected. Hadn't their relationship undergone a tremendous shift over the past few days? Was she wrong to believe that there was something new and fresh and different and rather terrifying between them?

He clearly didn't think so. And as much as she wanted to appear as calm and collected as he was, she couldn't do it. She whispered, "You kissed me."

He took a deep breath and exhaled. "I did."

"And, that night, everything seemed that it was somehow going to be different. Only it wasn't. It was all the same. In a good way . . . I suppose. But . . . I just . . ." She turned her large, clear emerald eyes on him and whispered again, "You kissed me. And you cannot erase that."

"You're right. I cannot take it back. I wouldn't even attempt to erase it. Because it would be impossible." He sighed, standing up straight. "But kissing you again would be one of the biggest mistakes I could make."

He saw the flash of pain in her eyes but, before he could explain, Vivi burst through the doors. "Oh, thank goodness you're here! Grabhands quite awkwardly cornered me on the way to the refreshment room. I had no choice but to escape — I saw you two on your way out here and made for you!" She offered a broad smile. "I hope I'm not interrupting, but I need a savior."

Alex's emerald eyes were glassy with unshed tears as she looked at Blackmoor. "Well, you're in luck. Savior is a role in which Blackmoor feels more than comfortable." Turning toward the ballroom, she continued, "If you're all right, Vivi, I have to get back inside."

And, with that, she fled.

seventeen

Alex pushed back into the ball, desperate for a spot where she could be alone to nurse her wounded ego. Of course, with more than five hundred people in her home, that desire wasn't the easiest to fulfill. She hadn't spent her entire life sneaking around this house on nights just like this one for nothing, however.

Slipping through the ladies' cloakroom to access the servants' passage that would lead her to the unoccupied part of the house, she wondered if she could simply take to her bedchamber without attracting notice. The idea hadn't even fully formed in her mind before she realized that she would never escape her mother's wrath if she did anything close to that. By her calculations, she had less than a quarter of an hour to be by herself before she would have to return to the ball.

She exited the servants' quarters into a darkened passageway, heading for the orangery, which had always been her favorite room in the house. The sounds of the orchestra faded into the distance as she moved quietly through the hallway, thanking her maker that the duchess had decided to keep these particular rooms free from visitors, only to be replaced with quiet murmurings coming from behind one of the closed doors of the corridor. Wondering who had snuck away from the ball and, more importantly, why they were behind closed doors deep in the inner recesses of the house, Alex paused outside the door, pressing her ear to the rich, dark wood, attempting to make out the voices inside, which appeared to be discussing politics.

"Napoleon gains strength. He's garnering support across France. If the Crown is going to strike, it will do so soon. We don't need informants to tell us that." The voice, laced with disdain, sounded foreign, but Alex couldn't identify it through the thick door.

"No, of course not. I wasn't suggesting that you did. I was simply pointing out that I have many strong connections that could prove useful in your search for information. If a strike is planned, I can help you predict it. I think I've done more than prove my commitment to your cause." Alex put a hand to her mouth in surprise, recognizing that she was eavesdropping on a particularly dark conversation. She stayed quiet, trying to hear over the pounding of her heart.

"Indeed. You have made your . . . commitment . . . more than clear."

"I intend to do it again. I expect to, within days, have very specific information about Wellington's movements." Alex's eyes widened as she realized that one of the men on the other side of the door was the worst kind of spy — one who traded secrets from British intelligence.

"I'm sure you think that's true. But you'll understand that we are unable to trust that you will make wise decisions any longer. We have come too far to risk losing ground. We simply cannot have you involved." The voice was cold, calm, and dismissive; Alex could hear that even through two inches of oak. "You have acted rashly . . . and to no avail. You have been unable to discover anything about what is known of our plans. And the knowledge is directly under your nose. Your involvement is becoming messy. And we simply don't have the time or the inclination to clean up after you anymore."

"Clean up after me? *I'm* the one who has done the cleaning." Alex started as the voice on the other side of the door shook with barely contained anger. "If it weren't for me, this entire operation would have been uncovered. You, and everyone else, would have been found and hanged. If it weren't for me, Blackmoor would still be alive."

Alex's mouth gaped in horror as she grasped the importance of what she was hearing. She knew she should run and fetch her father, Vivi's father, and any number of others. But she couldn't bring herself to move from her spot, waiting for the next revelation.

"And even with him dead, you cannot seem to retrieve the information he had. We're lucky that, by now, the young earl hasn't discovered everything and had us all strung up for treason. Between your botched robbery and your almost being discovered, this entire string of events has become far too risky."

"You need not worry. Young Blackmoor will very soon no longer be of concern. I plan to deal with him."

"Forgive me if I have little faith in your ability to follow through on that promise."

Alex was unable to keep the gasp from escaping as she realized what the villain on the other side of the door meant. The noise rent the air, jolting her out of her trance as silence fell on the other side of the door. She flew down the hallway, her soft calfskin slippers lending her a silent tread. Once she reached the orangery, she sank to the ground in the darkened room, allowing the sweet smell of citrus flowers to envelop her. Her heart was pounding with the realization of what she'd just overheard; she could barely think for the sound of her labored breathing.

The earl had been murdered. Gavin had been right. Alex shook her head, as though the action could erase her newfound knowledge. The elder Earl of Blackmoor was dead and Gavin was in danger. Blackmoor would no longer be a concern after this evening, they had said. She had to get to him first.

The thought had barely formed before she leapt to her feet, nothing considered except that she had to find Gavin. She started to exit the orangery when she heard a latch click along the hallway.

Pressing herself against the wall, she offered a silent prayer of thanks for the darkness and shadows that hid her position and she peered down the hallway as one man, then a second, emerged from the room. She couldn't identify either of the figures for a moment — they simply appeared as shadows clad in formal attire — but as they moved closer to the light trickling into the passageway from the ballroom, her eyes widened in horror.

While she wasn't entirely certain, she was fairly sure that one of the men was Lucian Sewell, Gavin's uncle.

She stood still for a moment, frozen by the gravity of everything she had overheard, combined with the weight of the probability that Gavin's uncle had murdered his own brother in cold blood. How was she going to tell Gavin that his uncle had killed his father? How was she going to tell him that, if he did not seek help immediately, he was going to be next? She had to get to him. They could be seeking him out right now.

After waiting a brief moment to ensure that the men had indeed returned to the ball and that she would not be discovered, she retraced her steps through the darkened corridor and back to the ladies' cloakroom, increasing her speed as she went so that she was just short of a run when she burst into the ballroom . . . where she was immediately stayed by the crush of people at the ball.

Looking around her, she was desperate for someone she knew. Her brow furrowed as she stood on her toes and searched for Gavin, one of her brothers, Vivi, Ella, *anyone.*

"Looking for someone?" The voice, close to her ear, startled her and she gave a small shriek, whirling to face a grinning Lord Stanhope.

"Oh! Freddie!" She put a hand to her chest in surprise. "You've no idea how happy I am that it's you!"

"As you can imagine, I hear that from women constantly," he jested, but the wicked gleam in his eye dissolved quickly into concern. "What's wrong with you, kitten? You look like you've seen a ghost."

"I'm afraid it's worse than that. But I can't discuss it. I need to find Blackmoor."

Freddie's tone turned dark and menacing. "Has the rogue done something to hurt you?"

The question would have amused Alex in the past, but this evening she ignored him, waving a hand in frustration. "No. I just need to find him. Help me?"

"I'll lay him out if he's done something inappropriate."

"Freddie. Stop being such a brute and help me. All right?" He nodded once, although he didn't seem happy about it. "Capital. Go that way," she said, indicating the direction of the orchestra. "If you see my brothers, or Vivi, or Ella, ask them to help find him. It's a matter of great import."

She started in the opposite direction, but he took hold of her arm and stayed her for a moment. "What's going on, Alex?"

"I — I can't tell you now. Please?" Her green eyes pleaded with him. "Please help?"

He locked gazes with her for a brief moment, as if attempting to read her thoughts. Something in her eyes must have convinced him. With a nod, he spun on his heel and disappeared into the crowd. She watched him go for a brief second, admiring his loyalty, before turning to find Blackmoor.

Only minutes later, she came upon Vivi and Ella, who had their heads bent in what looked like a serious discussion . . . or serious gossip. Alex approached them from behind, slipping her arms through theirs and interrupting, "Thank God I've found you. I need your help."

Both girls looked up at her in surprise before Vivi replied, "We've been looking for you everywhere! What happened out there? You looked like Blackmoor had said something awful, the rogue! Are you all right?"

"He did say something awful. However, that is all quite irrelevant now, as something much worse has come to pass. I need to find him."

"What kind of something much worse?" Ella spoke, concern in her blue eyes.

"I can't take the time to explain right now."

"Not even to us?" Vivi looked hurt.

"Not to anyone. I promise you'll be the very first to know . . . *after* I find Gavin. Which I must do. Immediately."

"Alex . . ." Vivi spoke with a warning tone in her voice.

"No. Vivi." Alex slashed a hand through the air. "I am asking you for help. I will tell you everything later. I promise. Please, help me find him."

"He left." This from Ella.

"What? Why? Where did he go?" Alex turned and grasped her friend's arms with both hands.

Ella gave Alex a startled look. “He left soon after you disappeared. Said something about balls not being the best places for him this season.”

“Did he say where he was going?”

“No. Although he left through the gardens, so I assume he went home.”

“I have to follow him.”

“I beg your pardon?” Vivi and Ella spoke in unison.

“I told you, I can’t explain. There’s no time. You have to help me. I’m going out through the gardens. If anyone asks, tell them I had a fallen hem and went to have Eliza repair it.”

“Wait. Are you all right, Alex?” Vivi looked concerned.

“I’m all right. Just do this for me? Oh . . . and find Freddie. Tell him thank you, I found Blackmoor.”

“This is becoming more and more curious as the moments pass,” said Ella.

“Alex, you can’t just go traipsing off to Blackmoor House after him. You’ll be ruined if you’re caught!”

“I’ll simply have to risk it,” Alex said, wishing she had time to savor their confusion. “I’ll tell you everything upon my return. I promise.” She kissed them both on the cheek. “Oh. And if I don’t return in three quarters of an hour, tell your father where I went, Vivi.”

“What?!”

“I’ll be fine. It’s just a precaution.”

“What kind of precaution involves my father?”

"I'll tell you everything upon my return," she repeated. And, with that, she exited the room, making her way to the music room, which had an entrance to the gardens that offered a better chance of her not being caught in her escape.

Rushing though the dark garden that connected Worthington and Blackmoor houses, Alex did not take any time to think about what she would do if she were to interrupt a dreadful event. Instead, she thought only of Gavin: his grey eyes the color of the winter sea; his bold smiles that heated her very core; his generous spirit. Thinking of him focused her mind on one thing . . . she had to reach him before anyone else.

As she broke through the trees and found herself in the Blackmoor House garden, she pulled up short and inspected the house. She could see dimly lit windows on the upper floor, reserved for servants, but the rest of the home was dark, appearing uninhabited and forbidding.

She was just deciding how to enter the house when she sensed movement nearby. Falling back to press herself against a tree and blend in with the shadows, she watched as a small, dark figure crept across the back garden toward the window she knew led to the Earl of Blackmoor's study. She focused intently on the figure, attempting to identify him. Try as she might, she couldn't make out his face, although his physique seemed vaguely familiar. She watched in surprise as he worked the latch on the window, quickly unlocking it from the outside and lifting the sash, pushing it open.

It was clear that he was breaking into the house. It was also clear that she had to do something to stop him.

She gathered her courage, prepared to rush at him and stop his actions, when a light beamed brightly from inside the study, surprising her and sending the intruder scurrying off like a rat — around the corner of the house and across the garden. As she watched him hurry off, she felt a jolt of recognition. She was certain that he was the Baron Montgrave.

"My God! Ella was right!" she whispered to the night air. She'd made light of her friend's overactive imagination and, this time, she should have listened!

Once the baron was out of sight, she followed his steps to the study window, which was still cracked open. Stepping into the soft earth beneath the window, she peered into the room to see Blackmoor at his desk, staring into nothingness, clearly lost in his own thoughts. She released an enormous sigh, grateful that he was unharmed — desperate to touch him and confirm his safety.

Reaching up, she rapped on the window pane sharply, startling Blackmoor from his thoughts. He stood up quickly, squinting at the window. Alex realized that he was unable to see her for the reflection of the light in the glass, so she called out softly, "It's me!"

His eyes widened in surprised recognition as he moved quickly toward her, saying, "I'm certain I must be dreaming. There's no way you'd risk your reputation quite so baldly."

He threw open the window and leaned down on the sill, peering out into the night, meeting her nose to nose and continuing drily, "Tell me I'm dreaming, Alexandra."

"I regret I cannot do that, my lord. It is indeed I standing in your flower bed . . . quite clandestinely." Placing her hands next to his on the windowsill, she continued, "I need to speak with you. Help me in?"

He considered leaving her in the garden and then thought better of it. Reaching down, he grasped her arms and hauled her through the opening and into the study, waiting for her to steady herself before turning and closing the window. She opened her mouth to speak, but he cut her off as he turned around. "You risked your reputation to follow me back here and, quite frankly, you had better have a decent reason to be skulking around my gardens instead of dancing the night away at your parents' house."

"I do. I've several reasons, actually, including the fact that it seems I'm not the only person skulking about your gardens this evening."

His eyes widened in surprise at her words. "I beg your pardon?"

She stole a glance at the clock on the fireplace mantel. "I cannot stay long, and neither can you. We have to return to Worthington House."

"Why? Haven't we been to enough balls this season?" he quipped.

"It's not the ball. It's that you cannot stay here by yourself. Someone is planning to kill you. I just watched an aborted attempt to enter the house through this very window. I think it was Baron Montgrave.

"He's gone now, and I can't be sure. You scared him off with the light." She pushed on, urgently. "I know that wasn't the most tactful way to tell you, but we don't have much time. You see . . . only moments ago at the ball, I overheard a private conversation between two men who sounded very much involved in what could only have been espionage. They made it quite clear that you have access to some very dangerous information or, rather, that your father was privy to some information that he should not have been privy to and, more importantly, that they were willing to kill to be sure that, first, you don't have the opportunity to share this knowledge you may or may not have with anyone else, and, second, you do not have the opportunity to learn this information to begin with." She grasped his hand and pulled. "We have to leave here. Now."

He did not move. "We're not going anywhere until you've explained slightly more than you already have."

She sighed impatiently. "I don't have time to explain any more! Someone could climb through that window at any moment and surprise us!"

"It does seem a popular entryway," he observed.

"How can you jest at a time like this?" she said. "Did you not understand me? Someone is plotting to do away with you!"

"Alex. Try to stay calm."

"Stay calm?" she burst out, frustrated. "You weren't there! You didn't hear them speaking as though killing you would fit in between breakfast and morning visitors!"

"You're not hearing what I'm trying to say, Alex," he said calmly. "I know. All of it. I know that my father had information damning enough to kill for. I know it related, in some way, to the war. I know that information is believed to be hidden somewhere in Blackmoor House. I know that whoever killed my father is out for me. I know, and so does most of the War Office. We're all waiting for the knave to make his next move, which we expect will be some time soon. Could have been just now, if what you say about an intruder running off is true. I assure you, we're all prepared for it."

"*What?* You know of it? But how? Why didn't anyone tell me?"

"I've suspected it to be the case for months — you know I never really believed that my father's death was an accident. The only other people who agreed with me were your father and Lord Langford, but none of us could prove anything, or so I thought. Once Blackmoor House was robbed and nothing of importance taken, I knew it must have been related to my father. Your father, Lord Langford, and I have been trying to root out the thief ever since."

"But you could be killed!"

He shook his head firmly. "While that is certainly a possibility, between my very frequent, very *public* appearances and the skilled Bow Street Runners who are patrolling the house, I don't think that's going to come to pass."

"Need I remind you that Baron Montgrave was skulking around the house just moments ago? Where was Bow Street then?"

"I thought you couldn't be sure it was Montgrave?" he asked, evading her question.

"I can't be. But I feel that it's better we are safe than sorry in this particular situation. I shan't be inviting the baron to tea any time soon."

"Alex. First, if indeed it was the baron, I assure you I could have easily held my own." He ignored her rolling eyes. "Second, there is no *we* in this situation. Part of the reason you were not apprised of this situation is because we all preferred you *not* know, as we understand you and Ella and Vivi more than you think. We knew that once you got wind of this, you would find it difficult to stay out of it. That said, I want you to remain out of it. *Thoroughly* out of it. This is no game."

"I *know* this is no game, Gavin. I'm not a child. And I cannot simply stay out of it. It's too late for that."

"No, it's not. I want you to pretend you didn't hear what you heard this evening. If ever there was a time for you to be a delicate flower, now is it. Is that understood?" He didn't wait for her answer. "Good. As it is, I should turn you over my knee for traipsing about in the darkness, but I shall refrain, because I cannot deny the fact that I'm rather happy you're here."

She opened her mouth to argue and he stopped her with a raised hand. "You see, I have rather a lot to say. I'm sorry that I hurt you earlier. I never meant for you to believe that I think kissing you was a mistake. In fact, if you asked me what I've wanted more than anything in the last week, what I want more than anything right now, I would answer, without question, not that I want to find the burglar who ransacked my home — not that I want to know the truth about my father's death — but that I want you."

She felt his gaze hot on her face as he continued, "I didn't use the term 'mistake' because of you. Never because of you. I used it because your brothers are the closest things I have to brothers, your father" — he paused, then pressed on — "the closest thing I have to a father now. They all trust me with you. They believe that you are safe with me. My behavior toward you is a betrayal of that trust. And a betrayal of your trust as well."

Distracted by his impassioned words, she asked, "Why a betrayal of *my* trust? I do trust you. Still. I trust you to be the same Gavin you've always been."

"That's the problem. The feelings that I have for you now are nothing like the ones I've always had. I'm not the same Gavin. I used to think of you as my friend. Now I think of you as something . . . more."

She wanted desperately to ask him to elaborate on his statement, but first, she had to know whether it was her specifically or rather the idea of her which was driving him to make such a confession. She blurted, "Are you planning to offer for Penelope Grayson's hand?"

The words were out of her mouth before she knew what she was saying. She dipped her chin, a blush spreading across her cheeks. She had no idea why she had asked such an inappropriate question. More than that, she had a sudden intense dread of his answer.

If she had been looking at his face, she would have seen the look of shock that passed over it and known his answer before he spoke it. "No. Alex. No, I have never intended to propose to Penelope. She's very beautiful, but . . ." He paused. "She's not you."

Her eyes flew to meet his as she realized just how monumental this moment — that statement — was.

"I confess, earlier in the season, I had plans to court Penelope. She seemed the ideal . . . candidate."

"Charming sentiment," Alex said, adding, "It's incredible that men think of finding a wife in the same vein as electing a politician."

Ignoring her pontification, he continued, "*However* . . . that's all changed now. I can't imagine being with Penelope. Because I seem only to be able to imagine being with you."

Attempting to ignore the lurch in her stomach that occurred in response to those words, she asked, "What does that mean?"

"It means that you've become the standard to which I hold all the other women in my life. Are they as humorous as you, as easy to speak with, as charming, as witty, as . . ." He stopped.

"Go on," she prodded.

He smiled at her shameless ploy for more compliments. "As wonderful as you. As clever. As beautiful."

She blushed shyly. "I'm not beautiful."

"Yes, love, you are." He stepped closer to her, pulling her close and tracing the curve of her cheek. "So beautiful that I rather wonder how I could have missed it before this season."

And, with that, he kissed her. She lost all her strength as his lips played over hers, but he held her in his strong arms without any difficulty. She lifted her hands to run them through his soft hair before wrapping her arms around his neck and giving in to the sheer pleasure of the moment.

After several minutes, he lifted his head and their eyes met. Neither of them could keep the broad smiles from their faces. Alex spoke, unable to keep her feelings quiet after his bold confession. "Gavin . . . I've never felt anything like this. You'll never be my friend again, never my surrogate brother. If I am the standard to which you hold the women in your life . . . then you are more than that for the men in mine. How will I ever find someone to compare to you? You, with your bold smiles and your brilliant mind and your handsome face . . ." She touched his cheek, running her fingers along his jaw. "You have quite ruined me for all others."

They kissed again, languishing in the feel of each other, before he raised his head and spoke, his voice deep and soft,

"Now that you've wheedled your way into my heart and mind and tricked me into confessing my feelings for you, don't you think you ought to be on your way . . . before someone finds us and I've damaged your reputation beyond repair? Although, I confess, right now I could think of worse ways to end this evening than betrothed to you . . . despite your opinions on the subject of marriage."

The words sent a thrill down her spine even as she realized that he was right. She stepped out of his arms, looking up at him with concern in her eyes. "Are you sure you are quite safe here? Will you not consider spending the night at Worthington House?"

He shook his head at her question, offering a reassuring smile as he tucked a loosened curl behind her ear. "No need. Don't worry about me, Alex. I would prefer you forget everything you heard this evening."

She rolled her eyes. "I cannot simply pretend I didn't hear it, Gavin. Your uncle plotting against you is not something I'm going to easily forget."

"My uncle?"

The surprised interest in Gavin's voice set off warning bells for Alex as she realized that he did not know everything there was to know about this particular evening. She had deliberately refrained from mentioning the fact that she'd overheard Lucian Sewell plotting against Gavin earlier — both because she hadn't been sure how to do it tactfully and because she was certain that if she explained everything, he would be unwilling to leave the house quickly.

"Alexandra. My uncle?"

She paused, unsure of how to proceed — of what words to use to share this terrible information. Taking a deep breath to shore up her courage, she plunged into her explanation. "The conversation I overheard, it was in the library annex of the house, on the way to the orangery?" She pushed on as he nodded in recognition. "There were two men in the room, but the door was closed, so I couldn't recognize them by voice alone . . . they were too muffled. I hid in the orangery, just inside the door, in the dark, until they emerged and, while I didn't recognize the first man to exit, I did recognize the second." She stopped, making sympathetic eye contact with Gavin before her final revelation. "It was your uncle Lucian."

He stood stock-still for a brief moment before speaking frankly, "You are mistaken."

It was Alex's turn to be surprised. "What do you mean?"

"I mean, there is no possible way that my uncle is plotting against the Blackmoor line. You did not see what you think you saw."

"But I did, Gavin. I saw your uncle exit that room."

"No, Alex, you couldn't have. My uncle Lucian is many things, but he would never betray his family. Of that, I am certain."

Indignation was rising in Alex's chest; she was beginning to feel warm with defensive ire. "With all due respect, my lord, I witnessed something that points to the opposite."

"I am sure that you believe you did, Alex. But I'm telling you that you were wrong. I don't doubt that you saw someone who appeared to be my uncle. However, it was not he. Of that I am certain."

"I know what I saw. You are in grave danger. And Lucian Sewell is a threat to you and to the Blackmoor line. He admitted to killing your father, Gavin." She saw the cool response in his eyes. "You do not believe me."

"I don't doubt what you heard. Only its source." Noticing her rising anger, he attempted to calm her. "Alex, my uncle Lucian adored his older brother — he was the first of the family to arrive at the Blackmoor estate once we found my father's body. He has been infinitely helpful in assisting me with the transition to earl. He has been an active part of the discussion relating to my father's death and the potential threat to me. He's an ally. Not a villain."

"But isn't it possible that all those things make him the *perfect* villain?" Alex's voice rose in desperation as she saw Gavin's expression darken. "Perhaps he was first to the Essex estate because he was *already there*. Have you even considered that his *assistance* in your transition to earl was merely a ploy to get closer to whatever information your father had garnered? And, Gavin . . . you must stop including him in any discussion of your safety. He is not to be trusted."

She watched him as he leaned against his desk, arms crossed over his broad chest, and her frustration brought tears to her eyes. She refused to cry in his study. Taking another deep breath, she spoke, her voice quivering, "I risked my reputation to come here tonight. I came out of nothing but the deepest concern for you and your family's well-being. I would never *ever* suggest something so damaging if I did not believe, with all my heart, that it was true. And you owe it to me — and to yourself — to at least consider it a possibility."

His expression was dark as he leveled her with a cool, grey gaze. "You are right that you have risked your reputation coming here tonight, Alex. It seems you have also risked my family's good name in doing so. I think it best you return to the ball and forget everything you saw. I assure you that we have this situation well in hand."

She was shocked by his cold dismissal. *Was it possible he was offended by her concern?* She opened her mouth to speak again, but he cut her off before any sound could escape. "I have heard what you have to say, Alex. You needn't repeat it. I encourage you to leave, and be quick about it. I would prefer that my uncle's character be the only one maligned this evening."

"Gavin —"

"Good night, Alexandra."

She watched him turn away from her, tears welling in her eyes. "Gavin —" He paused, not turning back, but clearly focused on her next words. "Be careful. Please."

And, with that, she turned and pushed the window open wide once more, enough for her to sit on the edge and swing herself out into the flower bed below. He made no move to help her exit and she landed off balance in the moist, soft soil, one knee sinking into the fresh dirt.

She didn't care about her ruined gown, or her filthy slippers, or the tears that were threatening to pour down her face. All she cared about was getting back home and finding someone who would believe her.

eighteen

She did not have to go far.

Once back in the Worthington House gardens, she retraced her steps to the balcony of the music room. She crossed the darkened space as though in a trance, not knowing to whom to go or what to say. She opened the door to step into the hallway filled with guests who had left the ballroom for quieter conversations or a moment's rest, and Vivi and Ella spilled into the doorway, barely catching themselves from falling at her feet. The two had obviously been standing with their backs against the door, waiting for her to return.

If Alex hadn't been so shocked by her encounter with Gavin, she would have burst into laughter.

Vivi righted herself first, whispering harshly, "Thank goodness! We've been worried to death!"

"And curious to death," Ella added.

Vivi looked at Ella oddly. "That's not even a phrase." Returning her attention to Alex, she continued, "We were just wondering whether we should call in the cavalry."

Ella drawled, "By that, she means her father."

"As angry as he would have been that we let Alex storm off into the night," Vivi pointed out, "I think 'cavalry' is a perfectly acceptable description."

The two looked up at Alex and spoke in unison, "What happened?"

And, with that, as she looked into the curious, concerned eyes of her best friends in the world, Alex did what she'd wanted to do since leaving Blackmoor on the balcony earlier in the evening. She burst into tears.

Ella and Vivi shared a quick anxious look before rushing forward and herding Alex back into the music room and closing the door firmly behind them.

"Are you all right? What happened?" Vivi asked urgently, guiding Alex to sit on a small tufted stool while Ella lit some nearby candles.

"I think we've established that she's not all right, Vivi," Ella piped in, crouching down beside her tearful friend. "Alex? Are you hurt? Has Blackmoor done something to deserve a thrashing?"

Alex sniffed and responded with a watery smile. "Yes. Would you go deliver it?"

Ella smiled back. "Well, I'm happy to see that you can still find humor in this situation. I would go try for you, you know it. But he is rather significantly larger than I."

"Yes, he is. But mainly he's just insufferable." Looking at her friends, Alex continued with pleading in her voice, "I don't want to go back to the ball. I want to go to my bedchamber and drown myself in my pathetic sorrow."

"Well, considering the condition of this dress, I don't think you would be able to return to the ball even if you wanted to. What on earth did you do to yourself? You're covered in dirt. And your slippers are ruined," Ella pointed out.

Vivi chimed in, "You look like you've fallen in a flower bed."

Alex looked down at her skirts with sadness, pulling them up to inspect her slippers. With a sigh, she spoke, her voice tiny, "I did fall in a flower bed."

"This sounds like a fascinating story," Ella teased, "but let's wait until we're abovestairs to tell it, shall we?"

"Indeed." Vivi whirled into motion, ever the problem solver. "Ella, you sneak Alex up and I shall take care of everything."

"How?" Alex asked. "My mother will be livid that I left the ball so early."

Vivi turned a regal look on Alex. "Never you mind. Have I not taught you yet that I never fail?" She kissed her sad friend on both cheeks and continued as she cracked the door to leave, "I shall see you soon."

And, with that, Vivi left the room, off to convince everyone in Alex's life that it was perfectly normal for her to have disappeared during a ball hosted in her own home.

Ella took her task very seriously and, within moments,

the two girls were in Alex's bedchamber. Ella had helped Alex strip down to her chemise so that the offending gown could be hidden from view prior to the extreme cleaning it was going to require. As for the slippers, Ella shoved them deep into the recesses of Alex's wardrobe, hoping that no one would come looking for them. Turning back to her friend, who had already crawled under the coverlet looking sad, Ella kicked off her own slippers and threw herself across the end of the bed.

She landed just as the door to the bedroom opened and Vivi entered, a smug smile on her face, announcing, "Problem solved. No one will come looking for you, Lady Alexandra, until the morning."

"You're a miracle worker!" Alex said with a shocked look on her face. "How did you manage that?"

"Easily enough. I enlisted Freddie's help in telling everyone that you'd felt sick just before your scheduled dance, and that he'd passed you off to us. That, combined with a quick chat with Kit, explaining that you hadn't wanted to upset or worry your mother, did the trick." Vivi's slippers joined Ella's in a pile on the floor just before she climbed onto the bed next to Alex. "Stanhope wants you to send him a note tomorrow to assure him that you are fine and, quote, 'that Blackmoor isn't a rogue who deserves to be called out.'"

Ella giggled and rolled her eyes. "Male bravado really is ridiculous."

Alex closed her eyes and said aloud, "I've had just about enough of the stuff tonight."

"Are you going to tell us what happened?"

"Which part? When Blackmoor told me that kissing me was a mistake? Or when he told me that he knew someone was trying to kill him? Or perhaps when I told him that the someone in question was his uncle Lucian and he didn't believe me?"

"What?!" The word came out on Ella's surprised exhale. Her wide eyes looked as though they would pop from their sockets.

Vivi sat up, eyeing Alex very closely. Slowly, she suggested, "Why don't we start from the beginning? You seem to have had quite a busy evening."

And so Alex started from the beginning, trying not to leave anything out — not that Ella would have allowed that. As she told her tale, Vivi and Ella listened intently, hanging on every word while she traced the events of the evening from Blackmoor's dance with Penelope to their argument and her ungraceful exit from his study.

As soon as she finished, they pounced, firing questions to obtain more details. "So you think the man who killed the earl was Lucian? Not the other?" Ella asked.

"I can't know for sure, as I couldn't make out the voices — but he certainly had a hand in it."

Vivi was next. "And Blackmoor knows someone is out to kill him?"

"Yes. Apparently he's known for a fortnight."

"And our fathers as well?"

"It seems that way," Alex said without emotion.

"But no one knows what information the former earl had?" Ella pressed.

"No." Alex shook her head before shrugging her shoulders. "At least, not that he told me. It seems they're waiting for the villain to lead them to whatever information the earl had."

"But couldn't Lucian have already found the information and all this be — a red herring?" Vivi spoke, searching for clarity.

"That wouldn't explain Montgrave's skulking about," Ella said to the room at large.

"Or the fact that the two men I overheard were clearly anxious about others beating them to the hiding place," Alex pointed out.

"You mean Lucian and Montgrave," Ella said firmly.

"I don't know it was Montgrave in the room. I didn't see him. And . . . if Gavin is to be believed —"

"Blackmoor is a dunderhead," Ella interrupted.

Vivi nodded in support. "Precisely."

Alex pushed on. "All the same — if he is to be believed —"

"He's not," Vivi pointed out.

"Quite," Ella agreed, adding, "Dunderhead."

Alex rolled her eyes. "Fine." Looking carefully at them, she continued, "You both believe me? You believe it was Lucian?"

"Absolutely!" Ella exclaimed.

"Without doubt," Vivi chimed in.

"Then why didn't he believe me?" Alex asked, falling back into the pillows on her bed.

Ella opened her mouth to speak from her spot at the end of the bed, but before she could get a word out, Alex raised a finger in the air and spoke in warning, "Ella . . . don't tell me he's a dunderhead."

Ella closed her mouth, then raised her head to look at Vivi for support.

"I rather think I understand," Vivi said carefully.

"I beg your pardon!" Ella sat up, leveling Vivi with a glare. "That's not exactly supportive, Vivian."

"Well, I do. After all, Gavin's uncle is almost all he has left of his father. Losing a parent is awful enough. I cannot imagine what it would be like to then, just as quickly, discover that a person you trust is behind all that pain."

"Even so . . . it doesn't excuse his complete stupidity in not believing Alex," Ella pointed out.

"No, of course not," Vivi allowed. "Although I imagine he'll come around to realizing that she is right."

"Of course he will," Ella said imperiously, "because we're going to prove her right."

Alex lifted her head from her pillows. "We are?"

"Indeed." Ella was in one of her moods — she was not taking no for an answer.

"I considered going to our fathers immediately," Alex said, shaking her head. "I wanted to pull mine away from the ball and reveal everything that I had overheard. But Gavin didn't believe me — what if my father doesn't either?"

"That's silly. Of course, your father will believe you," Vivi declared with certainty.

"I suppose so." Alex didn't sound as if she really believed her own words.

And she didn't. Gavin's response had thrown her off — upsetting her more than she could have imagined it would. She was hurt and confused by his cold reaction, as though she were an errant child who had fabricated the tale to garner his attention. She was devastated by his lack of trust and faith — even if Vivi was right and this was all a part of a larger issue that had little, if anything, to do with her. It didn't matter. She was desperate for someone to believe her; she had information that pointed to the murderer of the Earl of Blackmoor, for goodness sake! Wasn't that enough?

"There's only one way to be certain that everyone believes us," Ella said thoughtfully, reading Alex's mind. "We have to find the information before they do."

Vivi and Alex shared a surprised look. "How do you suggest we do that?" Vivi asked.

"I feel quite certain that, between us, we will be able to devise a plan. Once we discover what the earl knew, we will take it to our fathers — and Blackmoor, of course — and prove that Alex was right."

Alex smiled to herself. "I do like the sound of showing Gavin that I was right." She paused before asking, "Does it make me a bad person that I feel that way only in part because it will help to avenge the earl's death? The other part of me simply wants Gavin to see that I am, indeed, right."

Vivi shook her head and said matter-of-factly, "Absolutely not. His behavior was unkind and unpleasant. I would be worried if there *weren't* a small part of you that wanted to show him that you are right."

"Which brings us to the next question," Ella pointed out.

"Which is?" Alex was beginning to feel better about the entire evening.

"What was the kiss like?"

Alex thought for a moment, searching for the right word. Then, with a soft smile, she said, "It was wonderful. He was wonderful. The moment was . . ."

"Wonderful?" Vivi interjected with a laugh.

Alex grinned at her. "Quite." The smile disappeared as quickly as it had come. "But now he's furious with me. I doubt he's reveling in the wonder of the moment."

"Oh, I don't know," Vivi said supportively. "It seems that when something is that wonderful, it's hard to forget it. You're not thrilled with his behavior right now and *you* remember how fabulous it was."

"True," Alex replied on a sigh.

"Be careful, Alexandra, you're beginning to sound like the type of young lady who wants all those things typical young females want," Ella said with warning in her voice, her nose wrinkled, "marriage, children, a house in Surrey."

"What's wrong with wanting marriage and children?" Vivi asked. "I want those things. Not Surrey," she said with a raised finger, "but the rest."

"True, but with you, it's different. You're pining after The One." Ella said the last with an exaggerated swoon, which Vivi ignored.

"Well, maybe Blackmoor is Alex's One."

Ella turned an incredulous look on Alex. "Really?"

They both turned questioning looks on Alex, who thought for a moment before speaking. Was Gavin *The One*? Could she imagine spending the rest of her life with him? Certainly, his mere presence set her heart racing. When he flashed one of his private, conspiratorial grins, she wanted to stop whatever she was doing and just bask in the glow of his attention. And, if that wasn't enough, she couldn't imagine living a day without him in her life. Obviously, considering the events of the season, there was something between them. But was he The One? Did that person even exist? Shouldn't it be easier to communicate with The One? Shouldn't she understand him better? Shouldn't she be able to articulate what she wanted from him? When it came right down to it, she couldn't say *what* she wanted from Gavin Sewell, Eighth Earl of Blackmoor, except to say she wanted him with her. For now. And maybe forever.

Turning to her friends, she said simply, "I don't know. However, I would like to find out."

The three girls talked late into the night, eventually falling asleep on the bed long after the ball below ended and all the guests went home.

Alex had never been so happy to have her friends with her than she was that evening — they made the whole, horrible night seem tolerable. She knew without a doubt that, together, they would make this confusing, devastating situation right.

nineteen

Last night, everything had been so clear. His plans had been so well laid out, so perfect, so clean. He had returned home from the Worthington Ball to change clothes, planning to find young Blackmoor quickly and finally finish that which he should have finished long ago. As he changed out of his formal attire, he had imagined what it would feel like to eliminate the boy. How free and invigorated he would feel knowing that another high-and-mighty Blackmoor was gone from the earth. For moments, he had been giddy with laughter — eager to kill again. He'd allowed himself a few moments to fantasize about the manner in which he would dispose of the brat.

And then, everything had changed. A messenger had arrived at breakneck speed, barely able to breathe from the exertion. He had known before reading the missive that his plans for the evening were changed. Sadly, he would have to wait to exact his punishment on another Blackmoor, but the messenger had brought news of an unacceptable turn of events — one that must be rectified with all deliberate speed. He could not contain the hint of excitement that he felt in his new task — even though it increased a hundredfold his risk of being discovered. No matter. Here was his chance to prove his allegiance.

As always, he threw the note into the fire, watching the edges of the paper char and curl in the heat. He watched the lines of ink turn from black to brown and eventually become consumed by the flames. Long after the paper disintegrated, he remembered the message.

There was a girl in the orangery.
Find her.

He was going to enjoy this.

The next morning, Alex awoke to bright sunlight and the sound of fervent whispering. For a few seconds, she lingered in that moment between sleeping and waking when everything seems hazy and comfortable — until the memory of the previous evening's events came crashing down on her and she had an intense desire to throw the covers over her head and never leave her bed.

Instead, she rolled over and spied the source of the whispering. Vivi and Ella were sitting cross-legged on the chaise, facing each other, the tea tray next to them laden with a steaming pot, pastries, and jams. Vivi nibbled on a scone, nodding as Ella waved her hands in the air wildly to emphasize her hushed point.

"What are you two up to?" Alex said sleepily, sitting up.

They both turned to her with broad smiles. "Oh, excellent! You are awake!" Ella exclaimed.

"How are you feeling?" Vivi asked, pouring a cup of tea for her friend.

Alex stretched broadly, reaching out to accept the tea and biscuit Vivi brought to her. "What are you two plotting?"

"To be fair," Vivi said with a pointed look at Ella, "only one of us is plotting."

"Mmm. I see that. And what mischief have you devised for us, Lady Eleanor?"

"Not mischief so much as detective work," replied Ella.

"Ah. Of course."

"My theory is this: If we cannot prove Lucian's role in the plot to kill the earl, we can at least uncover the information that led to his death. Perhaps that in turn will lead us to the entire plot against the Crown! At the very least, it will prove to Blackmoor that he was wrong *not* to believe you."

"There's only one problem with that," Alex said.

"Only one?" Vivi interjected, earning a black look from Ella.

"Well, only one big one. If the War Office, Bow Street, and Blackmoor himself have not been able to find this information, why on earth would we be able to?"

"Ah . . . the voice of reason awakes," Vivi said with a smile.

"I'll tell you why. Because we have" — Ella ticked off the qualities on her fingers as she spoke them — "cleverness, a fresh eye for the problem, curiosity, superior instinct — as proven by my hunch that Montgrave was involved from the beginning — and —" She paused dramatically. "— the most important thing of all."

"Which is?" Alex asked.

"Desire to prove that we can," she added, with a measure of fantasy in her voice. "And think of the coup when they realize that three young women did something that a battalion of men could not."

At that moment, a knock came at the door and the duchess entered with all the poise befitting her position. She was wearing a day dress of rich purple satin and looked as though she had been up and fresh for hours, despite the fact that she'd hosted one of the greatest balls in London history the evening before. Stopping a few paces into the room, she looked suspiciously from one girl to the next, leveling each with a cool, blue gaze before finally speaking to her daughter. "Alexandra, I trust you are feeling better?"

"Yes, Mother. Thank you."

"What was it that befell you last evening?"

"I — uh —" For the life of her, Alex couldn't remember what Vivi and Freddie's excuse was. "I had a turned ankle after the dance with Freddie, and Vivi and Ella were nice enough to escort me here and keep me company."

A single brow of her mother's rose as Vivi coughed into her hand. "By that thoroughly unsubtle cough, I rather imagine that Vivian is attempting to tell you that it was not your ankle that bothered you last evening, but a touch of the ague."

Alex blushed under her mother's scrutiny. "Mothers always find out, Alexandra."

"I didn't —"

The duchess silenced her with a single raised hand. "I would prefer not to hear whatever excuse you have devised to explain your behavior last evening. Instead, I am here to tell you that, although you may have escaped the ball, you cannot escape me. As punishment for missing my ball, I am requiring your attendance at a country house party."

Despite her relief that her mother seemed to think they had schemed only to escape the ball last night and not for any more serious reason, Alex groaned, "Mother! You cannot!"

"On the contrary, daughter, I can. More so, I shall. You and your brothers are hereby required to be in attendance. They, I'm sure, will have a bone to pick with you when they hear." She turned to Vivi and Ella, adding, "I've invited both of your parents — so I expect you will be there as well."

Her statement elicited a wan smile from Ella and a slightly brighter one from Vivi. Alex piped in, "Well, at least you two will be forced to be there as well. That might help a bit." Turning back to her mother, she said grumpily, "Who else has been invited?"

"I have dispatched invitations to a number of influentials — including Blackmoor and Stanhope, the Salisburys, Lady Twizzleton, the Warings — I know your feelings on the young lord, but he is indeed a marquess — and a number of additional young, eligible men. The season is almost half over; it's time you girls turn your thoughts to finding a proper match."

She was so wrapped up in making her point, the duchess failed to notice the slight catch in Alex's breath when she referenced Gavin. He wouldn't attend, would he? Or maybe he would, simply to ignore her. She didn't know what was worse. Perhaps she could convince her mother to postpone this silly party? Alex opened her mouth to say something, when Ella beat her to the task with a bright smile and an "Oh, Your Grace! What a wonderful group of people! I, for one, am quite excited to attend. Aren't you, Vivi?"

Vivi gave Ella a strange look and answered warily, "Indeed."

Pleasantly surprised, the duchess smiled at Ella. "Thank you, Eleanor, I share your excitement and shall look forward to having you with us." Turning back to Alex, she continued, "You would do well to take a leaf from your friend's book, Alexandra. I shall expect to see you in a better humor when we leave tomorrow morning."

"Tomorrow morning!" Alex cried. "But that's impossible!" Her stomach dropped as she was flooded with reasons to dread the house party. Between Blackmoor's clear frustration with her, which could easily lead him to decline the invitation and stay in town, leaving Lucian and Montgrave with a much easier time finding and dispatching the young earl the way they'd done to his father, and the real possibility that he might join them in the country and plague her with his obvious dislike, her heart was racing and she was beginning to feel panicked.

"Well, I'm on rather an impressive streak of hosting excellent parties," Her Grace explained, "a fact you would be aware of if you had bothered to attend last evening's festivities. I see no reason to wait. The guests will join us on Saturday. I shall need your help to prepare the manor." Turning to the girls, she suggested, "Why don't you both join us? I'm happy to extend the request to your parents if you'd like. You would be welcome company for both Alexandra and myself."

Ella and Vivi nodded assent as Alex sighed heavily, drawing a smile from her mother. "There's no reason to be so dramatic, Alexandra. You like the country. Remember?"

"I know," she replied with reservation, "I just *hate* the season."

"Well, that's all the more reason to get yourself married — and avoid having to have another," her mother said with a broad grin that reminded Alex of her brothers on their most infuriating of days. She returned the smile with a black look as her mother kissed her on the forehead and turned on her heel to leave the room, saying, "Things will look better once you've dressed, my love. Girls, there's a beautiful breakfast spread in the dining room — Cook really has outdone herself. May I suggest you join us?"

And, with that, she departed.

As the door closed behind her mother, Alex worried her lip, wishing that she'd never escaped to the orangery the night before and swearing silently that she would never eavesdrop on another conversation again. Now she'd made a mess of everything. She had no idea to whom Lucian had been talking and no proof to share with anyone that she'd heard what she'd heard. On top of that, Blackmoor had all but pushed her out of his study last night. This was horrible.

"This is excellent!" Ella burst out after the door to the bedchamber closed behind the duchess.

Vivi and Alex turned shocked gazes on their friend. Vivi found her voice first. "I beg your pardon? This sounds the very opposite of excellent."

"You're not thinking about it in the right way! A house party in Essex will give us a chance to search for clues and information in Essex, where the crime was committed! If we don't return from the country with the whole mystery solved, I shall be quite surprised!"

"Ella, at the rate we're going, if we return from the country with all of our loved ones intact, *I* shall be quite surprised," Alex said, her words laced with frustration as she threw back her coverlet and got out of bed, ringing for Eliza to help her dress. "That's it. I'm going to tell my father everything. We can't do this alone."

"But, Alex!" Ella exclaimed.

"No, Ella. This is not a game. A man died. We're not in any position to solve this mystery ourselves. Blackmoor's life is at stake. And ours as well if we don't tell what we know."

Vivi nodded in agreement. "I think Alex is right, Ella. We cannot traipse off to Essex to save the day — we wouldn't even know how to begin to do that."

Ella pouted briefly until she recognized the truth behind her friends' words. Although she did allow herself a heavy sigh and a disappointed "Fine."

The rich, savory aromas of a traditional English breakfast were detectable even as they descended the massive central staircase of Worthington House. Alex's mouth was watering before the girls joined the Staffords in the dining room for breakfast.

The entire family was present for the meal, with the exception of the duke, who had clearly already been and gone; the seat always reserved for him at the head of the long mahogany table was empty save for an already-read newspaper. Alex tempered her disappointment — she had been hoping to catch her father before he left for the business of the day — and focused on the rest of the room. The duchess was seated in her traditional position at the foot of the table, listening to the chatter of Alex's brothers, who were dispersed amongst the eight places that had been prepared along either side of the long table. As was to be expected, the boys had filled their plates with mountains of food and were eating with gusto while they talked.

Noticing the entrance of the girls, all three stood to greet Ella and Vivi, as was expected of them as gentlemen, and the two, in turn, dropped quick curtsies in response. As the boys returned to their food, the girls made their way to the sideboard, where Cook had created a feast. There were eggs, English bacon and sausages, sautéed mushrooms, freshly baked bread and churned butter from Stafford Manor, and a dozen other choices in all manners sweet and savory. Alex's stomach rumbled and she smiled wryly to herself, thinking, *Anxious or no, it seems my appetite is very much intact.*

As she filled her plate, she listened to the conversation around her. "Mother, you cannot be serious. Four days in the country in a house teeming with as-yet-unspoken-for women and their cloying mothers?" Nick said. "Are you attempting to estrange your sons?"

"I cannot do it," Will said flatly. "Last night was enough — if I was introduced once as the 'Next Duke of Worthington,' I was introduced that way a thousand times. It's horrid. Those women want nothing more of me than my title . . . which I don't even hold as yet!"

"Nonsense," said Her Grace. "You are an attractive, charming, entertaining young man. Your title has little to do with your eligibility. They would be after you even if you were a farmer, or a butcher, or any other sort of untitled person."

There was a moment of silence during which the young Staffords looked at each other in shock before bursting into laughter. "It's true!" defended the duchess, indignantly.

"Mother, you cannot honestly believe that," Kit said. "Those mamas want money and land for their little angels. Ask yourself how you would feel if Alex came home wanting to marry a butcher. How would the Earl and Countess of Marlborough feel about that for Ella? Or the Marquess of Langford for Vivi?"

All three girls looked up from their plates, surprised to have been dragged into the discussion, and the duchess was saved from speaking by Alex, who had made her way to a seat next to Will. "Oh, no, don't bring our prospects for marriage into this. We have nothing to do with it."

"It seems, Scamp," Will said, "that you have everything to do with it, seeing as the three of you have secured the punishment in question for all of us with your behavior last night."

"Thank you all for that," Nick said. "I should tan your hide, Alex . . . and Freddie's, too, for his part in it." Looking at Ella and Vivi, he added, "You two are saved only because you are neither family nor male."

The duchess spoke, her place at the foot of the table making the statement seem more of a decree. "I am through with the four of you being so cavalier about your prospects for marriage and a future. You will all attend the house party and, more so, you will all enjoy it."

"You cannot force us to enjoy it, Mother," Kit said with a smile.

"You forget that I'm a duchess, Christopher. I can do whatever I like."

She flashed a bright smile as all four Stafford children groaned at her statement, a commonplace proclamation, sending Vivi and Ella into giggles.

"I still don't understand why we have to be punished for Alex's ills," Will said.

Alex looked her eldest brother square in the eye, saying tartly, "I assure you it's my punishment as well, Will. There is little I want to do less than be trapped in the country with you lot."

"Exactly why I'm guessing Mother is forcing all of us to attend," Nick pointed out. "Why not just suffer through the ball?"

Alex smiled sweetly. "Why, to make your collective lives more difficult, of course!" Three sets of male eyes narrowed as Ella went into a coughing fit and Vivi smiled into her teacup.

The sentence still hung in the air as the door to the room swung open, causing all heads to turn toward it. Alex's stomach dropped and her appetite vanished as Blackmoor stepped into the room. He was clad in traveling clothes — a chestnut topcoat over a crisp white linen shirt and buckskin breeches, tightly fitted to his long legs in a way she couldn't help but notice. The pants were tucked into tall leather riding boots that were freshly polished. He looked remarkably handsome, if slightly distracted, with his golden hair mussed and his eyes betraying his impatience. He was holding a riding crop and hat in one hand and a pair of lambskin gloves in the other.

Alex's gaze flew to Vivi, who met her gaze firmly and nodded almost imperceptibly, as if to say, *Be strong,* and then to Ella, who was looking at Blackmoor with narrowed eyes, making her displeasure with him clear to anyone who was looking. Thankfully, no one was, and Vivi poked her before it became an issue.

"Gavin!" Her Grace said brightly, offering up her hand for Blackmoor to bow low over. "You are a welcome addition to this motley bunch. Perhaps you can bring some calm to our table? There is plenty of food; have you eaten?"

"A pleasure, as always, Your Grace." Blackmoor's rich tenor sent a shiver down Alex's spine. "As much as I would like to stay, I'm afraid I have already eaten and am only here to take the male half of this gathering off your hands." She noticed that, as he looked around the table, he deliberately avoided her gaze. "We are off to Essex."

"Indeed." Will stood up from the table.

"Essex? For what?" Ella asked sharply.

"For an adventure that doesn't involve meddling females," Kit joked, then cleared his throat when no one laughed. He stood, moving toward the hallway to call for their topcoats and hats.

Nick stood last. "We had already arranged to use the house for hunting this week. Mother's party came as a surprise to all of us, but I suspect she chose to host one so quickly because she knew we would have no excuses to avoid it."

"Indeed," said the duchess. "Your mother possesses not only beauty, but intelligence as well. Lord Blackmoor, you will be joining us for the house party?" The words, while phrased as a question, were more a dictate.

An almost imperceptible color rose on Blackmoor's cheeks, something that Alex noticed only because she was so focused on him, waiting for his answer. "I shall endeavor to be there, my lady."

"Excellent," said the duchess, moving to exit alongside the young men. "We shall make a room for you and hope for the best."

The door closed behind the group, leaving the girls in the now quiet dining room. Alex let out a long breath — one she hadn't known she was holding. Turning sad eyes to her friends, she said, "He didn't look at me once. Did you notice?"

"I did," Vivi said softly. "You cannot expect him to get beyond the events of last night so quickly, Alex. It was a great deal for one person to take in."

"True," said Ella. "Men are not nearly as evolved as women are, nor as intelligent, evidently."

Alex offered a half smile but was lost in her disappointment. Vivi was right — she should have expected a cool response from Blackmoor, but his cut hurt just the same.

While she understood how difficult this situation must be for him, it didn't change the fact that she was tired of fighting with him, tired of always having to start over. She wished they could go back to the beginning and just be friends again. That would be enough. Almost.

She sighed and pushed back from the table. "I'm going to find my father. I need to speak with him about last night."

Ella stopped her from getting up. "Wait. Now, I know that we said we were going to tell the duke everything, but I have an idea."

"Ella . . ." Vivi's tone was laced with warning.

"I know, I know. But this is thoroughly harmless!" Ella defended herself quickly.

"Somehow I doubt that," Alex said, "but I shall endeavor to humor you."

"Thank you. All right. Blackmoor is gone from the house today, correct?" Ella's eyes were bright with excitement.

"So it seems."

"And we have little to do."

"No, Ella." This from Vivi. "I see where this is going. And it's a terrible idea."

"Why?! Why can't we just sneak next door, take a look around Blackmoor House, and sneak back? No one will ever know!"

Alex spoke quietly. "Ella, I know how much you want to be a part of this adventure. I do, too. But now we're at a point where we have to involve someone who knows a bit more about these matters than we do. We're not talking about the Dowager Duchess of Lockwood's walking stick going missing. We're discussing murder and treason. I'm sorry, Ella. I've got to tell my father."

With that, Alex stood and went to the door, pulling it open and calling out to Harquist, "Is my father free to speak with me, Harquist?"

"No, my lady, I'm afraid His Grace left early this morning," the butler said with a low bow. "He is at Parliament for the morning and will leave directly from there to join your brothers in Essex."

Alex tempered her disappointment. "Thank you. I suppose I shall wait and speak with him there, then."

She closed the door and turned back to her friends, who were watching her carefully, waiting for her next move — one they would support without question. She met Ella's eye, noting her friend's desperate attempt to hide the thoughts that were written, quite plainly, across her face.

"All right, Ella. You win. Blackmoor House it is."

twenty

Sneaking across the gardens to Blackmoor House felt very different by the light of day from how it had been when Alex was skulking around in the darkness the night before. In fact, it rather felt more like an afternoon walk than a clandestine activity. This could have been attributed to the fact that there were gardeners hard at work mere feet away who took absolutely no interest in their activities, or it could have been the fact that she hadn't just overheard a horrible conversation, but Alex had a suspicion that it was more Ella's glee at their activities. And her inability to keep quiet about it.

"How do we get into Blackmoor's study? Did you climb in?"

"No, he lifted me in."

"Hmm. Right, then. Vivi will have to give us a boost up."

"She will, will she?" from the booster in question.

"Well, how else do we sneak in?"

"I rather thought that we could knock on the front door and have Bingham let us in," Alex said matter-of-factly, referencing Blackmoor's ancient butler, as she led the trio around the corner of the house and toward the main entrance.

"What? We can't do that!" Ella stopped, indignant.

"Whyever not?" Vivi asked, following Alex. "It seems a perfectly acceptable way to enter. In fact, I believe I've been entering houses that way for my entire life."

Seeing that she had been outvoted, not to mention left behind, Ella scurried to catch up to the other two as they made their way to the door. "And what do you expect we'll say to him that will end in his leaving us in the house without a chaperone?" she whispered rather indelicately as Alex knocked on the door and put a finger to her lips, calling for silence.

"I imagine I'll think of something." The door opened, and she turned a brilliant smile on the older gentleman behind it. "Bingham! Good day!" She pushed through, Vivi and Ella hot on her heels. Once inside the house, she untied her bonnet, not allowing for a response. "Blackmoor asked that we pop over here and pick up some books from the study that he meant to bring over for my father before he left to go hunting with my brothers," she said quickly. "I find him to be very forgetful, don't you?"

As the butler began to speak, Vivi jumped in, picking up on the game, "Oh, I do as well — why, the other night, he left his walking stick at the Worthington House dinner. Nick had to return it the next morning, remember?"

"Indeed. So silly." She threw up her hands in a ridiculous gesture. "You don't mind if we just pop in and pick them up, do you, Bingham?" Alex was already moving toward the study, leaving the poor old man looking rather dumbfounded. "There's no need for you to wait for us. He gave us a rather long list. Didn't he, Ella?"

Ella turned surprised eyes on her. "He did?"

Vivi sighed, feigning exasperation. "Ella, you're almost as forgetful as Blackmoor. You put the list inside your journal, didn't you?"

Alex turned wide eyes on her friend. "You did bring the list, didn't you? Or do we have to go back?"

Ella caught on. Finally. "No. No! Of course not. I have it right here." She went digging into her reticule and brought out the book, opening it quickly and tearing out a page. She waved it under the nose of the butler, who was looking from one girl to the next, as if watching a game of lawn tennis. Ella buried her nose in the "list," saying, "*Agrarian Trends in the Counties of Essex and Staffordshire, 1750–1790.* Good Lord! Your poor father. Hopefully there's a novel somewhere on this list."

Vivi's mouth twitched in a desperate attempt to hold back the smile threatening to break across her face. She affected a feminine whine and said, "Let's go, Ella. The ribbon shop on Bond Street is receiving a new shipment of silks today. I shouldn't like to spend all day with Blackmoor's musty old books." Turning a wide, brilliant smile on the butler, she said, "Which way, Bingham?"

The butler pointed mutely in the direction of the study, and the three girls were off and through the door before he could say a word. Once inside, Alex called out, loudly enough for him to hear from his spot, "It's rather drafty in here. Ella, be a dear and close the door? I should hate to catch a chill."

The door closed firmly, leaving the poor old man on the other side, staring speechlessly at it, wondering at the silliness of females and thanking his maker that his masters had never had daughters, before taking himself off to continue his afternoon duties.

"The poor creature never had a chance of survival," Alex said, walking toward Blackmoor's desk. "You were both excellent."

"Although Ella almost ruined our chances," Vivi pointed out with a smile.

"Indeed," Alex agreed, "some investigator you make. You did rally, however. I confess I was quite impressed with *Agrarian Trends*. Nice touch."

"Thank you. I thought so, myself." Ella nodded in appreciation.

"We had better start finding a pile of books to carry out of here. We wouldn't like Bingham to think we were being untruthful." Vivi moved toward a bookshelf and started to do just that as Ella and Alex chuckled.

The girls tackled separate parts of the room working quickly but carefully, making sure to leave things exactly as they were found. Vivi checked the shelves as she searched for books that might seem relevant to the Duke of Worthington to anyone who cast a discerning eye, building a pile of them by the door that would topple if someone were to open it, to warn them that they were about to be discovered.

After several minutes of searching and turning up nothing, Alex sat in the earl's chair, announcing, "Everything here has been looked at, picked over, and considered. If there were something to be found in this room, it would have been found."

Ella blew a stray lock of hair from her face and closed a cabinet she had been searching through. "Agreed. But, then, where would it be?"

"I don't know, but we're not going to look for it now," declared Alex. "I promised you access to Blackmoor's study. Nothing else. We should go — as it is, when he discovers that we were here, we're going to be in a mountain of trouble."

"This is interesting," Vivi said from across the room, where she was holding a leather-bound book in her hands. "Someone has peeled the endpaper from this volume."

Ella asked, "Which volume is it?"

"*A History of Essex.* I selected it because I thought it would seem relevant to the nonexistent *Agrarian Trends of Essex* that we are expected to procure while here. But the binding is loose and —" Vivi broke off as the back page of the book peeled up off the leather cover. She gasped as a crisp, white square of paper popped out of the book. When they saw, Alex and Ella rushed from their positions across the room to join her.

"What is it?" Ella asked excitedly.

"Don't get too excited, Ella," Alex warned. "It's probably nothing. Remember this room has already been combed for information."

"Not this shelf," Vivi disputed. "These books are all covered in at least six months of dust." She carefully opened the paper as the other two girls leaned in to look at its contents. There, scribbled in a strong hand across the crisp parchment were the words they'd hoped — and feared — they would find.

27 December 1814

I suspect plans are being made for more war, and that there is an Englishman helping the plot. While I do not want to believe what I know to be true, I must act now, before others become aware of what I have discovered. If this letter is found and I have failed, use the book as your guide. Everything is at stake. Particularly the name. Keep it safe.

"My God." Alex breathed. "It's from the earl."

"We — We don't . . . we can't know for sure," Vivi said haltingly.

"We do know for sure, Vivi," Alex replied. "Who else would it be from? My God. He found proof of treason and was killed for it."

"'Everything is at stake, particularly the name'? What name?" Ella asked aloud.

"The Blackmoor name," Alex said quietly, almost to herself. She was recalling her conversation with Blackmoor from the previous night, one that took place in this very room. He had been concerned that her accusations about his uncle would risk the reputation of the Blackmoor name. *Just as his father had been.*

"My God, I was right," Alex whispered. She looked up and spoke quickly, grabbing the paper from Vivi's grasp and stuffing it back into the book, a feeling of dread coming over her. "We have to leave here. Immediately. I was right."

The words were barely out of her mouth when the books placed by the door toppled. The girls all spun toward the door, hoping it would be Bingham who was interrupting their conversation, praying it wouldn't be Lucian Sewell.

Their prayers went unanswered. There was a delicate straightening of all of their spines as he pushed his way into the room, looking distastefully first at the pile of books on the floor and then around the room until his gaze fell on the trio. Alex willed herself to smile and find a quick exit from this particular trap.

"My lord Sewell," she said brightly, "you gave us a fright!"

Vivi found her voice next. "Quite!" She rushed forward to the books strewn across the carpet and crouched to gather them. "I'm such a ninny. This was not the spot for a pile of books! Why, anyone could have knocked them over!"

Lucian's voice was slow and suspicious. "Indeed. An odd place for a pile of books. Odder even for a pile of books built by girls who are trespassing."

"Trespassing!" Ella laughed a touch too loudly, moving forward, *A History of Essex* clutched in her hand. "My lord, you are quite amusing. I assure you we would much rather be shopping for ribbon than picking up a selection of books for Alex's father that Blackmoor should have delivered himself. In fact, that is just where we are headed next." She took a stack of the books from Vivi's arms, adding hers to the pile before setting them on her hip. She turned back to Alex, saying, "I think that's all of them, don't you? Shall we have Bingham send a footman to help us?"

Alex moved toward them, keenly aware of Sewell's discerning eye and desperately attempting to appear nonchalant, "No. No. I don't think that's necessary. It will just take more time. We'll miss the best part of the day as it is."

Vivi nodded her head. "Quite." Turning on her heel, she offered a low curtsy and a warm smile to Sewell, saying, "My lord, again, apologies if we startled you."

He lifted a corner of his mouth in a false smile of his own. "It takes more than a few girls to scare me, Lady Vivian, Lady Eleanor."

He nodded to both girls as they left the room, and Alex felt a chill race down her spine. Was there a double meaning in his words? She took a deep breath and dropped into a curtsy identical to Vivi's, willing herself to get out of the room without betraying all she knew. "My lord Sewell."

"Lady Alexandra. May I have a word?"

No! Her mind screamed, but what was she to do? She had to appear nonchalant, and the only way to do that would be to humor the despicable man. Ella and Vivi were only feet away — how much harm could happen? "Of course," she replied with a look she hoped appeared to be curiosity.

He lowered his voice and spoke succinctly. "You care very much for my nephew, do you not?"

She nodded carefully and he continued, "Excellent. As do I. You seem an intelligent girl. You would do best to stop skulking about where you do not belong. You wouldn't want Blackmoor to get hurt because of you, would you? Or those lovely friends of yours who seem never to leave your side?"

"I — I don't know what you mean," Alex said, her voice wavering.

"Then this conversation was unnecessary," he said with an empty smile. "All the better." He moved past her, into the study, speaking as he went, "Have a lovely time on Bond Street."

She was terrified and furious and frustrated all at once. Terrified that he would follow them and somehow hurt them, furious that he would think to threaten those she held most dear, and frustrated because she felt so helpless and unheard. She turned to leave the room, her breath coming fast and hard.

"Oh, and one more thing, my lady?"

"Yes, my lord?" She willed the tremor from her voice, turning back to find him thumbing through a stack of correspondence.

"I so enjoyed myself at your parents' ball last evening. Do let them know, will you?"

"Indeed, my lord."

"And be sure to tell them that I was particularly enamored of the orangery."

Alex fled the room with a singular focus — to get Ella and Vivi as far from Lucian Sewell as possible. And quickly.

twenty-one

Alex awoke with a start as the carriage turned off the main thoroughfare and onto the mile-long drive that led up to Stafford Manor. Night had fallen and they had been driving for the entire day. They had left Worthington House at dawn and were arriving well after dark. For the first part of the trip, Ella and Vivi had kept her company, chattering about the odd things they witnessed on the long drive to the eastern edge of Britain. After the first break, when they had stopped for tea and a change of horses, the two had curled up on the seat across from Alex and the duchess and had fallen asleep, leaving Alex, unable to sleep herself, to talk quietly with her mother, who had been busy preparing activities for the house party that would begin late tomorrow with the arrival of the first wave of guests.

Within a few hours, even the duchess had succumbed to the lure of laziness that comes with long hours of travel in a warm, darkened coach, and Alex had found herself alone with her thoughts — thoughts that haunted her as she ran the events of the past two days over and over in her mind.

Of course, at the front of her mind was the confrontation she'd had the day before with Lucian Sewell; she could not pretend she was not thoroughly shaken by his words. He had all but admitted that he was not above hurting his nephew or anyone else who stood in his way — even Ella and Vivi. Alex had not missed his threats. He meant to hurt them if she told anyone her suspicions. She wrapped the travel blanket more tightly around herself to stave off the chill of the memory. *Was it possible that Gavin had recounted their conversation and her eavesdropping?* She couldn't imagine his doing such a thing, but she had to consider it an option.

She had risked Ella and Vivi's lives by bringing them to Blackmoor House. Before, Gavin's uncle hadn't given the three of them a second thought. Now, they were squarely in his sights. That was no one's fault but her own. Alex knew that she had only one task — to ensure her friends' safety without revealing to them any more of her suspicions, should there be any more. The less they knew of Lucian Sewell's part in whatever terrifying play this was, the better for them.

Their second stop had interrupted her somber thoughts, and while the grooms and coachmen changed the team of horses again, the four women had a chance to eat a warm, filling dinner in preparation for the longest leg of the trip. The food, combined with the already long day, had put Alex right to sleep when she returned to the carriage and cuddled under the traveling blanket until these, the last few minutes of the journey.

Alex inhaled deeply, breathing in the crisp air. To think, just a day earlier she'd been begging her mother not to force her to travel to Essex. Now she couldn't wait to be at the country house.

She would be lying to herself if she claimed that her eagerness to arrive was merely about protecting her friends. As she looked out the window into the blackness, she was keenly aware of the fact that she was staring blindly in the direction of Sewell Hall, the familial seat of the Blackmoor line. She knew that if Blackmoor wasn't in the billiard room at Stafford Manor with her brothers, unaware of her approach, he was at the hall, just a quarter of a mile away.

As time had passed since their confrontation in his study, she had grown less and less angry with Blackmoor. Instead, she found herself filled with sorrow at what their relationship — always comfortable and friendly — had lost. There had been a time when their tempers would not have flared, when hurtful words would never have been spoken, when he wouldn't have dreamed of asking her to leave his presence. That time had clearly passed, and she was devastated by that fact.

Perhaps Blackmoor had been right; perhaps the kiss had been a mistake. It had most assuredly made her life harder, because now she couldn't imagine her world without him. He'd been her fourth brother from the start, but now he was a great deal more. Yes, he was a friend, but she couldn't deny how thoroughly she was attracted to him — how much she ached for his approval, his affection, his love.

Love?

She started in the silence, surprised by the notion. It had always been such a laughable, ephemeral word — a concept she'd never understood and in which she'd never really been interested. It had been partner to The One . . . perhaps right for Vivi but never for Alex. But now, as she considered her feelings for Blackmoor — feelings that could only be defined as love — she could almost see herself embracing both of these notions.

There was only one thing to do. She had to find him, as soon as possible, and show him that everything they had, everything they'd said, was worth their taking the significant risks that faced them. She had to convince him that what she knew about his uncle and his father was true . . . that he was wrong not to believe her . . . that she would never hurt him without cause. She knew it was a risk, one that almost certainly would take her down a path that led to one of two things: either the happiness of sharing her life with the boy she was coming to realize she'd been destined for since the beginning; or the misery of living without him. It was a risk she had no choice but to take.

As she shored up her courage, telling herself she could manage this encounter and that she could overcome her disappointment if he were to dismiss her, the carriage entered the last, long curve on the manor drive. She could see the enormous stone house rising up in the darkness, and she was comforted by the fact that it had been the seat of the Stafford line for generations. If she were going to do such a nerve-wracking thing as confront the man she loved, there was no place in the world she'd rather do it than here.

She shook her mother awake, then reached across the seat and poked both Ella and Vivi, rousing them from their slumber. The three woke with the frustration of those who find sleep despite discomfort as she said, "We're here!" with a cheerfulness she didn't entirely feel.

The carriage rolled to a stop as Vivi yawned broadly and muttered, "Oh, excellent bed! How quickly can I find you?"

"I shall race you to it," Ella grumbled, drawing a smile from the duchess.

The door to the carriage opened and Alex clambered down with the help of a footman. As Vivi and Ella piled out behind her, she looked up at the manor house, smiling to herself at the welcoming light that was flickering in the windows of the rooms that had been prepared for their arrival this evening. The yellow light spilled into the night in a way that she had loved since she was a child, filling the darkness that was so much a part of country evenings.

Alex took a deep breath, taking in the "crisp Stafford air" — as her father would call it — remembering her mother's comment the day before. She did love the country. There was something about the way the stars shone ever so much more brightly here, about the way time slowed down, about the way it smelled on a cool May night. Everything seemed simpler here. Better.

The large oak door to the house opened, and Alex looked up to see her father, silhouetted by the bright lights of the entryway. He looked nothing like a duke — without an overcoat or a waistcoat, without a cravat. His shirt was tucked into his buckskin breeches, but his sleeves were rolled up on his bronzed arms, and Alex chuckled to think of what London's aristocracy would think to see him, one of the most powerful men in England, wandering about dressed like a "savage."

A flash of white appeared as he grinned down at the group on the drive. He called back into the house, "My word! It appears someone's left a group of orphans at the door!"

The four women laughed at his silly jest as he came bounding down the steps, taking Alex into his arms for a warm hug and a kiss on the forehead, and welcoming Vivi and Ella in turn. He then turned to help the duchess down from the carriage. When her feet touched the ground, she looked up at her husband and said, "Rather too old to be an orphan, I think."

Wrapping his arms around her, the duke replied lovingly, "Nonsense. You grow younger with each day," and kissed her soundly on the mouth.

Vivi and Ella turned away, blushing and leaving Alex shaking her head and teasing, "Your behavior really is too uncivilized. Shouldn't you be setting a better example for the next generation?"

"It looks like an excellent example to me."

The words sent a tingle up Alex's spine as she recognized the warm, friendly voice. She turned to find Blackmoor, clad as casually as her father, coming down the steps to greet them. In the darkness, she couldn't be sure, but he seemed to be looking straight at her. Her stomach turned over as she watched him approach, and she blushed deeply to think that he was discussing her parents' actions so openly.

"You could have this yourself, Gavin, if you would only take a wife!" her mother pointed out, kissing him on both cheeks in welcome.

Vivi's, Ella's, and Alex's jaws dropped in unison as they heard the duchess's cheeky response. There was most definitely something about the country.

They were soon inside, taking a brief late-evening meal with the entire Stafford family. The boys recounted their day hunting in traditional exaggerated fashion, and the girls played the part of remarkable audience, making appropriately appreciative noises.

"I caught a fish that weighed three stone if it weighed a pound!" Nick bragged, looking to Kit for approval.

"Indeed." Kit nodded in assent, supportively. "But mine was the real coup — I took down a rabbit with feet as large as my own!"

"Mmmm," Will agreed, taking a drink of wine. "Neither compares with the quail I bested . . . it was the size of a golden eagle! Wasn't it, Blackmoor?"

Blackmoor smiled broadly, leaning back and looking from one brother to the next. "I'm not certain I want to be involved in this particular conversation," he said with a laugh.

"Oh?" Alex asked with a twinkle in her eye, knowing exactly why he wouldn't participate. "Could that be because this generation of Staffords has been having this very conversation for years, since they were old enough to go hunting?"

Blackmoor smiled at her and replied, "It could be . . ."

"And perhaps because, for years, it is only after the Stafford boys have relayed their incredible feats of manhood that their father ruins their fun by telling the truth — that none of the three of them could catch a fish, a rabbit, or a bird if his very life depended on it?" the duke noted, drawing a laugh from everyone around the table.

"Alas, it seems the wildlife of this particular estate have nothing to fear from their masters," Vivi said.

"It's a good thing you're all fairly intelligent," Ella remarked.

"And don't forget attractive," added Nick, good-humoredly.

"Oh, of course!" Alex replied sarcastically. "How could we forget?"

The duchess stood on a laugh and spoke to the table. "I am afraid, my dears, that I must take to my chamber. It has been a long day, and tomorrow shall be another. May I suggest you all retire early?"

And, with that, the meal was ended, the duke and duchess taking their leave, followed closely by Vivi and Ella, who were looking more tired by the minute and were eager to find their beds. Alex silently willed her brothers to retire and give Blackmoor and her a moment alone together so she could say all the things she had decided to say during the carriage ride, but they appeared unmoved by her thoughts and did not accommodate her request. Realizing she would not have a private conversation with Blackmoor on this particular evening, she stood and announced her own intentions to find her bed. Leaving the room, she lit a candle in the hallway beyond and climbed the wide center stairway of the manor to the upper chambers.

She made it all the way to her bedchamber and had one hand on the door handle before she realized that Blackmoor had followed her abovestairs. She knew before she looked back that she would find him silhouetted in the light, and when she did, her heart began to pound.

"What are you doing up here?"

"Retiring to my chamber."

"Why aren't you doing that at your own home?" The question came out more harshly than she'd intended.

"Are you disappointed? I shan't bother you, Alex."

"No! No. I just thought . . . since . . . you live next door . . ." She stopped, feeling rather idiotic, then pressed on, "I . . . I don't care where you sleep."

"Excellent. Then if it's all the same to you, I think I shall stay here."

"It's fine with me."

"Good."

She turned back to her door and pushed it open as he moved down the hall. She started to step forward into the room; she meant to go in and close the door behind her. Instead, she turned just as he was moving past. "Wait."

He stopped just inches from her, so close that she had to step into the doorway to keep from burning him with her candle. His voice was no louder than a whisper when he spoke, "Yes?"

"I . . ." she paused again, mute with the flood of words that had rushed to her tongue. What should she say? Where should she start? Was this the place to take her risk? Did she really care? "I have something I want to say."

"I sensed that," he teased.

"Perhaps I'll just retire instead."

"I'd rather you didn't." He raised an eyebrow. "I apologize, Alex. Please. Go on."

"This just doesn't seem the . . . proper place."

"It seems proper enough to me."

"It's a darkened hallway. In the middle of the night."

"Do you have a better locale in mind?"

She looked from one side of the hallway to the other quickly, then reached out and grabbed his arm and pulled him quickly into her bedchamber, closing the door behind them. They both paused for a moment, equally shocked by her rash behavior.

He spoke first, saying slowly, "Well, I'm fairly certain *this* isn't the proper place."

She blushed. "It's well lit. That makes it more proper than the hallway." She hoped that sounding like she knew the rules would cover up the fact that he was absolutely right.

"And the fact that it's your bedchamber?"

"Irrelevant."

"Really." The word came out in a slow drawl. "Why do I have a feeling that if any one of your family members wandered in, they might feel differently?"

She held up her hand, effectively stopping him from saying anything more. "Either way. You're here now."

"So I am."

"I'll try to be quick."

"No need. I wouldn't like to be caught leaving this particular room. Suffice to say, I'm here for an hour or so, until your brothers have almost certainly retired themselves." He moved farther into the room and sat on a pink ruffled stool. Alex couldn't help but chuckle at the picture he made. Looking down at his seat, he joined her in laughter, saying, "Not exactly the portrait of lordliness?"

She covered her smile and shook her head. "Not exactly."

He leaned back and looked at her frankly. "I miss you, Alex."

Her breath caught at his words. "*I* was supposed to say something to *you*."

"You waited too long. I decided to speak first."

Alex sat tentatively on the edge of the bed, facing him. "All right, then. You go first."

"Happily." He paused briefly, and then plunged forward. "I miss you. Everything about you. Since that night at your house, at your mother's dinner, I've mucked up everything. I've lost a handle on how to be near you . . . how to speak with you."

"You appear to be doing quite well presently," Alex pointed out, teasingly.

He smiled. "Minx. I owe you a tremendous apology. In attempting to better understand everything that has happened in the last few months, I somehow lost my way with you. What can I do to find it again?"

Her heart began to pound as she detected the earnestness in his tone. She didn't know what to say. Earlier in the evening, she had wanted to force him to hear her thoughts on Lucian, but now she couldn't bring herself to draw his uncle into the conversation. She didn't want to risk his closing himself to her again.

She worried her lower lip, wondering if she shouldn't just forgo the topic with him. But what of her resolution in the carriage? What of her commitment to being honest and open with him to test the mettle of what they may or may not have together? She had sworn to herself that she'd speak to him about everything. Vowed that she would make him understand.

She didn't have to. He spoke before she could find her voice. "The things you were trying to tell me about my uncle . . . I should have listened."

Her eyes flew to his in disbelief. "Really?"

"I did not treat you fairly. I would have listened to your brothers if they had come to me with such a story." He smiled, continuing, "Perhaps not believed them, but listened nonetheless."

He rested his forearms on his thighs and leaned toward her. "I would like to make it up to you now. If you'd still like to discuss it."

She took a deep breath, looking into his clear grey eyes, and realized that choice had been removed from the situation. She was going to have to take the risk she'd promised herself she'd take.

"I would still like to discuss it," she said quietly.

"I am listening."

And so she told him everything, trying to be calm and relay facts rather than suspicions. She again recounted the conversation she overheard, again relayed what she had witnessed in the corridor beyond the orangery and in the garden outside his study, and then, steeling herself for his anger, told him about the trickery with Bingham, their reconnaissance of the Blackmoor House study when they knew he'd be away, her encounter with Lucian, and, finally, the note they'd found from the late earl.

He had remained silent, though his spine had grown straighter as she recounted her tale. When she was finished, he had only one question. "Do you have the note with you?"

She did, of course, and rose from the bed to find it in her trunk, which had arrived with them that evening, still tucked inside *A History of Essex*. She handed the book and note over together, not knowing what more to say.

Opening the parchment, his face was stony as he read the words of his father — words that seemed as though they'd come from beyond the grave. Alex winced, knowing what pain they must be causing him. He held still for a long moment, then looked up at her with a question in his eyes. "What name is at stake?"

"We could only believe that he was referencing the Sewell name. The Blackmoor line," she said carefully, uncertain of his thoughts.

He nodded, looking back at the letter. "And the book? *A History of Essex?* Every household in the county must own a copy."

"We don't know. There must be something particular to this copy. Do you remember your father ever speaking of it?"

He shook his head, turning the book over in his hands and studying it. After a few moments, he raised his eyes to hers. "Alex, I should have thought twice when you told me about the conversation you witnessed. I should have asked more questions, listened more carefully." Gavin's voice wavered, as he fought his emotions.

"Gavin —" She stopped, unsure of what she could say to help.

He stood and walked toward her, taking the spot next to her on the bed. He took her hand in a simple, beautiful act. She stayed quiet, waiting for him to speak.

Long minutes later, he did. "I believed in him. Believed that, despite his oddities, his coldness, he was first my uncle. My father's brother. My family. I suppose I wanted to believe in him because he brought me that much closer to the father that I no longer had. I searched for something about him that would remind me of my father. I was desperate to find that similarity. I haven't been able to. And now . . . I find that not only is he nothing like my father . . . he's the reason I lost my father."

The sadness and shock in his voice devastated Alex, and she wrapped her arms around him. He remained still, not responding to her attempt to comfort him for the first few seconds until, consumed by emotion, he caught her in an intense embrace, burying his face in her neck. They stayed that way, wrapped tightly together, sharing their strength in the silence.

And then, after what seemed like an eternity, he pulled back, loosening but not releasing his hold. Brushing a stray lock of hair from her face, he asked, "What should I do?"

She smiled softly, placing her hand on his roughened cheek. "You mean what should *we* do."

He shook his head. "No, Alex. It is too dangerous for you. He's already threatened you."

"Nonsense. I'm the one who discovered everything. We can do this together! We can discover his deeds and make sure he is punished for them, together! I've already been thinking about what we might be looking for at Sewell Hall."

He shook his head. "Absolutely not. You are forbidden from going within a quarter of a mile of Sewell Hall. Whatever I do, I shall do it alone. I won't risk anyone else I love."

Her voice shook with indignation. "And what am I to do? Simply watch someone *I* love sally off to save the day without helping you succeed? The concept is as ridiculous as it is impossible. I should like to see you attempt to forbid me from helping you. I am no delicate flower, Gavin."

He offered a half smile at her reference to her governess's lesson. "You are certainly no delicate flower right now, Alex. That much is true. We will discuss this in the morning, when we are both calmer," he said, ignoring her eyebrow raised in ire, and continuing, "Do you not think we should take this time to consider the minor fact that we seem to be in love?"

Her eyes widened slightly at the words and she played the last moments of their conversation over in her head. *We are in love.* He met her gaze, not letting her look away as he spoke. "You appear to have missed my meaning. Allow me to repeat myself more plainly. I love you, Alex."

She looked at him, shocked by his words, which chased all thoughts of their disagreement from her mind. She had been so wrapped up in making sure that he would include her in his plans that she had glossed over the meaning in his words. She opened her mouth, then closed it, scared to speak for fear of ruining this perfect moment.

He leaned forward and placed his forehead against hers, smiling as he spoke in low, liquid tones. "I adore you. I adore your laugh and your wit and your intelligence and your confidence. I cannot think of another woman I would rather have by my side than you. You are as brilliant as you are beautiful and I probably should have realized it years ago, but I seem to be rather dull-witted."

She shook her head, "I think that, at this particular moment, you are rather a genius."

"Oh, you do?" he said teasingly. "And what else are you thinking?"

She smiled softly at his obvious attempt to entice her into revealing her feelings. "I'm thinking you have the most beautiful eyes in the world. And that your shoulders have grown exponentially broader since last year. And that your smile is the only thing able to make me forget myself and do things that are thoroughly inexcusable.

"Mostly, however, I'm thinking that you've been my savior for years . . . since before I can remember . . . my friend for the same length of time. And I honestly believe that there is nothing that could have stopped me from falling in love with you. It was only a matter of time."

"Say the words," he prodded.

"I love you, Gavin. I love the boy you were and the man you have become." She had never been so certain of anything in her life.

"Capital," he pronounced, and kissed her roundly, threading his fingers through her hair, scattering her hairpins and setting her heart racing.

After several moments, she stopped the kiss, meeting his gaze directly for several seconds before saying firmly, "Gavin. Promise me you won't do anything rash about your uncle. Promise me you won't do anything by yourself. Promise me you'll ask for help."

"I promise. If you promise not to get yourself any more involved in this than you already are, Alex. I will tie you up in a linen closet if I think I must to keep you safe."

"All right."

"Say the words."

"I promise."

They sat together long into the night, basking in the glow of their newly professed love, talking until the light of day began to creep over the horizon in deep purple streaks and Alex was unable to keep her eyes open. Placing one final kiss on her forehead, Blackmoor snuck into the hallway and, unseen, found his own chamber.

twenty-two

He watched the Essex countryside roll past beyond the carriage window. He had been traveling all night — seething with anger.

He had lost everything. All because of that brat. His French partners had broken contact with him. Stopped using his services. It was only a matter of time before they came for him; he knew too much — their identities, their plans, their location.

The girls had to be dealt with. He would not be bested by a gaggle of irritating children.

He knew, without question, that they had been searching the study of Blackmoor House. They had been looking for the same thing he had been looking for — information that could lead to his capture and the capture of his contacts. Information that would see them all hanged.

While he was certain the girls hadn't found anything — after all, if he had failed to find the evidence designed to incriminate him, he was sure that three silly girls playing at investigators could do no better — but now he was concerned about Blackmoor's suspicions being raised.

He was growing more desperate. Everything he had worked for was lost. He could not risk losing his life as well. The ridiculous young earl was proving to be no sort of threat; he was just as much of a lapdog as his father had been. But those girls . . . they had to be silenced. Starting with that meddling Worthington chit, who seemed fearless. If anything happened to her, it would devastate the earl.

He smiled darkly, willing the horses forward.

Alex woke, stretching luxuriously, keenly aware of the sun high in the sky, marking the lateness of the hour. Outside her chamber, she could hear two maids chattering as they moved down the hallway, clearing away any stray dust that might take away from the imposing stature of the manor. One laughed, the sound tinkling through the door, and Alex felt a jolt of happiness at the sound.

Of course, it would have been difficult to dampen her mood on this particular morning, after such a wonderful night shared with Blackmoor. *Her* Blackmoor. She smiled to herself as a wave of eagerness coursed through her. She wondered if she'd missed the chance to see him at breakfast, if he was still in the house, if she could catch him before he left on whatever excursion her brothers had likely cooked up to avoid the arrival of her parents' guests. She threw back the covers and bounded from the bed, pulling the bell for Eliza.

She was deep in her wardrobe, poring through clothes, when the knock sounded on her door. She called out, "Enter!" expecting Eliza. Instead, Ella and Vivi entered, then stopped short just inside the room, surprised by the scene they had disturbed.

Vivi spoke first, unable to keep the curiosity from her tone. "Begging your pardon, whatever are you doing?"

Alex stepped back, exclaiming, "Oh! Thank goodness! I don't have any idea what to wear! You have to help me. What should I wear to make me look" — she waved her hand in the air as she searched for the word — "beautiful? The green walking dress? The lavender day dress? Something else? Help!"

"Whatever for? When have you ever been concerned with fashion?" Ella asked, unable to keep the confusion from her tone.

Vivi understood immediately. "Ella, you really can be dense at times." She walked toward Alex, pushing her way into the wardrobe beside her. "Looking to impress Blackmoor, are we?"

Alex blushed prettily, peeking around a cream-colored evening gown. "Yes. How did you know?"

"You've hardly been the model of discretion," Vivi pointed out.

Alex held up a turquoise-colored riding habit for Vivi and Ella to consider. "Am I that obvious?"

"Only to those who know you best," Ella said, wrinkling her nose and shaking her head at the dress and pointing, instead, to the buttercup-colored Empire walking dress that Vivi was holding. "That one."

Within minutes, Alex was dressed and the three girls had made their way to the terrace of the manor, where they joined the duchess and Will, who were seated under a large linen canopy, out of the sun. As soon as they dropped into the chairs set out for them, Alex announced, "I'm famished!"

The duchess reached for a nearby teapot and poured her daughter a cup of tea while continuing to list the tasks she needed to complete prior to the arrival of several early guests that afternoon. "I'm still not entirely sure how to arrange all the rooms — I thought I had it all complete, then realized that I placed Lady Twizzleton and Lord Vauxwell in adjoining rooms. That won't do." She placed two biscuits on the saucer and passed the makeshift breakfast to her youngest child.

"Why can't you just move one of them to an unused room?" Will queried.

"My dear boy, there *aren't* any unused rooms."

"Mother!" Alex exclaimed around a mouth filled with biscuit. "Whatever do you mean, there aren't any rooms? There are twenty-three bedchambers in this house."

"Twenty-four, actually. It seems the party has grown in size."

"It certainly has! How many young, eligible men did you invite?" Alex's exasperation showed.

"Not as many as I would have liked," the duchess replied. Will snickered, only to stop immediately when she explained, "I had to invite eligible young ladies as well . . . and their parents, of course."

Alex smiled sweetly at her brother. "Of course. Ah, sweet justice. You have to deal with girls *and* mothers."

Will scowled. "At least I'm not the only eligible male in attendance."

"To that end, where are Nick and Kit and Blackmoor?" Alex queried, attempting to sound casual.

"Christopher and Nicholas are still abed," the duchess replied, shaking her head. "I'm sending their valets to wake them in a quarter of an hour if they fail to emerge on their own. As for Blackmoor, he was up very early to go back to Sewell Hall and check on some estate affairs. I expect him back before this evening's dinner."

"Indeed," Will agreed, "Blackmoor *swore* he'd not leave me to face the wolves alone."

Alex sipped her tea to cover her disappointment that she wouldn't see Blackmoor until the evening. She had been hoping to spend some part of the day with him — she would have settled for seeing him at a distance. She sighed quietly into her teacup, wondering if he would come back sooner rather than later to see her.

Her brother gave her a wry look. "I feel exactly the same way," he said sympathetically, clearly thinking that she was accepting her fate as the unmarried daughter of an inveterate matchmaker.

Alex understood his meaning and smiled to herself, amused by his misinterpretation. "Somehow, I doubt that."

"Well, both of you will have to endeavor to overcome your disappointment," the duchess said distractedly, looking down at the list in her hand. "Eleanor, Vivian, do you girls mind my moving you to the adjoining rooms? That way, I can put Lord Vauxwell between Gavin's uncle and Lord and Lady Waring, and Lady Twizzleton next to the Stanhopes."

Alex's head snapped up at her mother's words. She met Ella's gaze to confirm that she'd heard correctly. Ella nodded mutely.

"Mother, did you say Lucian Sewell will be here?"

"Indeed, I did. I know he's an odd man, but I couldn't very well invite Blackmoor and leave him off the list. Especially since he's been such a help since the earl's death."

Vivi coughed to cover her innate response to the duchess's words. Alex, a chill running down her spine, spoke, choosing her words carefully. "Of course. I was merely surprised. When do you expect him to arrive?"

"My understanding is that they are on their way presently and should be here not long before dinner."

"They?" Ella blurted out.

"He and Baron Montgrave. They seem to be very close. I thought it might make Lucian more comfortable."

"I'm sure you did," Alex replied, her voice strained.

"Girls?" Her mother spoke, looking from Vivi to Ella. "You don't mind having adjoining rooms, do you?"

Ella shook her head as Vivi answered, "Not at all, Your Grace. We would be happy to share."

"Excellent. I'm off to make those changes, then." The duchess stood, then turned back to her children. "Do not go far, you two. And do not let your brothers disappear, should you see them. I may well require your combined assistance. In fact, William —" He groaned, knowing that he was about to be assigned a task. "Why don't you go and wake them?"

"I shall go as soon as I have finished reading this article." He nodded toward the paper he'd been trying to read. Seeming to accept that compromise, the duchess turned on her heel and exited the terrace into the house.

Alex watched her go, then turned to Will, buried in his newspaper. Cautiously, she asked, "Will, how do you feel about Blackmoor's uncle?"

"Strange fellow, but harmless," he said, distracted. "I suppose I understand why Mother invited him, but I find it very odd that he would attend. As helpful as the uncle has been, Blackmoor is thoroughly able to see to his duties himself by now. I think it's time for him to return to his prior life."

"Indeed," Ella said, meeting Alex's eye.

With a shake of the newsprint, Will closed the paper, folded it to its original position, and placed it on the table in front of him. Raising himself up to his full, looming height, he offered a short bow to the girls and spoke, taking two more biscuits from the tray. "I suppose I ought to raise the miscreants. Be warned . . . when we return, they shall devour everything in sight." Garnering a smile from the three friends, he entered the house to find his brothers.

Alex snatched another biscuit off the tea tray herself, nodding her agreement with Will's prediction. She needed to eat her fill before Nick and Kit arrived, or she'd have no chance of leaving this particular meal full.

Once Will was out of earshot, she spoke quietly to her friends. "Lucian Sewell and the Baron Montgrave are on their way here? I would guarantee they aren't coming because of my mother's reputation as a hostess."

"Likely not," Vivi said. "I think that when Blackmoor returns from the hall, we should sit our fathers down and discuss our next steps."

"Agreed."

Ella nodded, then pulled a familiar volume from her reticule, saying, "Well, I can cross one next step off of our list. I spent much of last evening reading *A History of Essex*. And guess what I discovered."

"What?" Alex leaned forward, hoping for a major revelation.

"Absolutely nothing. Aside from the fact that Essex has a thoroughly uninteresting history." She placed the book on the table between them.

Alex lifted the book and ran her fingers over the embossed letters on its cover. "I gave the earl's copy back to Blackmoor. Where did this copy come from?"

"Your father's library. It's incredible to me that there isn't a house in the county that doesn't have a copy of this exhaustively boring book. Even more so that the earl would have used it for his last missive."

"Perhaps it had something to do with his love of the land," Vivi suggested.

Ella shook her head. "Perhaps, but it simply seems too random. There has to be a reason he chose this book."

The two girls continued their hypothesizing as Alex turned the book over and over in her hands, reviewing the last few days in her mind, trying to remember everything she could about the book and where they had found it. Ella was right. This was not random. Yes, it had been luck that they had found it . . . but it was no accident that caused the earl to choose that book to carry his final words. What was special about a book that could be found everywhere?

Ella's voice echoed in her mind, *There isn't a house in the county that doesn't have a copy.* As the words turned over in her brain, she remembered Gavin saying the same thing — *Every household in the county must own a copy.*

"That's it!" Alex exclaimed, her voice filled with astonishment. She looked up at her friends, both of whom were wide-eyed. "The earl didn't choose the book because it was so close to his heart. He chose it because every house has a copy! It's not the volume in London that has the information. There must be a second copy at Sewell Hall!"

The words came in a flood of anxiety. The book held the information that would damn Montgrave and Lucian Sewell and save Blackmoor. She had to get to it — and to Blackmoor — before anyone else did. With the men set to arrive that evening, before dinner, she had only a few hours to do so. She stood from the table, so quickly that she toppled her teacup, leaving Vivi to right it for her. "I have to find Blackmoor. Now."

Ella stood. "We will help you."

Alex shook her head. "No. This, I have to do alone. I don't know what will be in that book but, whatever it is, it is bound to upset him. He has to face that without an audience." She clasped Ella's hands, looking from her to Vivi. "Help me by keeping my mother off the scent? Again?"

"Because we were so excellent at doing so the last time," Ella pointed out wryly.

Alex smiled quickly, already moving toward the steps that led down into the gardens. "Thank you! I shall be back soon — with Blackmoor in tow."

They watched her go, rushing through the garden and down the long, sandy path, which led through a field of bright yellow cowslips that separated the Stafford and Sewell lands. "She'll be ruined if she's not careful," Ella said.

"Nonsense. He'd wed her in a heartbeat if he thought she'd have him," Vivi replied.

"Quite."

A half an hour later, Will, who had been waylaid on his walk back from waking his brothers, rejoined them. He picked up his newspaper and bowed low to the girls, saying, "I'm afraid I must take my official leave. It seems a carriage has broken an axle on the main road and it falls to me to play rescuer."

"We shall miss your company, my lord," Vivi offered with a smile.

"And I yours," he returned. "My brothers will be down shortly, however, to entertain you until they are required to entertain the early guests."

"Are there guests here already?" Ella asked, curious.

"Indeed. The Baron Montgrave has arrived, but he has plans to visit Sewell Hall this afternoon, he says."

Vivi's sharp intake of breath was followed by Ella's quick response, "Why the hall?"

Will, who was pulling on his calfskin gloves and clearly distracted by the task he was about to undertake, shook his head and shrugged his shoulders. "I do not know. I imagine because Sewell has arrived early as well."

Both girls shot up from their seats at his words, the concern in their expressions shocking Will from his preoccupation. He asked sharply, "What is it?"

"I think we had better speak to your father," Vivi said, fear in her voice.

twenty-three

Alex pushed open the door to Sewell Hall and rushed inside, breathing heavily and wishing she hadn't worn her corset stays quite so tight this morning.

"Vanity be damned," she huffed to herself. "Loveliness will do me no good with Blackmoor if I drop dead from lack of air before he sees me." She had been so eager to get to the hall, to find the book and Blackmoor, that she had run the entire way — something she hadn't done since she had spent her childhood rushing about the heath, traipsing after the boys she so revered.

The hall was quiet and dark. Blackmoor had clearly not alerted his staff that he was coming this morning, so they were nowhere to be seen. She preferred the house this way, for it would give her a chance to find the book and find him without having to explain her visit or to risk being caught by anyone.

She had thought to find Blackmoor immediately but altered her plan once she arrived at the house, heading instead for the library to find the book. Somewhere in the dark recesses of her mind, she was reluctant to leave the volume unfound any longer than absolutely necessary. She paused just inside the front door, listening for any movement or conversation. Hearing nothing, she moved quietly across the central foyer of the hall, entered the library, and began her search.

The Sewell Hall library was designed for readers. Warm and cozy despite its high ceilings, the bookshelves inside the enormous room were filled to the brim with enough leather-bound volumes to make the space feel intimate. For generations, the Earls of Blackmoor had prided themselves on their literary appreciation. Alex could vividly remember Gavin's father holding her on his lap when she was knee-high and telling her tales from Shakespeare and Homer and Greek and Roman mythology.

Even now, years later, there were moments when she could hear the rich tenor of his voice alluding to Cupid and Psyche when she became too curious, or to *Much Ado About Nothing*'s Beatrice when she was becoming obviously headstrong. She breathed deeply, the memories flooding her as she inhaled the scent of the well-loved and well-cared-for inhabitants of this room — the aroma of oiled and leather-bound books.

Ordinarily, she would have spent her first few minutes in the room wandering aimlessly through the maze of shelves, marveling at the way the high windows were constructed to let just enough sunlight in for dust to dance in the rays without the light harming the books. But today, she had no time to dally.

The earl had always been thoroughly organized in regard to his library — the books were sorted by genre, then by title.

All Alex had to do was find the collection of books on the county history and she would discover that for which she was searching. She began poring over the shelves, pausing only long enough to identify the topic covered by the collection of books she was looking at — science, medicine, poetry, the classics of Shakespeare and Chaucer — she found the history collection quickly, running her fingers over the spines of books on the Far East, the Americas, the European continent, and, finally, British history with a whole collection of titles on the various counties in Britain. She crouched down to see them all clearly — identifying several volumes on Essex, but not the one she was looking for. She was certain her theory was right and the earl had a second copy of the book. Blowing back a lock of hair from her face, she spoke aloud to the empty room, "Where is the blasted thing?"

Perhaps he'd hidden it? Or, worse, perhaps he hadn't had the time to leave his final message. Perhaps he was killed before he could complete the task.

"No." Alex shook her head in frustration and sat on the floor, pulling books off the shelf one by one, opening them and running her hands across the endpapers, checking to see if he'd left his next missive in a different title. The stack of books on the floor by her side grew as she searched through the collection. When she had emptied the shelf on Essex, she sighed down at the pile she had made, wondering where else she could search. She looked back at the shelf in disappointment and there, hidden behind the other books, was a small volume bound in rich green leather. She knew the title before she looked closely at the book . . . *A History of Essex.*

Her heart pounding, Alex opened the cover, knowing with absolute certainty that she was about to find what she had been looking for. Looking down at the volume, she gasped. The book had been hollowed out and a stack of papers were tucked inside. She pulled them from their hiding place and was about to read them, when she realized that they were not her secrets to uncover. They were secrets that belonged to the Sewell line — to the Earls of Blackmoor. She had to find Gavin.

She burst from the room at a dead run, crossing the wide hallway, so intent on her mission that she didn't pause before throwing open the study door and rushing into the room. Gavin was sitting behind his desk, and she saw the surprise in his eyes at her entrance. She stopped just inside the door before exclaiming, "I found it! I found the information your father hid!"

It was only after she spoke the words that she noticed the harsh lines of his face, the clear tension in his mouth, and the anger in his eyes that had, for a fleeting moment, been replaced by shock at her presence. He was no longer looking at her. His gaze was fixed on a point behind her. She heard the door to the study close ominously and knew before looking that there was someone else in the room with them.

"Excellent, my dear girl. You are more intelligent than you appear, it seems."

Alex spun around at the words, her spine straightening when she took in the entire scene. There, standing just to the side of the now closed door, was Lucian Sewell. He was holding a pistol. And it was pointed directly at her.

Reaching one hand out to her, he continued, "Why don't you be a good girl and give the book to me, Alexandra? There's no need to make this any more difficult than it needs to be."

Alex looked back toward Blackmoor, but he did not take his eyes from his uncle, who spoke again, his tone vicious. "Don't be a fool, Alexandra. The rules of this game are very simple. You give me the book or I kill you."

This odious person had betrayed her country, murdered a man she adored, and was now threatening to kill her. She wasn't going to do anything he asked of her. Not without a fight. She didn't know where the defiance came from, but there it was, vivid and intense. "No."

"Alex." This time, it was Gavin who spoke. His tone brooked no discussion. "Give him the book."

"No. I won't." She held the volume tighter to her chest, glancing back at Gavin, who still wasn't looking at her. Turning back to Lucian, she met his eyes without fear. "You won't kill me. You'd have my father and every man in the county looking to see you hanged."

"You forget, child, that I am very good at making planned deaths appear accidental." Sewell smiled, evil in his eyes. "How sad it would be if the two of you took yourselves off to the cliffs for a private moment only to tumble, tragically, into the sea."

"I imagine you believe that if a plan worked once, it will work again?" Blackmoor asked.

Sewell's smile turned into a vicious sneer as he replied, "It worked perfectly the first time; need I remind you that we wouldn't be in this particular situation if you hadn't been so reluctant to accept the circumstances of your father's death."

"So you admit it. You killed my father. Your own brother."

"Those events were not in the original plan. Your father would still be here — very much alive — if he'd stayed out of my affairs. I never bothered him about the business of the estate . . . I fail to understand why he would think it acceptable to interfere in my life."

"Perhaps because you were using his land to break the law?" Alex said smartly.

"Ah, so you have looked at the information my brother left in the book. Something will have to be done about that."

"Actually, I haven't read anything in the volume. It's just a rather obvious scheme you've concocted. You can do what you want to me, but someone else will discover that you are selling secrets to the French. You cannot kill everyone."

"Once I destroy that book, I will have no need of killing anyone else. And to be clear, I *was* selling information to the French. Now I'm selling it to anyone who wants to buy. With no money and no land on which to make money, I have little opportunity to be discerning." He turned back to Alex and said, “Now give me the book, girl. I have no more patience for this conversation.”

“I will not.”

“And I will not ask again!” Lucian’s voice rose, filled with anger. Alex flinched in response as he lifted the pistol and began to pull the hammer back.

“No!” Gavin exclaimed, his voice heavy with emotion. “Give him the book, Alex. Please.”

At the sound of his voice, Alex turned back to him, witnessing the pain in his eyes for the first time. “Why, Gavin? This book holds all the information we need to link him to your father’s death. Why would I give it to him? Would you see him go free?”

He didn’t respond, but Lucian did, laughing darkly. “How very sweet. My dear,” he said, speaking to Alex, “I imagine he’s willing to give up the information because he fancies himself in love with you. Don’t you see? Your life simply isn’t worth the pleasure of avenging his father’s death. It’s touching, really.”

Alex looked back at Gavin, who was deliberately not meeting her gaze.

“Let’s see if the opposite is also true,” Lucian said, and before she knew it, he was pointing his pistol at Gavin and cocking the handle.

“No!” she cried, unable to stop herself from reaching out a protesting hand toward him.

"Ah, young love," he said with disgust in his voice. "So very predictable." He looked back to Alex. "I'm no longer playing games. Give me the book."

Alex stepped forward, tentatively, the book in her hands. She held the book out to him and he reached for it.

"Alex! No!" She turned her head, seeing Gavin jump up from his desk just as Sewell reached past the book and, before she could do anything, took hold of her wrist in a viselike grip, pulling her to him.

"Let go of her." The words came in a low growl from across the room just as she felt the cool iron barrel of the pistol press against the side of her neck.

Blackmoor moved toward them, stopping only when Sewell warned, "Don't do anything you'll regret, Nephew. You wouldn't want me to do something rash."

Gavin's fury was clear. "I have given you the benefit of the doubt throughout this ordeal, Uncle. But allow me to make myself plain . . . if you harm her in any way, you will wish it were you who had tumbled into the sea the day you killed my father."

"What big words for such a young pup," Sewell said viciously, gripping Alex more firmly, causing her to wince and Gavin to tense visibly. "I think I shall enjoy abducting your little friend. It's time an Earl of Blackmoor learns he cannot have everything he wants."

"So that is why you killed my father? Jealousy?"

"Your father had everything!" The high pitch of Lucian's voice sent a jolt through Alex, who paled at the sound and the lack of control it betrayed. "Money, land, title, the most beautiful woman in London. He was the perfect earl, and he couldn't stand having such an imperfect brother. He constantly sought out my flaws. Right up until the day he died." He pushed on, and Alex sensed that he was losing his temper. "For our entire lives, it was always Richard who was strongest, smartest, most revered, who was the heir to the great Blackmoor earldom.

"And now it's you . . ." he said to Gavin, with venom. "*You* who inherited the estate, the title . . . everything! *You,* the little brat who received all the love and acceptance that should have been mine!" Lucian's voice was becoming more and more hysterical as he spoke, making Alex wince every time he hit a shrill pitch. "And what of me? Nothing! I was given no title, not even a minor one. I was bequeathed no lands. Instead, when I came of age, it was suggested I join the Navy and go to war to make my fortune. I have no family, except my fellow soldiers from the battlefield. We went to war, where we received no recognition and a pittance of a salary . . . and then I came home to discover that my brother had been working at the War Office and turning himself into a legend!"

Alex could feel him coming unhinged; she was keenly aware of his anger and frustration as he continued, "You're no more than a child and now *you* are the earl? I fought for my country. Saved it! And I received nothing in return. So now I'm taking from you what you value most, because you deserve no more pleasure than your father did. *I'm* the one who deserves happiness. I'm the one who earned it."

"Earned it?" Gavin asked incredulously, unwittingly pushing his uncle to the breaking point. "How, exactly, did you *earn* it? By killing your brother? Your flesh and blood?"

"You insolent pup. You don't understand!" Alex felt him remove the pistol from her neck and saw him begin to point it at Gavin. In his anger, he had loosened his grip on her and she had enough space to move, but only to make a single attempt at saving them both.

Without pausing to consider the possibility of failure, Alex lifted her foot and slammed it down on her captor's instep with every ounce of her strength, spinning away from him as he doubled over in pain. She heard the report of the pistol and time stopped as she looked to Gavin, who was rushing forward with a roar, his face the portrait of anger.

He tackled his already off-balance uncle, bringing him to the floor and sending the pistol spinning across the room before landing two quick blows to his face. Alex turned to find something heavy that she could use to subdue Sewell but was interrupted by the door bursting open as the Duke of Worthington and Will rushed in, the Baron Montgrave quick on their heels, holding a pistol.

Taking in the scene before them, Will and the duke rushed to pull Gavin off his uncle and to restrain the older man, who squealed in protest.

"Montgrave has a pistol!" Alex announced to the room at large, alarmed.

"And thank goodness he does. We might have needed it," Gavin said as he approached her, concern in his eyes. "He's on our side, Alex." Taking her into his arms and running his hands over her extremities to find any wounds she might have incurred, he spoke softly to her, "Are you well? Did the bullet hit you? Did he hurt you?"

"I'm fine," she said, pulling away from him, embarrassed that he would be touching her so intimately in front of the room full of men. "Our side? He is?"

"Yes, my lady," the baron spoke up, from where he was tying Sewell's wrists behind his back. "You see, I have been working with the War Office to root out a network of French spies operating out of Essex, which we came to believe was related to the earl's death. I also knew Sewell from the war. Even then, he vilified his brother and talked of ruining the Blackmoor name. I never thought he would have the courage to do it, but when I heard from you that he was here, I had a feeling he was involved. Of course, I had no idea that the two situations were related until Lady Vivian told me everything this afternoon."

"But Ella saw you in the gardens at the Salisbury Ball! Discussing the robbery at Blackmoor House! *Before* it happened!"

"Did she? I *am* impressed, my lady. My informant and I had no knowledge of our being followed."

"If there is one thing women excel at, Baron, it is eavesdropping. Would you care to explain how you were able to discuss the future?" She still didn't trust this Frenchman.

"In fact, we were discussing the robbery as it was *in progress*, Lady Alexandra. I left the ball immediately and headed straight for Blackmoor House. Of course, you and Lord Blackmoor were close behind me, so it was he who entered the house, ending Sewell's search before I was able to do it myself."

Alex turned to Gavin. "But you didn't believe me when I told you about your uncle!"

"No, I didn't." Gavin appeared just as surprised as she was. "And I didn't know any of this either. Although I'm rather unclear about why I wasn't apprised of my uncle's wrongdoings."

"We didn't want to upset you unnecessarily," the duke interjected. "We didn't have any proof of Sewell's involvement in either of these crimes."

"Until now," Gavin said, retrieving his father's book from where it lay at their feet. "Alex has uncovered everything," he said with pride in his voice, handing the volume to the duke and congratulating Alex with, "Very well done, by the way."

Alex ignored the flash of pleasure she felt at his praise, and turned her questions on the baron, "But I saw you skulking around Blackmoor House!"

"That I *am* able to answer. You were not supposed to see Montgrave," Gavin interjected as the duke and the baron pulled Sewell to his feet. "You were not supposed to become involved at all. In fact, didn't you promise me that you were going to stay as far away from Sewell Hall as possible this weekend?"

She ignored his attempt to redirect her attention, instead exclaiming, "You *knew*? You knew Montgrave wasn't a threat and let me go on believing he was? You didn't tell me? What else did you know? What else didn't you share? Need I remind you that it was *I* who found your father's messages, *I* who uncovered the connection between the espionage and the murder, *I* who discovered the book here, *I* who saved *your* life just moments ago? Where were Bow Street and the baron during all those times?"

"Alex, calm yourself. We decided it was best you not know."

"Who decided?" Alex said shortly, her ire rising.

"Alexandra," her father interrupted, "contrary to what you believe, there are some situations in which young women should not participate."

"Like this one, for example," Will added, attempting to be helpful. "Vivi and Ella put everything together as far as what was happening here, but we came to rescue you. They stayed at the manor."

"I rescued us!" Alex protested, meeting Gavin's gaze. "Tell them!"

"Indeed. She did. I have a feeling my uncle might well be nursing a broken foot," he told the duke and baron, who seemed to have little concern for the pain their prisoner might be suffering.

"Truly? Well done, Alex," Will said, surprised. "Well, in any event, there's a reason we left Vivi and Ella behind."

"We're here!" Ella surprised everyone with her announcement from the doorway as the two entered, out of breath from their race across the heath.

"And we brought the constable!" This from Vivi, who was followed by the portly county constable, who had to pause to take great, heaving breaths and regain his composure before grabbing hold of Sewell and, with the help of the baron, removing him from the room.

Taking in the scene, Ella wrinkled her nose. "Drat. We missed the excitement!"

"It appears we did," Vivi agreed, disappointment in her tone.

"Ah, well. Next time!" Ella brightened.

Alex smiled as the duke and Will began to scold her friends, causing Gavin to lean down and whisper in her ear, "I am happy to see you smiling again."

She turned to him. "I remain vexed with you, my lord. I cannot believe you did not tell me about Montgrave!"

"Alex, I will not argue with you. You can be angry if you need to be, but I almost lost you today and there are other things I would prefer to do than spar."

"For example?" Alex asked.

"For example." He wrapped his arms around her again, and her heart began to pound as he continued, "I'd prefer to remind myself that you are safe. And that you are mine."

She smiled up at him. "I am yours, my lord. As much as you are mine."

He clasped her to him, holding her tightly until a throat cleared from across the room, and Alex and Gavin remembered that they had an audience.

"Blackmoor," the duke said, his casual tone belying his intent gaze, "perhaps you would like to explain exactly why your arms are wrapped around my daughter?"

twenty-four

Later that evening, Stafford Manor quieted as the guests took to their beds, and Ella, Vivi, and Alex curled up together on a wide, cozy chaise in the manor library where, for the first time that day, they were able to discuss the events of the afternoon. They had returned to the house just in time to change and welcome the first unsuspecting guests to the party and had spent the rest of the day and evening entertaining and pretending not to wish they were somewhere else.

Somewhere else, in this case, was with the duke, Blackmoor, Will, and the Marquess of Langford, who had holed themselves up in the manor study for the rest of the afternoon and much of the evening, poring through the documents that the former earl had secreted away in *A History of Essex*. They were still there now, hours later and, as exhausted as she was, Alex refused to go to sleep without hearing their findings. Ella and Vivi, equally curious, had agreed to keep her company.

Alex yawned broadly, relaxing into the seat. "It's hard to believe that everyone who arrived today was completely unaware of what had gone on all morning!"

Vivi stretched, then assumed a similar position on the couch, leaning her head against Alex's shoulder. "It's true. Your mother covered up the missing men extremely well. I just wish she could have covered up our sneaking in a nap. I thought I was going to fall asleep at the supper table this evening."

Ella lay down, placing her head on Alex's lap and saying, "A nap sounds wonderful! I think I'll take one right now . . . wake me when there is news?"

Alex smiled wearily and placed one hand on Ella's shoulder and the other on Vivi's knee, saying, "If nothing else, today taught me that you are the most wonderful friends a girl could ask for. Thank you for ignoring my instructions not to tell my parents about my heading to the hall. I don't know that we would have succeeded in capturing Gavin's uncle without my father, the baron, and Will."

At that moment, the door to the library opened and Will entered, looking surprised to find the trio. "I assumed you'd all be asleep!"

Alex straightened and said, "What happened? Are you through?"

"For the time being, yes," he replied. "There's much work to be done, but the earl left remarkably detailed logs of all the illegal activities taking place on Sewell land over the months leading up to his death — he thought someone was smuggling weapons to the French, then information as the war quieted. It appears that the earl had suspected the culprit was Lucian, but only very close to the date of his death."

"Why did he not tell anyone?" Vivi asked, "He was so close to our fathers — they were like brothers to him. They could have helped."

"Pride," Will replied. "Desire to protect his family name. Perhaps even a misguided belief that he could protect his brother."

"What about Sewell's partners?" Ella asked.

"There is enough evidence to incriminate several wealthy Englishmen and a few Frenchmen who have clearly been meeting with Sewell to exchange money for information. We received word from the constable that Sewell has already given up the names of a half dozen of his partners in the hope that he will receive a less severe punishment."

"No matter what he admits, he's still a traitor and a murderer," Vivi said, sounding very much like her father's daughter. "It's difficult to be lenient with such crimes."

"Indeed," Will said, relaxing into the large leather chair across from them. "Now, little sister," he said, allowing a teasing tone to enter his voice, "would you care to explain what exactly has happened between you and Blackmoor in the last few weeks?"

Alex leveled him with a frank look. "Not particularly."

"Come now! It's obvious you are . . . enamored of each other."

"Is it?" She attempted to appear bored, to little effect.

Will laughed. "You forget I have known you your entire

life, Scamp. I can tell when there is something of import in that lovely head of yours."

She stayed quiet, willing herself not to rise to her brother's bait.

"You also forget," he said in a deceptively casual tone, "that I spent the day with Blackmoor."

Alex sat up straighter, causing Vivi to lose her headrest. She was unable to hide her eagerness. "Did he say something about me? What was it?"

Will laughed, enjoying the power he held over his little sister. "My, my. Is this the same sister who spent much of her time prior to this season expounding on both the irrelevance of men to her future and her marked lack of interest in marriage and the trappings of romance?"

"I didn't say men were irrelevant to my future. That's ridiculous. Nor did I show a lack of interest in romance." She ignored the three sets of eyebrows that rose in a silent yet eloquent response to her statement. "What happened? Was Father difficult with him?"

"I thought you weren't interested in discussing Blackmoor?"

"Oh, William, I do wish you would be quiet if you have nothing to say," Alex growled in irritation, then sat back and said, "I'm not interested. I was merely being conversational."

All three of her companions snorted with laughter. "You cannot honestly think that he'd actually believe that, can you?" Vivi asked before turning to Will. "Take pity on her, my lord. Have you never wondered what a girl thought of you?"

"Never." He lied baldly, a broad smile on his face, then pressed on. "Well, I shall simply say that our father and he are currently having a serious conversation."

"What?!" She leaned forward, squashing Ella's head on her lap, causing her friend to cry out and sit up. Alex's "I beg your pardon, Ella" was followed immediately with, "William! What are they talking about?"

"I haven't any idea." Will leaned back in his chair and stretched his long legs out in front of him. "It seems to me that it would likely have something to do with your inappropriate display this morning."

Alex stood. "Oh, no! Do you think Father is angry? Do you think Gavin is being lectured? Do you think I should go to him?"

"In order: No, I don't think Father is angry. Yes, I do think Gavin is being lectured — that's what Father does, remember? And no, I definitely do not think you should go anywhere near the study while they are locked in there. I think you should sit down and attempt to relax," Will said, finally sounding more like the brother she loved and less like the one she wanted to murder.

"You might try lowering your voice as well," Vivi suggested. "You'll wake everyone in the house if you keep on like that."

She sat. And lowered her voice. "I'm sorry. I simply . . . well, I seem to be rather overly excited."

"Really?" Ella said sarcastically, leaning back on the couch, one hand over her eyes, exhausted, but still managing to elicit a laugh from the others in the room.

"What is it that is amusing you all?" The voice came from the doorway of the library, drawing the attention of the entire group. Four heads turned toward Blackmoor, who entered with a tired, curious smile on his face.

Alex drank in the sight of him, thoroughly disheveled — somewhere he had lost his waistcoat and his cravat, his blond hair was unruly, falling into his face after hours of his running his fingers through it in concentration, and she could detect the hint of a beard on his face, which he had not shaved since that morning. He had never looked more handsome, more remarkable. She had never wanted to be near him so very much.

His grey gaze fell on her from across the room, and she could feel his inspection as he studied her. She longed for five minutes with a looking glass as she touched her hair nervously, knowing that he was seeing the stray auburn locks that had come loose from her topknot, her tired eyes, her wrinkled dress. Pushing a strand of hair behind her ear, she looked into his eyes and recognized the intensity there. It was the same emotion she'd seen that afternoon, and the night before. Her breath caught. He loved her.

She was shaken from her reverie by Vivi and Ella, who stood up in unison.

"I find myself exhausted," Vivi said, making a show of a wide stretch.

"Indeed. It has been a long day for me as well," replied Ella, who did not have to fabricate the yawn that followed her words.

They looked to each other with a nod, and then to Will, who was still seated comfortably in his chair. "And you, my lord?" Vivi said politely. "Are you not tired after your long day?"

"No. I find myself feeling rather energized."

Ella and Vivi looked at each other, and Vivi tried again, with a slightly firmer tone, "Perhaps you would feel differently if you found your chamber, my lord."

"I don't think so." The corner of Will's mouth twitched, betraying his amusement.

"William, you would try the patience of a saint," Vivi said with a smile. "Must I ask you to escort two young women frightened of the dark upstairs?"

He laughed aloud. "You two? Frightened of something? I find that very difficult to believe."

Ella lost her patience with the entire conversation. "Will, just leave the room. Go wherever you'd like. But give Alex and Blackmoor some peace, please?"

Will winked broadly at her. "Now that's a request to which I cannot help but respond." He stood, waiting for Ella and Vivi to kiss Alex good night, then motioned them to precede him from the room.

When the trio had left, Gavin started across the room to Alex, who felt a sudden wave of nervousness. To cover it up, she said, "We seem to have a connection with libraries in the evening, don't we?"

He paused, cocking his head, contemplating her statement. She loved that about him. He really did think about what she said. Even when it was inane. And about libraries. "Indeed, we do," he replied finally, joining her on the chaise and taking her hands in his.

"It's interesting, really, when you think that the library isn't a room typically used in the evening, what with the difficulty of reading by candlelight and the high ceilings. They simply devour light usually. Not my parents' libraries, of course, as you can see. They can also be rather drafty but, again, not these. These are —"

He kissed her, interrupting her rambling. Within moments, she had forgotten what she was saying.

"Alexandra," he said, pulling away slightly and staring deep into her eyes. "My God, I love you."

She dipped her head, made shy by the comment.

"I don't know what I would have done without you today," he said, his voice rich with emotion. "I don't know how I would have handled my uncle and I can't imagine how any of us would have found the information left by my father, but, most importantly, I don't know how I would have survived the last few hours — poring over that information until I finally understood the reasons behind my father's death — if I hadn't known you were here, waiting for me."

"I'm so sorry, Gavin. About everything. I'm sorry it happened to you."

"I'm not," he said, kissing the tip of her nose lightly.

"You aren't?" she asked, surprised.

"I'm sorry my father was killed. I would do anything to get him back . . . and I imagine I shall feel that way forever. But the rest of the events . . . those I don't regret. You see, they brought me to you."

They embraced for a long moment, breathing each other in, savoring this end to such a harrowing, exhausting day. Minutes later, Blackmoor pulled back from her and asked, "Don't you want to know what your father and I discussed?"

"No. I mean, not unless you want me to know. I understand that you might want to keep that conversation private."

"Really? That's very mature of you." He leaned back on the chaise, closing his eyes, a hint of a smile playing across his lips.

"Thank you." She folded her hands in her lap, not knowing what to say. She couldn't ask. That wasn't very ladylike. They sat in silence for what seemed like an eternity, until she was certain she would go mad with curiosity. "Fine! Yes! Of course, I want to know!"

Before the words had left her lips, he had started to laugh. "Nine seconds. That's how long you could go without asking."

She smiled. "Truly? It felt like much longer. A quarter of an hour at least."

He laughed again, pulling her to him, letting her rest her head on his chest. She could hear his heartbeat beneath her ear, slow and steady. When he spoke, she felt the words as much as she heard them. "We talked about my being in love with you. And about my wanting to court you."

Her heart began to pound. "And what did he say?"

"He launched into a remarkably detailed lecture regarding the proper order of events when making this kind of request. Specifically, he thought the father should be consulted before the daughter runs any risk whatsoever of being ruined."

She winced, flushing with embarrassment at the idea that her father thought she might be ruined. She looked up at him and said, "What did you say?"

"You have beautiful eyes."

"You told my father that he has beautiful eyes?"

He smiled. "No. You distracted me. I told your father that, while I was very grateful for the lesson, I doubted I would ever have need of it again — because I was planning to court only one woman in my lifetime."

Her breath caught. "And what did he say?"

"Does it matter?"

"Not entirely, no."

"You realize that if you allow me to court you, all your opposition to marriage is going to have to be reconsidered."

She smiled, feigning innocence. "What opposition to marriage?"

"Excellent."

"But I am thinking we should have a long courtship."

"Why?" He looked surprised.

"Because I find I've developed a taste for adventure."

"That sounds dangerous. Not at all in character for a delicate flower."

She laughed. "We know I've never been good at being a delicate flower. Besides, it shan't be too dangerous."

"How can you be so sure?"

She smiled brilliantly at him, taking his breath away. "Because, on my next adventure, I'll have you by my side."

He pulled her across his lap and they kissed, the emotion of the day and the promise of the future making it soft and sweet and wonderful. She sighed as he lifted his lips off hers and offered her one of his wide, beautiful smiles. Overcome with happiness, she threw her arms around him and laughed, wondering just how it was that she had come to be so lucky.

the peerage

Peers of the Realm are those who hold one or more of five possible titles of nobility, bestowed upon them or their ancestors by a sitting British Monarch. In most cases, these titles are hereditary, and are passed down to the eldest son. Peers' wives receive titles upon marriage. The title becomes extinct if there is no male heir or relative to inherit, although some of the longest-standing families in the peerage have provisions that allow the title to be passed to a female relation in the extreme case.

The five titles, in order of rank, are:
Duke/Duchess, addressed as His/Her/Your Grace or Duke/Duchess
Marquess/Marchioness, addressed as Lord/Lady
Earl/Countess, addressed as Lord/Lady
Viscount/Viscountess, addressed as Lord/Lady
Baron/Baroness, addressed as Lord/Lady

courtesy titles in *The Season*

Depending upon the age and longevity of a particular line of the peerage, as well as his connections to the royal family, a peer of the realm might have multiple titles. He uses the highest rank.

The Duke of Worthington's full name and title is: Garrett Stafford, 6th Duke of Worthington; 8th Marquess of Weston; 4th Earl of Farrow; 11th Baron Baxter. A mouthful! His Grace uses the title of Duke, which William, his eldest son and heir, will assume upon Garrett's death. As British Dukedoms retain a courtesy title for their eldest sons, Will is given the title of Marquess of Weston—the next most prestigious on the list. Will, as eldest son to a Duke, has rights to all of the courtesy due a Duke.

Things in the Worthington Dukedom are a bit uncommon, but not unheard of. Because the Duke also holds two other titles, at the birth of Nick and Kit, he requested permission from the King to bestow those unused titles upon his younger sons. Nick became the Earl of Farrow; Kit became Baron Baxter. Upon Garrett's death, these titles will revert to the Dukedom, and Nick and Kit will become Lords Stafford, which is why they rarely use the titles anyway.

acknowledgments

As much as I would like to say that my characters sprang from my forehead fully formed like some kind of literary pantheon, the truth is that Alex, Ella, and Vivi would never have come to life if it hadn't been for a group of truly remarkable people. Thank goodness for acknowledgments, or I would feel very much a fraud.

First and foremost, thank you seems too little to say to my brilliant editor and wonderful friend, Lisa Sandell. Lisa, you have my unending gratitude for believing in Alex, in Gavin, and, most of all, in me. You are the greatest editor an author could ask for — the perfect combination of insight, ideas, and inspiration. Lisa came packaged with the incredible team at Scholastic, including Susan Jeffers Casel, Jody Corbett, Elizabeth Parisi, and Chris Stengel, all of whom worked tirelessly to bring these girls to life. I must give a special thanks to the unparalleled Corporate Communications team, who were so very encouraging from the earliest days of this journey.

The Season is, at its core, a story about the power of female friendship, and I have been blessed with a group of amazing women who have supported me from day one: Susan Lawler, Cynthia Noble, and Gayle Jacobson, who set my standards of friendship so very high at the beginning; Lindsay Thibeault and Beth Jarosz, who enthusiastically shared my obsession with historical fiction in the early days; all my friends from Smith College; Lynn Goldberg, who taught me everything I know about the publishing world and so much more; and, of course, my girls — Lisa, Meghan Tierney, Sarah Gelt, and Amanda Glesmann, who understood when I let all calls go to voice mail during those final months and loved me anyway. They — and countless other remarkable women — were my inspiration. I can only hope the book does them justice.

There will never be enough words to tell my family how instrumental they have been in this journey or how much I love them. Enormous thanks go to my sister, Chiara, who taught me the power the written word can have in shaping one's dreams; to my mother, Gylean, who has never wavered in her encouragement of my wild ideas; to my father, Zeno, who has always championed my eccentricities; and to Baxter, who sat quietly by my side as I wrote — my most loyal companion.

And finally, to Eric — you already have my heart, but now you have my eternal gratitude for your patience, your strength, your insight, and your love. This book would not exist without you.

about the author

As the daughter of a former British spy and a jet-setting Italian who met in Paris and lived, at one point or another, in Rome, London, San Francisco, and New York, I feel that I should tell you that I'm a real-life Lara Croft who spends her days haggling in the bazaars of Morocco, shopping on the Champs-Élysées, riding a motorbike across the Gobi desert, and scaling ancient Mayan temples.

Unfortunately for all of us, however, that would be a gross untruth. My parents settled down in Rhode Island long before I was born and left me little choice but to turn to books to find my own romance and adventure. And turn to books I did. When I was in elementary school, I must have read Roald Dahl's entire catalog five or six times, I was addicted to The Baby-sitters Club, and I can vividly remember reading Judy Blume and feeling like I had *finally* found someone who understood me.

By high school, thanks to my older (and much wiser) sister, I was thoroughly obsessed with historical fiction. I would become enamored of whole eras and read anything and everything I could get my hands on that related to them. I went through phases — the Civil War, medieval England, the Vikings, the Italian Renaissance.

Then I found Jane Austen. And I was hooked. Here was an author (a woman, no less!) who went against everything that had been written before and who birthed a genre of literature. She cast aside the melodramatic gothic romance that had dominated "literature for women" for decades and that the Brontë sisters (whom I could never quite stomach) would eventually canonize, and instead made romance fun . . . and funny . . . and real. Austen's heroines were cheeky and ironic, her heroes dark and brooding and arrogant to a fault. The combination of the two, for the teenager I was then and the twenty-something I am now, was electric.

That's when I fell in love with Regency England. I imagine that I — and everyone around me — thought it was just another one of my historical phases . . . but I never seemed to grow out of this one. I spent much of my teenage years, nose buried in historical romances, bemoaning the fact that I was born more than a century too late to enter the swirling *beau monde* that waltzed its way through the glittering ballrooms of London for my own season.

All was not lost, however. Through a stroke of very good luck I found myself at Smith College, where I was free to explore my wild obsessions. I had a group of friends who shared my love of historical fiction; we traded romances, talked Austen, and imagined what it would be like to be courted . . . *really* courted. I majored in history and somewhere along the way learned a rhyme that lists the Kings and Queens of England in order. After graduation, I went on a trip across Britain with my mother. We stopped in Hampshire, where I sat in the gardens of the Austen home and breathed the air of Aunt Jane.

Next, I found my way to New York, where I took a job in publishing and all those years of reading paid off. I bounced through several jobs and a graduate degree, amassing an unfathomably large collection of Regency fiction along the way, which fills the bookshelves of my Brooklyn home to bursting. I am lucky to have a husband and dog who overlook my eccentricities and, sometimes, love me better for them.

And now, I'm happy to say that, through writing, I have the chance to put my crazy, eclectic life to good use and, while I may never be able to live up to the British spy and the jet-setting Italian, my characters are certainly making a go of it.